D1434874

Under His Wings

Rosemary Fisher

ISBN 978-1-0980-8315-1 (paperback)
ISBN 978-1-0980-9072-2 (hardcover)
ISBN 978-1-0980-8316-8 (digital)

Copyright © 2020 by Rosemary Fisher

All rights reserved. No part of this publication may be reproduced, distributed, or transmitted in any form or by any means, including photocopying, recording, or other electronic or mechanical methods without the prior written permission of the publisher. For permission requests, solicit the publisher via the address below.

Christian Faith Publishing, Inc.
832 Park Avenue
Meadville, PA 16335
www.christianfaithpublishing.com

Printed in the United States of America

ACKNOWLEDGEMENTS

Dedicated to—My husband John, who never complained about the time I spent on this Pandemic-driven endeavor. He let me ramble on, even gave me some ideas! He was the first to suggest publishing and encouraged me every step of the way.

In Memory of Wilma Williams, who always requested 'Under His Wings' during Sunday night Singspirations when I was growing up, and who's sweet alto voice inspired me to learn to sing in harmony.

With Greatest Respect to all the pastors through the years who taught me well from behind the pulpit

AND

With Newfound Regards to many 'regular people' who taught from in front of it. You may not have known it, but you made an impact on me. You demonstrated. Christian love by the way you lived your lives and quietly mentored me. Thank you.

With Special Thanks to my family and many friends, who read my first manuscript, helped with proofreading and gave suggestions from time to time. I can't name you all, for fear of omitting someone, but you know who you are. Your encouragement kept me going, and made me feel loved and supported. I appreciate you all so much!

With Appreciation to my sister-in-law Nancy and her brother Fred, for helping me understand life on a family farm.

With Love and Thanks to Mom, Wanda Gossell, for insisting that I change the ending—Your right mom, it IS better this way.

And lastly, I should thank my High School English teacher, Mrs. Betenbender. She encouraged me to aim for the stars.

Above all, I thank God for giving me the idea for this story in the middle of the night! It must be something He wanted me to do, because I wouldn't have come up with this on my own. To God Be The Glory!

CHAPTER 1

─── ✼ ───

All in the Family

Benjamin Cooper Smith jumped down from the tractor and landed with a splat. He groaned and slowly looked down at his boots, knowing full well what he would see. Sure enough, his left foot had landed in a fresh cow pie. Swearing softly under his breath, Coop did the cattleman's two-step as he headed toward the barn. A sudden breeze hit his face as he rounded the corner of the corncrib. He stopped, took off his hat, and let the cool air rustle through his sandy blond hair. Banging his dusty black cowboy hat against his leg, Coop stretched and tried to work some kinks out of his achy back. Farm life had some disadvantages, that's for sure. He was dirty, from his head to the tip of his stinky boot. Every muscle in his twenty-six-year-old body was tight. Four hours on the tractor had rattled his bones. His lips were parched, and he was thirsty. Mom had given him a thermos of lemonade, but it was long since gone. And now he had to pee.

There were advantages to this somewhat isolated farm life too. He stood beside the corncrib, glanced quickly over his shoulder to be sure his sister wasn't anywhere nearby, unzipped, and relieved the pressure in his bladder. The cows did it, and Coop saw no reason why he shouldn't if he needed to.

The barn was musty and smelled pleasantly of hay and manure. Coop chuckled at the thought. Pleasantly! Not a word most people would use to describe hay and manure. But he liked it, always had. The barn was his second home. Even as a young boy, he had found a peace there among the stalls and feeding troughs. Even now, the barn was a place of refuge when things got tough. When he needed to get away, Coop often found himself in the haymow, sitting on a bale of hay, lost in thought. Usually he had a cat or two curled up on his lap. Animals always soothed his mind. Sometimes he prayed. Sometimes he cried. Sometimes he even yelled at God. But mostly it was a place of quiet, a place where he could think. It was safe here, in the peace of the barn.

No time for sitting and thinking now, though. He was hungry and thirsty, and he needed to wash up for supper. Dust particles, stirred up when Coop passed by, danced through the sunbeams. As he walked past the feed bins, he rattled and banged on the wooden lids. It was an old habit, from his childhood, when rats inhabited the storage bins. As a child, the rats frightened him. He thought that banging on the lids would make the rats fear him. It helped him, back then, to feel a bit braver. The cats took care of the problem now. They could be vicious. Funny to think of a cat as a protector. Funny how old habits never die.

He closed the side door of the barn and walked through the chicken yard. His feet crunched on the gravel walkway.

He stuck his head into the chicken house and counted. Six hens sitting on nests. He knew they'd have lots of new chicks any day now. If he could keep the possums away. Last year they had lost several good sitting hens. Hopefully never again. But that was the way of nature. Sometimes, no matter what he did, some things were out of his control. Even begging God didn't change everything.

A sudden movement near the fence caught his attention. Riley, their rough collie, came sauntering toward him. Riley was twelve years old and didn't move very quickly anymore. He still had enough energy to herd the chickens into the henhouse every night, but that was about it. Coop knew that Riley's days were numbered. Another truth of nature. He gave Riley a pat on the head and a scratch behind the ears, and they walked together toward the house.

When Riley was younger, Coop's sister Dana had entered him in dog-agility competitions through 4-H. Riley had excelled in weave poles and hurdle jumps, but for some reason he never did learn how to catch a Frisbee. Dana still had a bunch of ribbons and certificates hanging on her bedroom wall. Coop wondered if they would get another dog once Riley had passed. He couldn't imagine life on the farm without a collie. But puppies required a lot of work and training. With Dana concentrating on college classes, she wouldn't have much time anymore.

As he approached the house, Coop stooped to pick a big blue hydrangea blossom from his mother's bush along the sidewalk. His mom loved gardening. She used to spend a lot of time caring for her flowers. Lately she hadn't had that much time. The flower beds had to take a back seat to more important things that needed to be cared for. She'll like that he picked her this pretty flower. Just for good measure, he picked two more.

The screen door slammed behind him as he entered the back porch. He smiled, knowing that his mom would have something to say about that. She always did. He hung his cowboy hat on a peg near the door and kicked his boots off and set them beside the door. He'd have to get them cleaned up a little later. The smell of supper was already pulling him toward the kitchen. He was guessing pot roast with potatoes, carrots, and onions. His mouth was watering. Mom was a good cook, used to cooking for hungry, hardworking men. Lately there were a lot of leftovers. Coop's dad didn't eat much nowadays. This pot roast could stretch for several days.

Marla Jean Cooper-Smith was standing at the kitchen sink, hands deep in soapy water. She didn't turn toward Coop as he came up behind her, but she did say, "Just in time for supper. Better get cleaned up. Then call the others please."

Coop reached his arms around his mother and presented her with the bouquet of hydrangeas. She chuckled and said, "Thank you, son. But if you think flowers will make me overlook the slamming of the screen door, you are sadly mistaken."

Coop kissed her on the top of her head and said, "Love you, Mom. Supper smells great."

"Kisses and sweet talk won't work either. Now put those flowers in a vase and go get cleaned up."

When he left the kitchen, she dried her hands and turned to set the table. Marla Jean had just celebrated her fiftieth birthday, and she was starting to show some gray in her auburn hair. She liked to call it highlights, not gray hair. She was short and a bit on the heavy side. She described herself with words like *solid* and *substantial*, not *heavy* or *overweight*. She had a cheerful disposition and an easy smile. She played the piano for church and was usually singing around the house. She prided herself with being what she called "a good farmer's wife." Married right out of high school, she and Walter Smith worked side by side to get the farm up and going. She knew how to muck the barn, she'd bottle-fed baby calves, and she had even assisted with calving a time or two. Once her own babies came along, Marla Jean split her time with gardening, housework, and childcare. Walter took care of the farming, even hiring help as their farming operation grew. But things were different now. Walter was not able to do much of the work, and Coop had pretty much taken over those responsibilities.

They had three children. Well, four actually, but only three grew to adulthood. Michael was nearly thirty and had been born very shortly after she and Walter were married. In fact, almost exactly nine months after the wedding. He had enlisted in the Marines on his eighteenth birthday, and he had already served two tours overseas. While he was stationed in San Diego, he had met a cute little waitress, and they were married a year later. They had no children yet, and they were enjoying seeing the world, or parts of it, on Uncle Sam's dollar. They had never made it back to the farm, and Marla Jean and Walter had never even met Stacy. Pictures and phone calls now and then helped keep them connected, but Michael had made it clear that farming was not the life for him. Marla Jean prayed for him and Stacy every day. Walter used to pray for them too but now prayed silently.

Then they had Benjamin Cooper. That boy came out kicking and howling. Marla Jean didn't know if it was because he was mad to be pulled out of his comfortable living quarters, or he was just announcing to the world that he was here. He seemed to have a lot to say. Once he could talk, he was full of questions, and by the time he got to high school, he was a deep, rather philosophical thinker. Marla Jean thought he might decide to be a preacher, but that wasn't in the cards. He had completed three years of college, but seminary had been put on hold.

Patrick was next. He was born when Benjamin Cooper was just a year old. Walter joked about having *My Three Sons*, but Marla Jean had secretly hoped for a girl. Years later she wondered if her longing for a girl had been a bad thing, an omen, or a jinx. She never expressed that fear to anyone, of course. It was a crazy thought but one she had pondered nonetheless. Patrick was injured in a sledding accident the winter he was seven. His bones could heal, the doctor had told them, but the trauma done to his brain would be long lasting. Ultimately, that's what killed him. He had a massive stroke and died during surgery to put metal rods in his broken leg. Just seven years old. It wasn't fair. It was a tragedy that left a big hole in the family, one that every family member had dealt with in an individual way.

Walter's way of dealing with it was to insist on having another child as soon as possible. To fill the gap, maybe, or to get Marla Jean's mind off her loss. Either way, Marla Jean finally got her daughter. Dana was born the very next year, oddly enough, on what was originally Patrick's birthday. They thought about naming her Patricia, but Benjamin Cooper, at the wise age of nine, had overruled that suggestion by saying it would be just wrong. Patrick was Patrick, and this new baby was, well, *not* Patrick. So Dana Jean came to be. She had blond hair and blue eyes and had grown into a beautiful young lady. She was a senior in high school, about to graduate, but she had already started taking classes at the local community college. She had excelled in English in high school, and she had been accepted to take a college-level English class. She still had plenty of time to decide what she wanted to major in at a four-year school.

Dana Jean came into the kitchen just then, and she took the plates from her mother. Dressed in knee-length cutoff shorts and a T-shirt, she had been home from class just long enough to take a shower before supper. Her damp hair was pulled into a neat French braid, and she wore no makeup. Her face had a natural, healthy glow, and she seldom wore anything but a light lipstick. "I really wish this house had another bathroom," she said. "I barely got my shower done, and here comes Cooper, banging on the door." It was an ongoing discussion, the need for another bathroom.

"I don't see that's a big problem," Marla Jean said. "You've done fine all these years, even when Michael was here. And now that you're in college, and maybe moving out in a few years, I doubt we really need to spend our hard-earned money putting in an additional bathroom." She lifted the roast out of the pan and set it on the cutting board. Dana began to cut it into thin slices. A little pink juice oozed from the meat, and Dana let out a sigh.

"Mmmm. Just the way I like it, Mom. Nice and tender." She continued slicing the beef as she listened to sounds coming from the living room. Cooper and Dad were making their way slowly toward the kitchen. They were talking, but Dana had to strain to hear their words. Something about plowing or soybeans or the cows, probably. That topic occupied most of the conversation between the men. What little conversation there was, anyway. Cooper did most of the talking. Dad managed to ask a few questions now and then.

Cooper helped his dad into his chair at the head of the table. He hung his cane over the back of the chair and took his own seat at his dad's right. Dana sat to Dad's left, and Mom was at the other end. They joined hands and bowed their heads for prayer before eating. "We thank you, Lord, for the blessings of this day. We praise you for the fine weather you have sent for plowing. We pray for your merciful blessings of rain and sun to continue through the growing season. We ask that you help us remember that all good gifts come from you, the maker of Heaven and earth. Keep us in your care. Mind our tongues and our thoughts. May they always be pleasing to you. And now we thank you for once again providing this wonderful food for our supper. Bless the hands that prepared our meal. Be with those who have little to eat tonight. Send your people to help feed and comfort them this day. And Lord, guide us in paths of your righteousness. Show us your will as we make decisions. Lead us with your strong right hand. In your holy name we pray. Amen."

The family joined in with a soft amen, and Dana chuckled. "Jeez, Coop. Could you have prayed a little longer? Everything's going to be cold by now!"

"Stop now, Dana Jean! I love hearing your brother pray." She passed the bowl of potatoes to Coop and smiled at him. "The Lord speaks through your words, son. Sometimes I just get touched. I do wish you could have gone into the ministry. You'd make a fine preacher."

"I don't know about that, Mom. I think God put me right here, right now, to serve him just where I am. You don't have to stand behind a pulpit to be used by God, you know. In fact, I think some of the best preachers preach by actions, not sermons." Coop had mulled this over a lot lately, and he had come to a contentment regarding his position on the farm and his future here. He had a peace, knowing this was the place God wanted him to be. His family needed him here. Besides, he loved farm life, and he could see that God was using him here. God seemed to have given him the desires of his heart. Or at least one of them. He would wait on the Lord for more desires to be met.

Everyone got down to the business of eating, enjoying the meal, and chatting about the day's activities. "Did anyone save room for dessert?" asked Marla Jean. "I made a chocolate cake this afternoon. Chocolate frosting too." She picked up a small bowl holding Walter's evening medication and passed it to Dana. As was their routine, Dana turned with the pills toward her dad and helped him take them, one by one, followed with sips of coffee. "I think I'll have my cake later, Mom," she said. "Maybe before bed, with some ice cream."

Coop agreed. "I'll wait on the cake, Mom, but I would like another slice of beef right now. I think you outdid yourself tonight. This is the best roast we've had in a long time. My favorite meal, actually! It's really wonderful to come in from the fields and have good food like this on the table. I'm a growing boy, you know."

Marla Jean passed the platter of meat over to her son with a smile. "Well, I know you work hard. I'm happy to feed you. That's what I'm here for! Chief cook and bottle washer!"

"And we love you for it, Mom. You know you're the glue that holds this family together. I thank God for you every day."

Supper was almost over when Walter rapped his knuckles on the table for attention. Coop reached over and held his hand still. "What is it, Dad? What do you need?"

Walter nodded toward the backyard and asked in a quiet voice, "All done?"

Cooper picked up dishes from the table and took them to the sink. "No, Dad. I'm not quite done. I'll get out there soon, and get it finished before sundown. The weather's great, the dirt is easy to turn. Not dry and hard. Not messy and muddy. Just perfect. I'll be done in a couple of hours."

"That's good. You do good, son." Then Walter stood slowly, grabbed Cooper's arm, and looked intently into his eyes. "Thank you, Coop." He turned, found his cane, and moved slowly away from the table. He walked toward the living room, ready to take a seat in his recliner, where he would sit with the newspaper until he nodded off to sleep.

Dana and her mom chatted away as they cleaned up the kitchen. Marla Jean sliced up some of the roast to make sandwiches for Cooper's lunch the next day. She also made up a big pitcher of lemonade and another of iced tea. Coop would need it tomorrow; the temperature was climbing a little every day and soon would be full-on summer. Time to get the corn in the ground. It was a lot of work, and Marla Jean was proud of Cooper for taking it on so willingly. She was pretty sure he did it because he wanted to, but she hoped it wasn't out of a sense of obligation. Or guilt.

Coop grabbed his black cowboy hat and headed out to the tractor. He was careful to catch the screen door before it slammed.

CHAPTER 2

⸺ ❦ ⸺

Tribulation Times Two

The corn got in right on time. The day after planting was complete, Coop woke up to the sound of a gentle rain watering the earth. "Thank you, Jesus," he sighed, as he rolled over and pulled the comforter up around his ears. It was early yet; maybe he could get a little more sleep. Sound from his parents' bedroom kept him from drifting back to sleep. His dad was coughing again. It had been happening more and more often, and with every coughing episode it seemed that Walter grew weaker and took longer to recover. Coop knew that was why his dad had pulled more into himself, had withdrawn from most conversations, and slept so much. Talking wore him out.

Walter had started smoking in high school. Marla Jean didn't really like it, but it seemed that all the boys were doing it. She loved Walter, even with his habit. After they were married, she dropped hints now and then that she wished he would quit, yet she acknowledged that he was a good husband, and if this were his only fault, then she could put up with it. But that all changed after Patrick died.

That fateful afternoon, Walter had taken all three boys out to the big sledding hill west of town. There were usually a lot of kids sledding here, and today was no exception. Several cars and trucks were parked along the road, and there was a lot of laughter coming from the top of the hill. It was the perfect day for sledding: bright sunlight and cold, crisp air. The boys were bundled up in snow pants, winter coats, boots, hats, and gloves. They went flying down the hill several times while Walter stood with other parents and watched from the top.

As they trudged up the hill through the deep snow, the boys were laughing and cheerful. Walter patted his coat pocket, looking for his cigarettes. Then he realized that he had left the pack on the dash of his truck, so he turned back to go retrieve it. Leaning over the steering wheel, reaching for the cigarettes, he heard shouts from the hill. Michael was yelling, "Turn! Turn hard!" Cooper was calling out Patrick's name. Walter turned from the truck to see his older boys racing down the hill. Some of the other dads were charging down to help. With dread, Walter took off running too.

Patrick's sled had hit a tree at the bottom of the hill head-on. By the time Walter reached him, blood had already soaked through Patrick's green woolen cap. By the time Walter got him into the truck, it was obvious that Patrick had some major injuries. Another dad drove Walter's truck, and they got to the hospital as fast as they safely could. Another family agreed to take Michael and Cooper home, where they quickly told Marla Jean what had happened. She drove toward the hospital, praying all the way and calling out to God for help. The boys prayed from the back seat.

News of the accident spread through their little town. Soon their pastor, Reverend Long, arrived to sit with the family. Other church members gathered in the chapel to pray. As the afternoon turned to evening, the pastor's wife came to take Michael and Cooper to the parsonage for supper, though neither of them ate much. Reverend Long returned just as the boys were climbing into the double bed in the guest room. He told them that their brother had broken bones and other injuries. Together they joined hands and prayed fervently for the Lord to give wisdom to the doctors, for complete healing of Patrick's body, for the family to rest in the assurance that God was in control.

The next day, Reverend Long drove the boys back to the hospital, where their parents had spent the entire night. Patrick was in surgery, repairing his broken leg. The family sat in the waiting room, numb and fearful. After a couple of hours, the surgeon came out of the operating room and asked to speak privately to Walter and Marla Jean. The boys watched as their mother let out a gasp and collapsed into Walter's arms. Patrick had died on the operating table.

Benjamin Cooper wondered why they had even bothered to pray. It didn't do any good. Was God even listening? Was God even real? Why would he have let this happen to Patrick? It wasn't right.

After the funeral, which was on a numbingly cold February day, Walter took his small family home to a house that seemed extremely empty. He wandered from room to room, as the older boys closed themselves into their own rooms. Before long, he put his arms around Marla Jean and said, "I've gotta get out of here." He got in his truck and drove back to the sledding hill. He parked near where he had parked just a few days before and walked slowly up the hill. No one was sledding today; everyone seemed to be staying away since the accident. It had become a frightening, painful place, no longer a place of joy and laughter. Walter stood at the top of the hill. He looked up to Heaven and yelled out, "Why, God? Why did you take him? Why not me? He was so little. So young and innocent. Why? Why?"

Walter was overwhelmed by a sense of guilt. He wished he had never left the boys alone on the hill that day. He should have been there. He should have been watching more carefully. If only he had been there, Patrick might not have gone down at the angle that sent him crashing into the tree. All for the sake of a pack of cigarettes. His baby boy was gone, all because his irresponsible dad had wanted a cigarette.

Walter collapsed into the snow and sobbed. His shoulders shook, and cold tears rolled down his cheek. He knelt there, hands to his face, and prayed for answers. After a bit, his prayers changed to pleas for help, for assurance, for peace. He knew he had to be strong, to help the rest of his family get through this. A cold chill ran through his body, and he shuddered. He sat up and looked down the hill, toward the tree. For the first time, Walter noticed that there was a green ribbon tied around the tree, and someone had placed flowers at the base of the tree. He carefully made his was down the hill. Several sets of footprints led through the snow to this makeshift shrine to his son. Besides flowers and notes tacked to the tree, he also found a small teddy bear and a plastic dinosaur.

He took a deep breath and read every note. Despite his young age, Patrick had been loved by many. And many people were praying for his family. Words of peace and comfort warmed him. God spoke through the sincere writings of neighbors and friends, and even people he didn't really know. Walter was touched. He raised his hands toward Heaven and thanked the Lord for making his presence known. As he turned to go back up the hill, a bird began to sing. Walter turned back to Patrick's tree and easily spotted a bright-red cardinal, sitting on a low, leafless branch. He remembered the old saying about cardinals being a sign from the lost loved one. He smiled, grateful for the sighting.

Snow was beginning to fall as Walter neared his truck. Something caught his eye near the truck's front tire. It was a pack of cigarettes, his pack, the one he was reaching for when Patrick went careening down the snowy hill. In one quick movement, Walter stomped on the cigarettes, twisting his foot to smash them and grind them into the snow. Never again did he long for a smoke. He quit right then and there.

Unfortunately, the damage had been done. At the age of forty-six, Walter had gotten the diagnosis. Lung cancer.

Cooper had been in his third year of college at the time. He had been majoring in business, with a minor in religious studies. The degree was put on hold, and his plans for seminary vanished. He hurried home to help with the farmwork, while his dad dealt with chemo and radiation treatments. Cooper kept his disappointments at bay by focusing on the cattle and chores. Marla Jean took Walter to appointments, sat with him during treatments, and attended to him with home care. She prayed unceasingly.

Eventually Walter showed signs of improvement, and his care required less of her. Marla Jean never stopped praying for his complete recovery. She rejoiced when the oncologist declared that Walter was in remission. Soon he was able to climb up on the tractor, and could help with the farming, albeit his movements were slower than usual. But he was trying, and he was managing. They all thought he had turned the corner and complete recovery was on the horizon. Cooper was thinking about going back to school to finish that business degree.

But then winter came. And Kansas winters can be relentless. The weather was miserable, cold and damp, and the whole family caught colds. Coughing, runny noses, sore throat, they had it all. But whereas Marla Jean and the kids recovered with some over-the-counter meds, Walter did not. His cough lingered and became deeper. He didn't feel like eating a thing. He spiked a fever and had shortness of breath. When it became obvious that he was not responding to the OTCs, Marla Jean took him to the doctor. Listening to his lungs, the doctor feared pneumonia and sent him for a chest X-ray. That's when they discovered that the lung cancer had returned with a vengeance, and they found cancer in other places as well. The battle began again. This time Walter was weaker, and he didn't respond to the treatments.

As Cooper lay in his bed that morning, listening to the comforting, gentle rain outside and his father's rasping coughs and gasps for breath on the other side of his bedroom wall, he cried out to the Lord. "Father God, we need you. We pray for healing, we pray for comfort, we pray for hope. Lord, hear my prayer. Touch Dad's body. Breathe air into his lungs. Help him, God. And give us peace as we all struggle through this dark valley. Guide us, we pray. Help us know how to proceed. Hold Mom's hand and comfort her too." He took a deep breath, let it out slowly, and whispered, "May your will be done. Amen."

Cooper sat up in bed, shuffled his feet into his slippers, and stretched. He went to the window to look out at the barn. He needed to check on the cows and milk Bessie. She was the cow they kept for their own milk. She had had a calf a year ago, but the calf didn't survive. So the Smiths were able to continue milking her for their own family. It was one way they had found to turn a tragedy into a blessing.

The rest of their herd, usually about fifteen cows, was being raised for meat. They hoped to have at least a dozen calves born soon. If their bull had done his duty, they should almost double their herd size. Then several would be sold off to the slaughterhouse, or auction barn, or stockyards. The cattle raised on the Smith farm were grass fed throughout the spring, summer, and fall. Only during the winter was their food supplemented with grain. Grass-fed beef definitely tasted better than corn fed, and was a lot healthier. Consumers were starting to be educated as to the benefits of grass-fed beef, and the demand for their meat increased every year.

The Smiths planted about two hundred acres in corn, winter wheat, soybeans, milo, and alfalfa. They also raised cattle in pastures of another hundred acres. In addition, they had several barns, storage silos, and other outbuildings. Their farmhouse, though adequate for the family of five, was small in comparison to the barns. But that was typical for Kansas farmers; most of their money was put into the buildings and equipment needed for their business. Farmers usually had a lot of assets, but not a lot of cash on hand. Income wasn't steady, either; it fluctuated with the harvest seasons and could be greatly affected by weather.

Despite the uncertainties, the Smith family farm was doing pretty well. It did take a lot of work, and a lot of prayer, and a lot of faith. The Smiths believed in all three.

Before he went to the barn for morning chores, Coop made coffee for his mom. She came into the kitchen just as he was grabbing his rain jacket to dash out the door. "Oh, wonderful," she said. "Thanks for making the coffee."

"Yeah, I heard you busy with Dad. His cough sounds really bad this morning. Anything I can do to help?"

"You do so much already, Cooper. Just having you here helps me so much. I don't know how we'd manage without you." She sighed and reached for a mug. The coffee was strong and steaming hot. She took a sip and gratefully whispered, "Thank you, Lord. This will help." Then she turned to Coop and said, "He had a really bad night, tossing and turning and said he couldn't get comfortable. I know he has trouble breathing, even with three pillows to elevate his head. I think we might try having him sleep in the recliner tonight. It might help."

"Do you think you ought to call the doctor?"

"Well, he already has an appointment set for tomorrow, so we'll see if it can wait till then. I'm going to see if he can eat a little oatmeal. He just hasn't been eating well. He needs to eat, to keep his strength up."

"Okay, well, I'm headed out to the barn. Be back in a bit." Cooper pulled his collar up around his chin, hunched his shoulders, and dashed out the door. As usual, most of the cows were in the barnyard or milling around in the pasture. But not Bessie. She stood near the barn, knowing that she would soon be called for milking. Coop pushed open the heavy sliding door to the cow barn and said, "Good morning, Bessie. Are you ready to be milked?" Bessie calmly came into the barn and took her place in the milking station. He marveled at the intelligence of God's creatures. Even cows understood routines.

Going about the morning chores had become routine, and Cooper went through the motions quickly. His mind moved easily to a place of praise. As he often did, Cooper recited verses of comfort and hope. Today, the verse that came to mind was Philippians 4:6. "Don't fret or worry. Instead of worrying, pray. Let petitions and praises shape your worries into prayers, letting God know your concerns." Out loud, Coop said, "God, I know that all things work together for good, to those who love you and are called to your purposes. And I know that even though I don't understand it, you are going to work this out too, and we are going to be okay. I trust you. I know you keep your promises. And I also know that doesn't necessarily mean that you will heal my dad. But you will be with us as we struggle and get through whatever lies ahead. I want to rejoice in that, knowing that you are with me, you will never leave me or forsake me. Thank you, Lord Jesus. I praise you for your faithfulness and your promises. This tribulation is going to bring us to a place of hope. And I thank you."

Coop had long ago learned that praying was as easy as talking to a friend. He didn't think twice about expressing himself and calling on the name of Jesus at any time. It had taken a while for him to get to that point. After Patrick died, Cooper had been angry at God. He had questioned why God would do such a terrible thing to his little brother. It was a difficult time for Cooper, and he struggled for months. Pastor Long had helped a lot, giving Cooper a shoulder to cry on, and a chance to voice his questions. Pastor Long told him it wasn't unusual to have these feelings, and everyone worked through these issues at some time or another. He found a verse that helped a lot, and Cooper memorized it. The words came back to him now. Romans 5:3: "We rejoice in tribulations, knowing that tribulation works steadfastness, and steadfastness, approvedness, and approvedness, hope."

"Well, God, I guess this is tribulation. Watching Dad suffer like this, struggling to breathe, sinking into himself a little more day by day. Yeah, this is what I would call a big trouble, a tribulation. And you tell me to rejoice? That sounds crazy. What is there to be happy about?" He thought a minute. His dad was a good man, a hard worker, a role model, a leader at church, and a loving father. His dad had helped him a lot when Patrick died. In fact, his dad showed him about the way to salvation. Now there was something to rejoice about! And if rejoicing in tribulation would ultimately lead to hope, then he would have hope. Hope. Coop would cling on to hope.

CHAPTER 3

◦ ❧ ◦

Hope on the Horizon

The rain had stopped by early afternoon. Cooper was working in the office when he heard a car pull into the driveway. Glancing out the window, he saw Dr. Larson's black pickup. Coop closed down his computer and met the doctor at the door. "Hi, Doc," he said, reaching out to shake the older man's hand. "What brings you out our way? We didn't have an appointment I forgot about, did we?"

"Oh, no, I was just in the neighborhood and thought I'd stop by. Wanted to see how Walt is doing. Is he awake?" Oliver Larson had gone to school with Walter and Marla Jean. He had become a veterinarian, specializing in large animals. He came to the Smith farm to look after the cattle and sometimes just to catch up with the family.

"Yes, he's awake. Sitting in his recliner in the living room. Come on in." As Coop ushered him into the house, he noticed that there was someone sitting in the truck. He turned to Dr. Larson and asked. "Who's that?"

"Oh, that's Becky. She's my new vet tech. She's really good with animals. She was helping me with a well check of the new calves over at the Hennesseys. Why don't you go over and introduce yourself? She's a little cutie!"

Coop gave him a raised eyebrow look. It wasn't the first time someone had tried to hook him up. Not like he had a lot of free time to spend on girls. But just to be nice, Cooper went outside to talk to her. She rolled the window down as she saw him approaching. Becky had shoulder-length brown hair, pulled back into a ponytail. Her cheeks were rosy pink, and her smile was bright and friendly. She leaned a little out of the window and said, "Hi. You must be Cooper. I'm Becky. Becky Emerson. Doc Larson has told me a lot about you."

"Is that right? I hope it was truthful. What did he say?" Coop smiled, and Becky caught herself looking closely at his nice teeth. Teeth are important, a sign of good health. It was true with animals anyway.

"Well, he told me how you've been working the farm for the last few years, taking over for your dad, who's been sick. And he told me that you were in college, but didn't get to finish your degree." She looked past Cooper, to where Riley was coming across the yard. She smiled as the dog came and sat at Cooper's side, looking patiently up at her. "But he didn't tell me you had a collie! That's my very favorite breed of dog!"

"Yes, this is Riley. Would you like to pet him?"

Becky eagerly got out of the truck and knelt down to pet the collie. Soon Riley was licking her hand. Cooper said, "Looks like you have gotten the Riley seal of approval."

"I've grown up with collies. In fact, my sister and her husband breed them. My mom and dad did for years, but after Dad died, Mom decided to move here, and Joyce and

Stephen took over the farm and the collie business. The farm is south of Wichita, and they have a whole bunch of rough collies. Several females and a few males. And puppies all the time. I used to help with their training and socialization, until I left for college. I sure miss them. There's nothing like a collie! Smartest dogs ever. How old is Riley?"

"He's twelve. Starting to slow down. But he's still just as sweet as ever. He's really smart. Sometimes it's like he can read my mind. I think collies are intuitive too. I mean, he knows when someone is having a bad day. Sometimes he'll just go and sit near my Dad when he comes home from a chemo treatment. It's like Riley just knows Dad needs a little extra comfort."

"That's why they make such great therapy and emotional-support dogs. I think they can really connect with their people." She held Riley's face in her hands and looked into his eyes. "You're a good boy, aren't you? You love your people? Oh, I know you do. Good Riley."

"So Doc Larson told me you have been over to the Henneseys to check their calves."

Becky gave Riley one last ear rub and stood up. Cooper noticed that she was quite short, maybe only five feet or so. Though of course, most everyone looked short to his six foot one. Her cowboy boots had a little heel, but it didn't really make her much taller. Coop had to agree with Doc Larson: she was a little cutie.

"Yes," Becky answered. "They had quite a few calves born recently. How many head do you have here?"

"Usually fifteen to twenty. We had eight calves this spring. A couple more still to come." Cooper liked looking at Becky. She seemed younger than him, but he sensed a maturity and wisdom in her eyes. And her gentle nature with Riley was an indication of kindness and compassion. Cooper had always thought that you could tell a lot about a person by the way they treated animals. Becky treated them just fine.

They both glanced up when they heard the screen door squeak open. Doc Larson and Marla Jean came out on the porch, deep in quiet conversation. "We'll see what the doctor says tomorrow," Marla Jean was saying, "I'm just praying for some more time, and less pain. When he gets those coughing fits, I can tell his whole chest hurts. It's hard to watch."

"You all are in my prayers, Marla Jean. Let me know if you need anything. And I mean it. You two have been my good friends for a long, long time. I'm here if you need me. For anything." Then he raised his voice a bit as they walked toward his truck. "I see you met Becky," he said to Coop.

"I did. And you were right." He winked at Doc. "She obviously loves animals. She'll make a great vet."

Marla Jean walked over to Becky and said, "Welcome, Becky. So you want to be a vet, huh? It's a great occupation. Where do you go to school?"

Becky shuffled her feet in the gravel a bit and then looked at Marla Jean. "Well, I was going to Wichita State, but I only went one year. I am taking some classes online now, but it's a slow process. For now, I'm enjoying working with Dr. Larson, and honestly, I think I'm learning more from him than from my textbooks."

"I know what you mean," Marla Jean said comfortingly. "Hands-on learning is always the best. And Doc is a good teacher."

"Well, Becky, we better get going. We have another stop to make before our day is done." They opened the truck doors and climbed in. Cooper tapped on Becky's door as she buckled her seat belt. "See you around."

Becky smiled and said, "I hope so." Doc Larson started the engine and pulled out of the driveway. Marla Jean looked over at her son, raised her eyebrows, and said, "Now, she seems like a real nice girl."

"Yeah, Mom, she does. She sure likes Riley, and Riley likes her." Coop turned toward the barn. "Time to do some chores, Mom. I'll be in before supper." He shook his head and smiled as he lifted the latch on the gate near the chicken house. Mom wasn't exactly subtle.

Coop climbed up the steep ladder to the haymow. He needed to bring down a fresh bale of straw for bedding in the calf nursery. That's what he called the area of the barn where newborn calves could be brought, with their mothers, if they were struggling in some way. One of their pregnant cows, Lolly, was at least a week overdue, and Coop wanted to have the nursery ready in case there were complications. He threw the straw bale down through the drop door, but before he went down the ladder, he sat on a bale to pray. This was his custom, whenever he was in the haymow. His dad had done it, and he had taught Coop the importance of spending time with God in solitude. Today's prayer had to do with Coop's future. There was one desire of his heart that he wanted to offer up to God. It involved finding a wife, a Christian soul mate who would share the farming life with him. Coop had witnessed firsthand the love and companionship that grew daily between his mom and dad. He longed for that as well. He wondered if he would ever have that in his life. Day by day, it didn't bother him that he was no closer to finding the right girl. But as the months rolled into years, Coop wondered if he was destined to be alone. "Lord, I'm waiting on your timing. I'm trying to be patient. I'm listening for your still, small voice. But sometimes I wish you would talk louder!"

CHAPTER 4

———— ❧ ————

Mac and Cheese

Becky pulled into her carport on the side of her rental home. From the back seat, four-year-old Jennifer Hope Emerson unhooked her seatbelt, grabbed her backpack off the seat beside her, and jumped out of the car. "Race ya, Mommy," she said and took off running.

"Oh, honey, you win. I just can't run this time. It's been a long day."

Jenny continued to run up and down the sidewalk while her mother got two bags of groceries out of the trunk of the car. "Can we have mac and cheese for supper? Please?"

"What did you have for lunch at Grandma's?"

"Mac and cheese," Jenny answered with a grin.

"That's what I thought!" Becky chuckled as she unlocked the door and went in, holding the door with her foot while Jenny entered. "You know, you can't eat mac and cheese for every single meal. You're gonna turn into a bowl of pasta!"

"You're silly, Mommy! I can't be pasta! I'm a human!"

"Right you are. And humans need protein and vita-mins, which you get when you eat meat and vegetables. So how about we have some salmon and rice and broccoli?"

Jenny hesitated a minute, and then said, "Well, okay. And after we eat, can we go to the playground?"

Becky put the grocery bags down on the kitchen counter and starting putting things away. "Yes, but we can't stay too long. I have to finish up a paper for my class, and I don't want to be up all night doing it."

Sometimes Becky thought her life was one big balanc-ing act. Working thirty-five hours a week, online classes, and single parenting were enough to keep her head spin-ning. She felt like she never stopped, running from one focus to another, always trying to keep one step ahead of potential disaster. Fortunately, her mom lived nearby, so she did have help with Jenny. Grandma had been caring for Jenny since she was six weeks old, when Becky had gone back to work. Job after job had not worked out, until three months ago, when Becky had finally gotten this position with Dr. Larson. Becky was happy there. She loved work-ing with all kinds of animals. The hours were good, and the commute to work wasn't bad. With Grandma providing free childcare, Becky was finally able to relax a little. Things were really starting to work out.

After Jenny was tucked into bed, Becky turned on her computer and began to proofread the paper she had writ-ten for school. She was getting tired, and her mind seemed to drift. She found herself remembering the smile of a tall blond man in blue jeans and cowboy boots. He seemed like a nice guy, and he did have that nice smile. But looks could be deceiving, she knew, and first impressions were not always accurate. People could fool you: she'd been fooled before. "Not gonna let that happen again," she said to herself. She turned back to her computer, pressed *print*, and listened to make sure the printer clicked in. She sent an e-mail to her professor, with her paper attached, and shut off the computer. Tomorrow was another day.

CHAPTER 5

Final Arrangements

Walter decided he was done. Done with chemo. Done with radiation. Done with fighting. Done. He'd tried everything the doctors proposed, and it had bought him a couple more years. But now he was tired. And he was ready to go. He'd had a good life, he was ready to meet his Savior, and he wasn't afraid of dying. He was sorry he couldn't do any more to help his family, but he felt that Cooper was ready. And he didn't want to drain their already depleted finances with more hospital bills. He talked it over with Marla Jean that night, lying in bed with their arms wrapped around each other. With tears, they prayed together, asking that God bring them peace. They no longer prayed for miracles of healing. They prayed for comfort, assurance, and contentment. And they prayed for their children.

Six months to a year, the doctor had said. It was time enough to get things in order, make sure all the legal angles were covered, say his goodbyes. Walter knew that he was just a few steps from Heaven. Marla Jean knew it too, and it brought her comfort. They would all be together again, for eternity. Getting through the valley of the shadow might be difficult, but they could have hope. And they believed, strongly, that God kept his promises.

CHAPTER 6

Beware the Lion

Winslow was a small but growing town in the middle of farm country. Most of the activity in town centered around the high school, which drew students from throughout the county. The Winslow Wildcats had been state champions in football and did well in basketball too. Their marching band had won awards in competitions at the state level.

The town had a grocery store, a tractor-supply store, grain elevators, and a couple of gas stations. There was also a diner and a new fast-food restaurant. Doc Larson had his veterinarian office on Main Street next to the post office. Most people traveled twenty-five minutes to Atkins, the next town over, for medical care. Sheriff Bert Bertell was Winslow's only law officer, and his office was just a small room with a desk, some filing cabinets, and a single jail cell. There wasn't much need for more in Winslow. It was a quiet and sleepy little town. The sheriff had noticed a trend of trouble coming from people living on the edge of town in the trailer court. Most of them were short-term residents and didn't stick around town long.

Winslow had two churches, both of which had been there for close to a century. The Catholic church and the Methodist church had coexisted for years, but the Methodists had built a new, larger, more modern building just a few years ago, and the congregation had grown rapidly under the leadership of Pastor J. D. Green. He was a friendly young man, with a real passion for missions and evangelism. As teenagers, Walter and Marla Jean had grown up in the Methodist church. They were married in the little old sanctuary and brought their children up in Sunday school and vacation Bible school and youth group. Now they attended at the new building and were active on the church boards, choirs, and mission teams. Farm life and church life seemed to go hand in hand.

Cooper drove Dana into town to do some shopping. Dana had a list of groceries, and Cooper dropped her off at Hy-Vee and agreed to pick her up in an hour. He headed toward the hardware store. There was always something on the farm that needed fixing, or building, or cleaning, or redoing. Never-ending chores. Not that he minded, really. It kept him busy, kept his mind off Dad's failing health and his decision. He knew it was probably the right decision, but it was still hard. Hard to imagine life on the farm without Dad. Hard to imagine all the responsibility resting on his shoulders alone. It was a big load. He prayed that he would be strong enough.

Coop entered the hardware store and walked down the aisle, looking for a hose clamp. He was going to repair a hose so that his mom could water her flowers and small vegetable garden. He hadn't gone far when Jerry, the store manager, came up to him and said, "Hey, Coop! Good to see you. How's your dad doing these days?" Everyone in town knew that Walter had cancer. It was a small town, and everybody knew everything about everybody. But in this case, there was a true concern for Walter's well-being. Jerry really cared about his customers, and Walter had been a regular for a very long time.

"Hi, Jerry," said Coop. "Dad's doing okay. Taking one day at a time."

"That's all any of us can do, if you think about it," said Jerry. "You tell him I said hello, ya hear?"

"Sure, I'll tell him. Stop by and see him sometime, if you want. He always perks up a little when he has visitors."

"I'll do that," Jerry said. "Now what can I help you find?"

Coop bought the hose clamps he needed, and he also looked around to price out a new kind of fertilizer for his mom's tomatoes. He decided to get that too, knowing that they were almost out at home. Marla Jean didn't have time for a large garden this year, but she insisted on having a couple of tomato plants. She couldn't have a summer without fresh homegrown tomatoes. Store tomatoes just had no taste. Dana had planted some green beans and cucumbers. They'd have enough for several meals but probably wouldn't do any canning this year.

He drove up to the entrance of the grocery store and saw that Dana was already standing there, with several bags of groceries in her cart. He parked and helped her put everything into the back seat of the truck. "Get everything?" he asked, as he lifted a watermelon from the cart.

"I did. I even got that watermelon, even though it wasn't on the list. I know Dad loves watermelon. Thought he might enjoy some." Her voice caught slightly, and she turned away.

"Hey, I was thinking we should maybe go over to the diner and have some lunch. What do you think? We haven't really had a chance to talk much lately."

Dana wiped a tear from the corner of her eye. "Sounds good. I'm in the mood for a Reuben."

The diner was the town's gathering place. Breakfast was the big meal, when a lot of the older farmers would stop in to meet with friends, talk weather and crops, and gossip about goings-on. But at lunchtime, the place was almost deserted. Everyone had gone home, or off to work, or back to the fields. Only a few customers were seated along the counter, chatting with the waitresses. Coop and Dana chose a booth near the window. Before long a waitress came over carrying glasses of water.

"What else can I get you to drink?" she asked. The question was for both of them, but she was definitely focusing her attention toward Cooper. When he glanced up from the menu, she exclaimed, "Oh, I know you. You're Benjamin Smith. I was in your class at Winslow High."

Coop looked at her name tag. "Misty. Hmmm, I don't remember anyone named Misty. You do look a little familiar, though."

"Well, in high school, I was called Melissa. I went to college in California and decided to change to a cooler name. Changed my hair too." She turned around so they could see the back of her hair, which was extremely long and was jet-black with several thick purple highlights. "Cool, isn't it?" She leaned in close to Cooper and said, "I don't think these Kansas farmers quite know what to think of me, though. I get some pretty strange looks sometimes." She giggled and shook her head so her hair swirled around her shoulders. "The tattoos throw them too." Misty thrust her right arm forward, so Coop could see the tattoo that twined around her from wrist to shoulder. It was a vine, with leaves and flowers, colorful and artsy. "I have more too, but I can't show you right now."

He smiled at this little attempt at humor. "I go by Cooper now. Or Coop. Not that I exactly changed my name. It's my middle name and what my parents always called me. This is my sister Dana."

"Oh hi. Nice to meet'cha." She turned quickly back to Cooper. "So, Coop, what have you been doing with yourself since high school?"

"I did a few years at Wichita State. And now I'm back home, working the farm."

"Farm, huh? Good old Kansas farm boy! What's that they say? 'You can take the boy off the farm, but you can't take the farm out of the boy.' Or something like that! Not me, oh no, not me. I went to Cali right after graduation, got a major in fashion design, and I'm headed to New York City. Just stopped by home for a while, to live free and save up some money for city life. Do you know how expensive it is to get a decent apartment in New York? Oh my god! It's just crazy!"

A sharp bell sounded, and Misty looked toward the counter, where the shift manager was giving her a look that said "Get back to work." So she took out her notepad and sweetly asked, "Now, what can I get you for lunch?"

When their plates arrived, Dana reached for Coop's hand and prayed quietly over the meal. Misty watched from behind the counter, shook her head, and said, "Farmers."

Over Reuben sandwiches and french fries, Cooper and Dana had some time to talk about their dad's decision. "I understand why Dad doesn't want any more treatments, I really do," said Dana. "It's just going to be so hard to watch him go through that. And it seems like he's so young. He should have a lot of life left in him. I don't think any of my friends have lost a parent. It seems like it's not fair."

Coop took a drink of water, paused a moment, and said, "Fair or not fair, right or not right, it's just something we are all going to have to adjust to. We know this cancer is going to take him, sooner or later. There's just too much of it. Short of a miracle, he will die, even with treatments." He stopped talking long enough for that thought to settle across the table. "I think we just have to be strong, and as supportive and positive as we can be. He is really determined that this is the way he wants to go. At home, with family, no hospital, no machines. I just pray that he doesn't have a lot of pain, doesn't suffer."

Dana put down her fork and looked directly at him. "But that's the thing I'm having trouble with. This idea of prayer. It seems like prayer is demanding that God do something. Like we're telling him what we want and expecting that he do it. I mean, we prayed that Dad would be healed. We prayed that the medicine would work. We prayed that the cancer would go away. We got our hopes up and praised God for answering our prayers. And then the cancer came back. So now we pray that Dad won't have pain. And what if he does? Does that mean that God doesn't answer our prayers? That he just does what he wants anyway? Then what's the point of prayer, if it doesn't make any difference?"

"You sound a lot like me when I was little. Remember the preacher we had when Patrick died? Reverend Long?"

"Um, no, I don't remember him. I wasn't born yet, remember?"

Cooper chuckled. "Oh, yeah, that's right. Well, anyway, I asked him almost those same questions. I remember him saying that that's one reason we should include 'Thy will be done' in our prayers. That we should acknowledge that God's understanding of a situation is far beyond our human understanding, and his ways are not our ways. He sees the whole picture, knows what is best for everyone. And even though 'the fervent prayer of a righteous man availeth much, all things work together for good for them that trust the Lord and are called according to his purposes.' We just have to trust that God knows best because he does, of course, and rest in the assurance that we are in his care. And Dad certainly knows that, and he's trusting Jesus to lead him across the river."

Dana sat back in her chair, wiped her lips with her napkin, and sighed. "Mom's right. You really should be a preacher. You do know how to put the right words together. Thanks for helping me think of it a new way."

Misty appeared with the check and said to Cooper, "It was sure good to see you. Come by again, and we can talk about old times. I want to hear all about our classmates. Hey, get your cell phone and take down my number. And then give me yours. We should go hang out sometime."

Dana looked at Coop with a little smirk as they exchanged numbers. After they left the diner, she elbowed Coop and said, "So you're gonna go hang out with Misty, huh? She doesn't strike me as your type."

"The world is made up of all types of people, little sis. God loves them all. I should too. You never know, her heart might be ripe for the gospel, and I might be the one to bring it to her."

"You better be careful, Cooper. The devil can be disguised in many forms. And Peter says sometimes he's a hungry lion, ready to devour. She's just a lion with a black-and-purple mane!"

Misty walked down the block, up an alley, and down a gravel road to the trailer park. She walked past several run-down trailers, one with boards on the windows, one with a broken-down old car parked in front. Several of the trailers had one or two motorcycles on the parking pad. She knocked on the door of an old trailer. She didn't wait for an answer but let herself in. The smell of weed greeted her as she walked into the dark room. "Hey, baby, I'm here. Where are you?"

A gruff voice came from the back of the trailer. "Well, since I'm not out there, I guess I must be in the bedroom, brilliant."

"What'cha got to drink?"

"There's beer in the fridge. Bring me one when you come back."

"A please would be nice," she murmured as she pulled open the refrigerator door. There was beer in there, for sure. That's all that was there. A half-eaten pizza sat on the table, still in the box it came in. She grabbed a slice and took a bite, washing it down with a swallow of beer. It was cold, but it would do. She'd had some chips and salsa at the diner not long ago.

Patch was sitting on the side of the bed, smoking. He glanced up as she came into the room. She handed him the beer and kicked her shoes off. She sat on the bed beside him and snuggled up to him. With his free hand, he took hold of her long black-and-purple hair, and pulled her head back. He took a mouthful of beer, turned to kiss her, and emptied the beer into her mouth. She swallowed it, licked her lips, and kissed him deeply.

An hour later, Misty pulled her T-shirt over her head and smoothed down her hair. Sex with Patch was rough but could be satisfying. She had met Patch a few months ago, at the diner. He had come in with some biker friends, and as she often did, Misty struck up a flirtatious conversation with them. Patch seemed particularly interested in her, so she played along with him. Before long, she was in his bed, and they were an "on again, off again" item. She liked riding with him on the back of his motorcycle. He always had alcohol and drugs available, and although Misty didn't consider herself an addict, she did like to relax with weed now and then. Well, maybe more often than now and then.

Patch was a mystery man. He didn't talk much, he drank a lot, and he had a gruff manner with most everyone he met. He never wanted to talk about his past, or how he got the injury to his eye, which resulted in his nickname. Misty assumed it was from a brawl, but he never said.

Misty had left town for college in California, and she never planned to come back. Her major in fashion design left her with big student loans and no assurance of a good job, especially not in a small Kansas town. So here she was, waiting tables in the diner, trying to make some money but really going nowhere. Her mom and dad had divorced shortly after Misty had graduated from high school. Mom packed up and left, and Misty hadn't heard from her in years. They had never been really close, but it was awkward being at the house without her there. Living with her dad was uncomfortable, so she spent a lot of time at Patch's place. She hadn't moved in with him, but it was a good place to hang out.

She finished off another slice of cold pizza, said good-bye to Patch, and walked to her dad's place. It was getting dark, and the house was not in the best part of town, so she hurried in and locked the door behind her. "I'm home, Dad," she called, and headed up the stairs to her room. "Just gonna get ready for bed."

Misty dumped her tip money out onto her bed and starting sorting coins and bills. She counted it all up and sighed. Twenty-seven dollars and eighty-six cents. Not too bad for a weekday. But not enough to get her to New York City. She knew that flirting with customers at the diner, and sometimes even showing a little extra cleavage, was getting her some big tips, but she couldn't get ahead on minimum wage and tips. Something's got to give.

She jumped in the shower and washed the smell of Patch off her. He wasn't the cleanest guy she'd ever been with. As she lathered up her hair, she thought back to Coop and his sister. What was her name? Oh well, it didn't really matter. Coop, formerly Ben, was a clean-cut, good-looking man. He'd turned out mighty fine. She liked how he looked in tight jeans and cowboy boots. He wore a plaid shirt, a farmer's shirt, she called it. But his arm muscles were obviously toned, and his shirt sleeves fit tightly. She wondered about other muscles and how toned they probably were.

"If he doesn't call me in a day or two, I'm definitely gonna call him. I need to explore my options. There might be something worth digging into."

CHAPTER 7

Cowboy Boots

Mrs. Emerson called Jenny to come in from playing in the backyard. "Mommy will be here soon. Wash your hands and help me set the table."

Jenny took her shoes off at the door, washed her hands in the powder room, and gave her grandma a hug. 'I love the new swing set, Grandma. I can swing real high."

"I'm glad, honey. It's your birthday present, a little early. I wanted you to have lots of time this summer to swing a lot before school starts. Your mommy used to love to swing. She would be in our backyard swinging and singing every time she got a chance. She and Aunt Joyce would have contests to see who could swing the highest."

Elizabeth Emerson loved having a chance to spend so much time with her granddaughter. She didn't mind that she had had to step up as day-care provider ever since Jenny was a little baby. She was happy to help. Becky was a good girl. She just got lost for a little while. She made some bad errors in judgment, that's all. That's easy to do. Out on her own for the first time, pushed into things by peer pressure and the desire to fit in, she just forgot her upbringing and made some poor choices. Jenny was the result. And once Elizabeth got past the shock and disappointment, she came to accept the situation and wanted to support her daughter in whatever way she could.

She was so thankful that there had never been a discussion of abortion. Becky had owned up to her mistake and taken responsibility right from the start. She had finished her freshman year of college, moved in with Mom, gotten to the obstetrician, and taken birthing classes. Being Becky's birthing coach had been an amazing honor. Holding newborn Jenny for the first time, well, there was just nothing like it.

Now that Jenny was nearly five, and headed off to kindergarten soon, Mrs. Emerson knew that her responsibilities would be changing. She prayed that she and Jenny would remain close. Jenny would be coming to Grandma's house every day after school. Mrs. Emerson would watch her until Becky got off from work.

Every Wednesday afternoon, the three of them had supper together. Becky got off work early on Wednesday. They would eat together, then head off to church. Elizabeth went to choir practice, Jenny went to a children's Bible class, and Becky attended a single-moms' Bible study.

As they sat at the table, eating tacos and refried beans, they had a chance to talk. Elizabeth asked Becky, "So what's new? How is work going? Seen any interesting animals lately?"

"Well, the most interesting was a collie, Mom! He was just beautiful. Kinda reminded me of King that we had on the farm. He was a sable, with a white blaze. His name was Riley."

"Really? That's terrific. It doesn't seem like there are many collies around anymore. Does Dr. Larson have any others in his practice?"

"Not that I've seen. We were at a farm west of town. I assume this dog was one of Dr. Larson's patients, but I don't really know. We weren't there to see him. We were there because Dr. Larson wanted to visit with Mr. Smith, who's been really sick. They were friends way back in high school."

"Smith? That wouldn't be Walter Smith, would it? We've been praying for him. His wife is our choir pianist."

"I think that's what Doc said. Walter and Marla Jean Smith. I met their son Cooper."

"I've met him too. He dropped his mother off at church a few weeks ago. I met him in the parking lot. Nice-looking young man."

"Yes, he is. He has good teeth. Nice smile too."

Elizabeth gave her daughter a little smile and said, "Well, maybe if we're lucky he will be in the church parking lot again tonight. Then you can talk some more."

"Oh, Mom, please don't go pushing. I just met the man. And believe you me, if I ever get involved again, I'm taking my time. It's got to be slow and natural. No more jumping ahead. I've come so far, and I don't want to make the same mistake again." She looked to Jenny and asked, "Do you remember your Bible verse for tonight?"

"Joshua 1:9B. 'God is with me wherever I go.' It's easy. Is it time to go?"

Becky stood and cleared the dishes. "As soon as I get these dishes in the dishwasher. Go and brush your teeth, okay?" Elizabeth put the leftover taco fixings into the refrigerator, then left to gather her choir music. Becky's Bible and study book were in the car.

As it so happened, Coop was letting his mother off at the church door as the Emersons crossed the parking lot, headed to the sidewalk. Coop waved as they crossed in front of his truck, and took notice of the young woman holding the little girl's hand. She looked familiar. Short. Brown hair. Nice neat shirt tucked into skinny jeans.

Cowboy boots. Oh ya, he recognized the boots. *That's the new vet tech*, he thought to himself. "She looks a little different, cleaned up and with her hair down. Becky, that's her name. So she has a little girl. I didn't realize she was married. Doc didn't mention that. All he said was that she's cute. Hmmm."

After choir practice, Elizabeth waited up a bit until Marla Jean was ready to leave. She made a point of walking out with her. "I hear that my daughter met your son the other day. She said she and Doc Larson had been out to your farm."

"Oh you must mean Doc's new assistant, Becky. I didn't realize she was your daughter." Down the hall they could see Becky and Jenny coming out of the children's area.

"Yes, here she comes now." Elizabeth waved and motioned for Becky to join them. "Becky, look who I ran into. It's Marla Jean Smith."

"How nice to see you again, Becky!" She looked down at Jenny, who was proudly holding a memory verse certificate. "And who's this little cutie?"

The little girl said, "I'm Jenny. And I said my memory verse. 'Joshua 1:9B, God is with me wherever I go.' See?" She showed her certificate to her grandma.

"Very good, sweetie," said Elizabeth. "I knew you would do it perfectly." Then she turned to Marla Jean and said, "This is my granddaughter. She's four."

"Almost five, Grandma. Don't forget."

"Oh don't worry, Jenny. We will not forget your birthday," Becky said. "It's a very special day for Grandma and me. Besides, you keep reminding us about it!"

They walked on out the door and found Coop waiting there in his truck. He jumped out and opened the door for his mom and was prepared to help her climb in, but his mother had a different idea. She smiled brightly at Coop and said, "Look, Coop. Look who I ran into. It's Becky, Doc Larson's new assistant. And this is her mother, Elizabeth Emerson. And this is her daughter, Jenny."

Jenny said, "Hi. I'm almost five. My birthday is coming." Becky rolled her eyes, and the older ladies chuckled.

"Five, huh?" said Cooper. "That is a fun time. Are you in school?"

"I'm going to kindergarten soon."

"Kindergarten? That's great. What you got there?" Coop pointed to the certificate Jenny was holding.

"My Bible-verse prize. Wanna see it?"

"Sure." Coop took the paper and read it. "This says you can say Joshua 1:9B. Can you tell me?"

Jenny proceeded to recite the verse, and Cooper congratulated her. "That's a very important verse. Don't ever forget it. God will be with you always, wherever you go." He gave the paper back to Jenny and turned to Becky.

"Hi, Becky. It's so nice to see you again. So it looks like we go to the same church."

"It looks like it! How long have you been going here?"

"Only all my life!" Coop laughed. "How about you?"

"Just a few years, really. We used to just come on Sunday mornings, but I joined the single-moms' group a year ago, and we meet on Wednesdays. Jenny has a kid's class too, so it works out just perfectly."

"I go to the young-adult Sunday school class. You should come sometime. Bet you'd like it. It's guys and girls, some married, some not. We're studying Romans right now."

She hesitated just a bit. It was sometimes hard for Becky to go into a group of people. Sometimes she felt judged. She had a history that many people did not understand or approve of. It wasn't easy to expose herself to strangers. But then she thought, *These are church people. They should accept me, and love me without judgment. If I'm being judged or criticized, then obviously they aren't demonstrating Christ.*

Becky was so glad she had joined the Wednesday-night single-moms' support group. Now there were some women who accepted her, understood her fears and struggles, and supported her through some hard times. Many of them were going through some of the same things as she was. The insecurities. The financial worries. The guilt. But the leaders of the group had taught about God's unconditional love. They had helped Becky recognize her sin, ask for forgiveness, and trust God to lead in the future. Like Jenny's Bible verse said, Becky believed that God was always with her.

"Thanks. I might try it," she said to Coop. "What time?"

"We start at nine thirty, but if you think you can come this Sunday, I'll meet you in the lobby about nine twenty, and we can go in together. Then I can introduce you to a few people before we get started."

"Do you know if there's a children's class at that time for Jenny?"

Marla Jean interrupted and said, "Oh yes, there's children's Sunday school. And a lot of the kids in Jenny's Wednesday-night class will be in Sunday school with her. She'll feel right at home."

"Well, sure, okay. I'll be here at nine twenty. Thanks for inviting me." Becky and Jenny walked to the car, but Elizabeth lagged a bit behind, talking to Marla Jean and Cooper. When she finally got into her seat and buckled her belt, she smiled and said, "I'm so happy. That's a wonderful family. You would do well to get to know Cooper. He's such a nice young man."

"Mom, take it easy. Let's not go making big plans, all right? I hardly know the guy."

From the back seat, Jenny piped up, "I like him, Mommy. He has cowboy boots like you."

CHAPTER 8

Messages

Misty called Cooper. He didn't answer. She left a bubbly, giggly message. He didn't call right back. So she called a couple of hours later. Left another message.

Clearing away the dishes after the breakfast rush at the diner, Misty let her mind wander. She was thinking about Coop more and more often. He was so tall. And those arm muscles were so defined. *I bet he works out a lot. To get arms like that, he'd have to. I bet he's got some abs too. Sure would like to see his chest with no shirt.* And in her mind, she pictured him with even less clothes on. She pictured them together, enjoying time in bed.

As she walked through the dining area, daydreaming, she bumped into the corner of a table and jostled the dishes she was carrying. A coffee cup crashed to the floor and shattered. "Damn," she whispered under her breath but loud enough for an elderly lady at the counter to hear her. The lady shook her head and turned away, obviously disgusted. The hair, the makeup, the tattoo, and the language. This girl should go back where she came from, she obviously doesn't belong here.

Misty's boss, Al, called out from the back, "Hey, take it easy. You break any more of our stuff, and you'll be losing your tips. Pay attention to what you're doing."

Misty carried the tray more carefully to the sink. She felt like using some other words, but said sweetly, "Oh I'm so sorry. I'll clean it right up. And it won't happen again, Al. I'll be more careful." She hated bowing down to him, but she needed this job and didn't want to blow it. There weren't a lot of job openings in this hick town, so she had to hang on to this one as long as she could. Though honestly, it wasn't like she was making tons of money. Just enough to get by, and yet there were those school loans hanging over her head.

Misty told Al she needed a bathroom break, and she took out her cell phone to call Cooper once more. Why wasn't he answering? Was he ignoring her? *Oh well,* she thought, *I'm always up for a challenge.*

When she recorded her message this time, her voice was pouty and childlike. "Oh, Cooper, you're making me so sad. Please call me back. I really want to see you. We could go do something fun. Dancing, drinking, driving around, whatever you like to do. Please call me."

CHAPTER 9

✺

Into the Valley of the Shadow

Coop felt the phone jiggle in his pocket, and knew he needed to call her back. But he had been busy out in the pasture, looking for Lolly, the cow that was overdue in delivering her calf. Hopefully there wasn't going to be a problem with the birth. Although he had assisted his dad with a couple of troublesome deliveries in the past, he certainly didn't wish to do it again anytime soon. Calving could be a risky business, and he didn't want to lose even one. They needed every head of cattle they could raise. Each one was income they depended on. It was hard enough to keep the farm running, to buy seed and repair equipment, and to hire extra help during harvesttime. Their income came from selling cattle and crops, and they depended on every new calf and every bushel of harvested grain. Farming was a struggling business. Weather could make or break them. Market prices for soybeans and wheat were unstable, and depended on so many variables.

Coop's dad had taught him years ago to put the farm and all its ups and downs into God's hands. They could do their very best, but so much depended on just the raw facts of nature. Weather was certainly out of their control. Even the death of a calf or cow was something they didn't have a lot of power over. And the markets, well, that was dependent on so many things. So learning to trust God, to know that he would be with them, no matter how dire things might look, to seek his peace in the dark times, those had been very important lessons for Coop as a young boy. And now, with the situation with his dad, and knowing that there was little he could do to control or change the outcome, Coop found himself resting in those truths. He was still seeking God's peace in the dark times.

Just then Coop noticed movement behind some bushes. He turned his four-wheeler toward the movement, and sure enough there stood Lolly. Beside her stood not one, but two, newborn calves. The larger of the two was already nursing, but the other one was just trying out his new legs. He seemed weak and wobbly, but that was always the case with a newborn. Lolly was nuzzling him, licking him, and welcoming him into the world. Twins! That was great news.

He took his phone out of his pocket and called Misty.

As soon as she saw his number show up on her phone, Misty snatched it up off the counter and answered on the second ring. "Hi, Coop. I'm so glad you called. I thought maybe you were mad at me or something."

"Of course not, I have no reason to be mad at you. I've been out in the pasture all morning, looking for a cow that was about to deliver. And I finally found her, and guess what? She had twins!"

"That's cool, I guess. Hey, when can we get together? I really want to hang out with you."

"Well, I don't know." Coop thought for a bit. "Things are pretty busy at the farm right now, but maybe I could get a couple of hours free on Friday, and we could do something. What time do you get off work?"

"Well, it just so happens that Friday is my day off. I'm free all day. What would you like to do? Could we just go somewhere and talk?"

"Okay. How about we go to the lake? Maybe we could get some food and take it out there. They have picnic tables." He added, "I have to warn you, though. I'm not completely sure I'll be available. That's the way it is with farmwork. Things come up and plans get changed all the time. But if I can, I'll take you to the lake, and we can sit and talk."

"Sounds fun. Hey, call me with details, okay? I gotta get back to work." Misty hung up and smiled. She had a date with Cooper Smith! Her mind was already working on what to wear.

Coop put his phone back into his pocket and started up the four-wheeler. As he drove back to the house, he remembered Dana's warning. She had as much as said that Misty might be the devil disguised as a lion, seeking to devour him. He chuckled at the thought, but then he realized that he really didn't know much about Misty anyway. Other than high school, what did they have in common? Well, maybe this picnic at the lake would be a good opportunity to find out more about her. At first glance, she was not someone he would have been interested in. But Coop knew that judging a person by appearance was shallow, and he knew God judged on the heart. Wanting to be like God, Coop had been trying to see people for their inner qualities. He was willing to give Misty a chance. There were lots of things he wanted to learn about her.

Coop wondered about Misty's knowledge of the Savior. He was glad to have the opportunity to share his testimony with her. Maybe he could explain to her about salvation and eternal life.

Riley was sleeping in the shade under a tree as Coop drove the four-wheeler down the driveway and parked it alongside his truck. Riley lifted his head slightly when Coop called to him, but he did not get up. Coop sat in the grass beside him, rubbing his head and talking soothingly. "What's the matter, old man? Are you tired today?"

Riley looked up at him sadly. He laid his chin across Cooper's knee. He let out a sigh and closed his eyes. Coop sat with him for several minutes, but then he said, "Sorry, Riley, but I have to get up. I want to go tell Dad about the twins that were born this morning."

Cooper gently moved Riley's head and stood up. Riley struggled to stand also. He had more difficulty than usual with rising. As they walked to the house, Cooper saw that Riley was limping. His left front leg seemed to be in pain with each step. "Oh dear," Coop said to Riley. "It looks like your arthritis is acting up again. Maybe it's time to increase your meds. I'll call Doc Larson today."

Cooper found his dad sitting in the recliner in the living room. He was covered with an afghan, even though it was comfortably warm in the house. Walt stayed cold most of the time. His afternoon pain medicine was sitting on the end table near him, with a full glass of water.

"Dad, don't forget to take your medicine. Here, let me help you."

Walt shook his head and waved Coop off. "Don't need it. I feel okay."

"But, Dad, you know how it goes. You need to keep ahead of the pain. Taking your meds at the right time will prevent you from having another episode of really bad pain." He picked up the pills and offered them to his dad, who took them begrudgingly. Cooper lifted the water glass to Walter's lips and held it for his dad. He was happy to be of help, but this was more difficult than he had envisioned. He was watching his dad growing weaker every day, almost helpless now.

Walter swallowed and pushed the water glass away. He started to cough, then began to choke. The coughing fit left him struggling for breath. He slumped back in his chair, held his hand across his chest, and gasped for air. Cooper sat with him, gently massaging his shoulders, until his breathing eased. Tears fill his eyes. He was glad his dad couldn't see him.

Standing in the doorway, Marla Jean watched what had transpired. Her eyes were glistening with unshed tears too. She loved those men so completely, and hated to see either one of them suffering. Coop was trying so hard to be strong. Walt was trying not to show his pain and discomfort. They were both doing the best they could.

When Walt had recovered a bit, Cooper moved in front of him and sat on a footstool at his feet. "Guess what, Dad. One of the cows had twins. I had to look all over the pasture, but I finally found them way out in the back, down by the creek. Cute little calves. One's a girl, one's a boy. The boy is a little small, but I think he'll be okay. He was just getting his feet when I found them."

"That's good. Keep watch." He had to pause for breath before going on. "Call Doc if you think you need to."

"Well, I am going to call him, because it looks like Riley is having a hard time walking. He could barely get up off the ground. Hindquarters are weak, and he's limping."

"Don't let him suffer, son."

Coop looked at his dad's face, shallow and drawn, dark circles under his eyes. He said, "Oh, I won't, Dad, but I think he just needs a different dosage of his arthritis medicine. I'll call Doc and see what he says."

Marla Jean came to stand beside her husband. She adjusted the afghan up around his shoulders and said, "There you go. Are you warm enough? Why don't you take a nap now? It's still a while before supper."

Walt patted her hand and said, "Not hungry. You all eat."

"Well, you sleep now. Maybe you will be hungry when you wake up."

Walter was already asleep.

CHAPTER 10

—— ✑ ——

Back to the Bible

"Larson's Animal Hospital. This is Becky. How can I help you?"

"Oh hi, Becky. This is Cooper Smith. Remember me?"

"Yes, of course I do. I'm looking forward to visiting that Sunday school class with you this weekend."

"Great. Me too. But that's not what I called about. It's our dog, Riley. He's limping worse, and struggling to get up off the ground. I think he probably needs an increased dosage of his arthritis medicine."

"Oh no. I'm so sorry to hear that. I'm sure Doc Larson will want to see him. Can you bring him in first thing in the morning?"

"Sure. Thanks for working us in so quickly. What time do you open? Seven?"

"Yes, seven. For tonight, be sure he rests. Limit his activity, no running or jumping. Make sure he's getting enough to drink this evening, but don't feed him or give him any water after midnight, just in case Doc wants to run some labs. He might need to order some X-rays too."

Becky was efficient, Coop thought, and he appreciated her thoroughness.

"Do you think I'll need to leave him overnight?"

"I couldn't say for sure, since it depends on what Doc wants to do. It is possible, though, especially if he has X-rays. He'll need to be sedated, and Doc usually likes to keep them overnight after sedation, for observation. But like I said, I don't know at this point."

"Okay, well, thanks. See you in the morning."

"Well, no, actually, I don't come in until nine o'clock," Becky said.

Cooper was surprised to realize that he was a little disappointed. It would have been nice to see her again, even under these circumstances. "Oh, that's too bad. Okay, then at least we're still on for Sunday school, right?"

"Yes, definitely. I'm looking forward to it," Becky said, and she had to admit to herself that she really was.

It had been a long time since Becky had considered the possibility of having any kind of relationship with a man. Her past experience had scared her, and she wasn't sure, even now, that she could ever trust a man again.

She had been so young and foolish. Away from home and on her own for the first time, she had gone a little crazy. She'd gone to a college party, met an extremely good-looking upperclassman, and been swept off her feet. It felt good to be seen around campus with a popular, handsome man. It built her self-esteem and gave her confidence. She was in love.

And being in love, she gave herself to him completely. Shortly into her second semester, she found herself pregnant. And alone. He wanted nothing to do with her now, and she was devastated. Self-esteem was replaced with guilt, and confidence turned to embarrassment. She was hurt, angry, and worried. She managed to finish the semester without anyone knowing her condition, though she felt eyes upon her as people whispered and wondered. She was just beginning to show when she packed her things and left school.

Fortunately, her mom had welcomed her home and, although a bit disappointed, offered to support her any way possible. The pregnancy progressed normally, and Becky managed to focus on her health and preparing for delivery. The obstetrician said the baby was on the small side, but not to worry. Becky was amazed when she felt the first kicks, and she shared the joy with her mom. They found out it was a girl, and they started thinking of names. Becky and her mom went to birthing classes. They got the basics and set up a nursery. They were ready for this new stage of life.

Mrs. Emerson did not condemn her daughter for her risky behavior. She was sorry that this changed a lot of things for Becky, but she saw no point in chastising her for her mistakes. Becky had made some poor choices, and now she would have to live with the consequences. It wasn't going to be easy, but they'd get through it together.

Becky, however, was dealing with guilt. She felt stupid, used, reckless, worthless, and immoral. She couldn't forgive herself for her sinfulness. She put on a cheerful, confident front when she was around her mom, but she often cried herself to sleep, worrying about what people were saying about her, and how her life got so messed up. And it was all her own fault. She was so stupid to let this happen.

And she considered herself damaged goods. She thought she was no longer worthwhile. She'd messed up her life, and now no one would be interested in her. She and this baby girl would be on their own. Mom wouldn't be around forever, and anyway, it wasn't her responsibility. It was Becky's fault and Becky's responsibility and Becky's messed-up future.

In her sixth month, Becky's obstetrician had picked up on her depression and suggested that she should go to a counselor. The doctor told Becky that her mental health was as important as her physical health, and that depression and stress could affect the baby, not just now but also after the child was born. Becky saw the wisdom in that, and she agreed.

The counselor was Dr. Lauren Whitefield. She had an office in her home. Becky saw her once a week. Dr. Whitefield was a plump, jolly woman with mousy brown hair pulled into a bun and glasses that sat on the tip of her nose. She could gaze over the tops of her glasses and look directly into Becky's heart. She wasn't judgmental, but she asked probing questions and made Becky think.

Becky was a little surprised when Dr. Whitefield asked her if she believed in God. "Well, yes, I do. I've gone to church most all my life. And I should have known better than to fall into this sin. I must be a real disappointment to God. I mean, I should have resisted the temptations. I should have been a good girl. God must be disgusted with me. I mean, I am. He surely is."

"Becky, I'm going to give you some verses to look up, and I want you to do some journaling before next week. Write down your thoughts about the verses, and how they can relate to you and your situation. We'll talk about them at our next session."

Becky wasn't sure how this was going to help her deal with her depression and self-loathing, but she did as Dr. Whitefield requested. She found her old Bible, got a notebook and pen, and set about her task. Looking up verses took a bit of time. She hadn't done much Bible reading before. The church she had attended with her parents wasn't really into that. Her mom was going to a new church now, but Becky hadn't wanted to go because of her pregnancy. She thought they would look down their noses at her.

One of the verses Dr. Whitefield had given her was Romans 8:1, "There is therefore now no condemnation for those who are in Christ Jesus." The word *condemnation* jumped out at her. Yes, she was feeling condemned. She condemned herself, and assumed that others would condemn her too. And of course, God condemned her. How could he not? The first part of this verse said there would be no condemnation. That sounded promising. But the next part said there was a condition, a big *if.* You had to be in Christ Jesus. What in the world did that mean?

As she pondered this, she wondered if Dr. Whitefield could help her understand, and if it would make any difference anyway.

CHAPTER 11

Honorable Intentions

Coop took Riley into Doc Larson's office early Friday morning. As he had rather expected, he was told he needed to leave Riley for some testing. Blood work, X-rays, and observation were necessary to make a complete diagnosis. Doc Larson was calm and reassuring as he spoke with Coop about the situation, reminding him that because of Riley's age, they might have to make some difficult decisions. Coop left the office in a mix of emotions. He knew he could trust Doc, and he knew Doc's recommendations would be accurate. But he also knew that, if it came to that difficult decision, it would be heart-wrenching. "Dear Lord, creator of Heaven and earth and all that is in it, I know that all of our days are numbered. But, God, this dog has been an important part of our family for so long. We'll all need your strength and comfort to get through this. Thank you for every day we have had with Riley. And thank you for every day yet to come. Help us, Lord. He is in your hands. May your will be done."

Dana had been worried about Riley too, so Coop talked to her as soon as he got back to the farm. She got teary-eyed when she thought about losing him. She had done most of Riley's training when he was a puppy. They had a special relationship because of it. She could hardly imagine life without Riley. And at the same time, she didn't want him to struggle or be in pain for his last days. Whatever time God allowed, she would want Riley to be comfortable.

"Doc is going to keep Riley overnight. He and Mrs. Larson will check on him several times through the night, and he'll call us in the morning to tell us what's going on."

Dana said, "It's sure convenient that their house is right next door to the office. Makes it easy for them to watch over their patients."

Coop's mind was preoccupied with Riley the rest of the morning as he went about chores on the farm. At lunchtime, he noticed that he had a text message on his phone. Misty didn't sound too happy. "Hey, you haven't called me about details about tonight. Did you forget? Well, thanks a lot. Are we still on? You wouldn't bail on me, would you? Better not! Call me. Or text me. I need to know what's going on."

He called her, preferring to really talk, instead of texting, which seemed so impersonal and could often be misinterpreted. She answered on the first ring.

"Hi, Coop. Please don't tell me you forgot. Or did you change your mind? I've been waiting to hear from you."

"No, I didn't forget, and I didn't change my mind. I just got a little distracted with an emergency I've had to deal with. I'm still planning on taking you out to the lake, if you still want to go."

"Of course I do, silly! I've been thinking about it for days. What time?"

"How about I pick you up at five o'clock? But where should I meet you? I don't know where you live."

"I can meet you at the diner at five. That will be fine. Are you going to bring food?"

"Yes, I will. I'll bring some sandwiches and chips. Do you like watermelon?"

"I do. Can I bring something? Drinks, maybe? I could pick up some beer."

"Well, you can bring drinks, but I don't drink beer. Except root beer. Or any kind of soda. Or tea. Whatever you want."

"Wow, I've never known an adult man who didn't drink beer. But okay, I'll bring some sodas. I have a little cooler that should work perfectly. I can't wait to see you."

"Okay then, I'll pick you up at the diner at five. See you then. Bye."

"Don't be late. Bye."

Coop set about making some chicken sandwiches. He put them into sandwich bags, got a bag of potato chips, and packed some of his mom's bread and butter pickles into a small container. He was just slicing up some watermelon when his mom and sister came into the kitchen.

Dana asked, "Is all that for your lunch? Save some chicken for me please."

"No, it's not all for me. I'm packing supper for two." Coop turned to his mother and said, "Oh, Mom, I won't be here for supper tonight. I'm taking a picnic out to the lake."

Marla Jean said, "Oh, really? This is kinda sudden, isn't it?"

"Well, yes, kinda. We just decided a day or two ago."

Dana turned quickly to face him. "We? And who exactly is the other part of 'we'?"

"If you must know, Miss Snoopy, I'm taking the waitress from the diner, Misty. We're going to have some picnic food and talk about old times."

"Misty? Don't you mean the purple-haired lion? You better be careful. I'm warning you, she's not your type. I do not think this is a good idea."

"Oh, stop," Coop said. "It's just a picnic and some conversation. You're reading more into this than you should. And besides, don't you think I can take care of myself?"

"Well, I sure hope so. But before you pick her up, I want you to recite I Corinthians 10:13. You might need it."

"I don't know this girl," interjected Marla Jean. "But remember what your dad has always said. If he were awake, he would remind you. Every girl you date is a potential marriage partner. Be very careful who you get comfortable with. Why start a relationship with a girl you have nothing in common with, don't share beliefs with, or wouldn't fit well with for the long haul? We always told your brother Michael that, and only hope and pray that he made a good choice when he married Stacy. Just be smart, Coop. I do know you, and I'm sure you will make good decisions."

"Well, that's the thing, Mom. I don't really know her either. But how will I ever learn about her beliefs or what we have in common, if I don't spend time with her to find out? I'm only talking about some conversation, some time to get to know her."

"I know we shouldn't judge on appearances," said Dana. "But honestly, she wears tons of eye makeup, has tattoos, and purple hair. I would think that right there would tell you that you don't have a lot in common."

"Purple hair?" repeated Marla Jean.

"Not really," said Coop. "It's just purple in stripes."

"Well, I understand that you might want to get to know more about her before you jump to conclusions," said Marla Jean, and she looked toward her daughter with raised eyebrows. "But think about what your dad said, and be listening to the Spirit's nudging. You'll know how far you should take this relationship. You're a good boy, a fine young man. You'll know what to do about it."

"Just remember, Jesus hung out with prostitutes and tax collectors and robbers and all kinds of questionable characters. And if he didn't, we wouldn't have the conversion story of the woman at the well, or Zacchaeus, or the thief on the cross. Following Christ's example, we are to love and witness to all people, regardless of how they look, or what they do, or their ungodly behaviors. That's how the gospel will be spread."

"You're right, son, of course you are. But just be careful. Sometimes temptations come disguised as honorable intentions."

"Thanks, Mom. I'll be fine. It's just a picnic and some conversation."

"Like I said," Dana put in. "Quote I Corinthians 10:13 before you go. Better pray over it too."

CHAPTER 12

———— ❧ ————

The Three Rs

Misty didn't know what to wear. She tried on several different outfits. Shorts and halter tops. Cutoff jeans and T-shirts. Capris and tank tops. Capris and button-down shirts. A skirt? No, definitely not a skirt. Bra or no bra. No bra. Definitely no bra.

Cooper stepped out of the shower and dried off. He stepped into a clean pair of jeans and draped a towel around his shoulders. He walked down the hall to his bedroom and dug a Wichita State T-shirt out of his dresser drawer. He tossed it aside and reached for a short-sleeved, button-down shirt instead. Then he put on his socks, good boots, and a belt. Back in the bathroom, he towel-dried his hair and shaved. He thought about splashing on some aftershave but decided against it, then at the last minute put some on anyway. He ran a comb through his damp hair, put his wet towels into the hamper, and turned out the light.

As he passed through the living room, he saw that his dad's afghan had slipped off him as he slept. He picked it up off the floor, shook it out, and gently laid it back over his dad. Walt made a smacking noise with his mouth, settled deeper into the recliner, and resumed his nap. Coop thought he looked small in that big chair. He didn't used to.

Coop glanced over at the empty dog bed next to Dad's chair. He wondered how Riley was doing, after his X-rays this afternoon. He put in a quick call to Doc Larson. Becky answered, and she assured him that Riley was coming out of sedation just fine. It was the truth, but not the whole truth. She said Doc would call him in the morning.

"Okay, thanks, Becky. I'll see you Sunday morning." Coop walked into the kitchen to get the bag of picnic items he had packed. His mom was peeling potatoes, and he said goodbye to her and kissed her on the cheek. She smiled and said, "Have fun, Coop. Be careful. I love you."

"Love you too, Mom. I won't be out late."

Cooper walked to his truck and opened the passenger door. He brushed some straw off the seat and put the bag of food on the floor. He noticed a folded piece of paper taped to his steering wheel. He walked around to the driver's door, opened it, and brought the paper out to read. He recognized Dana's handwriting right away. On the outside it said, "In case you forgot." When he opened up the paper to the inside he read, "I Corinthians 10:13, There hath no temptation taken you but such as man can bear: but God is faithful, who will not suffer you to be tempted above that ye are able; but will with the temptation make also the way of escape, that ye may be able to endure it. READ. REPEAT. REMEMBER." She signed it with a smiley face.

He smiled, shook his head, laid the paper on the passenger seat, and drove off to town.

CHAPTER 13

No Holds

Becky checked on Riley one last time before she locked up the office for the day. He seemed to be recovering, but it was slower than was expected. He hadn't tried to stand yet, and he seemed content to sleep and rest. She filled his water bowl and placed it near him. He hadn't eaten yet, but every once in a while he would raise his head enough to drink. But that was all right. He would start to eat when he felt more like himself. Doc Larson and his wife would come over several times in the night to monitor his recovery. In the morning, Doc would call Cooper and give him the news.

She had seen the X-rays. She knew the diagnosis was going to be hard on Cooper and the Smith family. There weren't very many options for care, and since Riley was already approaching old age, well, Doc would have to talk with Cooper about side effects, quality of life, and even life expectancy. It was going to be a hard conversation.

Becky backed her car out of the parking spot and headed across town to her mom's to pick up Jenny. Friday nights were always special. She and Jenny would go out for supper, then rent a movie and watch at home, with popcorn, or maybe root beer floats. Tonight, it was Jenny's turn to pick the restaurant and the movie. That would probably mean a Disney princess, but that was fine with Becky. She found those princesses strong characters, and she didn't mind that Jenny used them as role models.

She noticed a red pickup parked outside the diner as she drove past. It reminded her of Cooper's truck. She wondered if he was having supper at the diner. *Don't be silly*, she thought. *There are lots of red pickups in this town. Chances are it isn't Cooper at all.*

She was stopped at the stoplight and saw him leaving the diner with a woman. The woman was tall, with long legs made to look even longer by the briefness of her cut-off jean shorts. She had very long black hair caught up in a ponytail on the top of her head. They were laughing as Coop held the passenger door open for her. Becky thought they made an odd-looking couple. He was tall and blond, nicely dressed in jeans and a cotton shirt. She was tall, very dark, and dressed in almost nothing.

Becky couldn't help but feel a twinge of disappointment. Then she again chastised herself. There was absolutely no reason why she should feel like this. Jealousy and insecurity were totally out of place at this point. She had no holds on Cooper Smith, and to even imagine that she did was childish and ridiculous.

She couldn't stop herself from wondering, though. Was he serious about that woman? Was it a long-standing, ongoing kind of thing? And why did it matter to her?

Jenny was excited to go out to eat. Friday was her special day with Mommy. She loved having time together, just the two of them. She already knew which Disney movie she wanted to pick. *Beauty and the Beast* was her favorite, and she didn't care that she had seen it at least half a dozen times already. She hadn't decided where she wanted to eat, though. Usually she asked for chicken nuggets, but tonight she thought maybe she wanted something different. Her next choice would be pasta, but Mommy wasn't fond of mac and cheese too often. So maybe lasagna. Yes, lasagna would be great. Maybe they could take a trip to Olive Garden, in Atkins, the next town over. They had been there once, but Mommy said she wanted to save it for a special occasion, because it cost a lot of money. Well, she would ask anyway. It would be fun to pretend that tonight was a special night.

But Mommy said no. Instead, they went to Fazolli's. It was a new place that had just opened in Winslow, and they decided they wanted to try it out. They had lasagna and salad and lots of breadsticks. They laughed about silly things and talked about things important to a four-year-old. They started making plans for Jenny's birthday, which was coming in a few weeks. Then they went to rent a movie from the Redbox. Jenny was happy that *Beauty and the Beast* was available.

Jenny got into her pajamas, and Becky changed out of her work clothes. They snuggled together on the couch watching the movie and eating popcorn. Jenny concentrated on singing along to all the songs. Becky's mind wandered to Coop once again. She wondered where they had gone and what they were doing.

CHAPTER 14

A Way to Escape

Misty picked up a piece of paper that was lying on the passenger seat of Coop's truck. As he walked around the truck to get in, she read what Dana had written. "What's this?" she asked while Cooper put on his seatbelt.

"Oh, that's just a note my sister Dana wrote to me. She wants me to memorize that verse. What she doesn't know is that I already memorized it years ago."

"You have this memorized? Then say it," Misty challenged him.

Cooper quoted the verse to her, but using the King James Version instead of the American Standard that Dana had written. Misty corrected him, "You got it mostly right, but some of the words are not exactly the same."

"That's because when I memorized it, I was using the King James Bible. Dana likes American Standard better. Which version do you prefer?" He started up the truck, checked for traffic, and pulled out into the street.

"I don't. They're all the same to me. Boring. Pointless. Not much of a story. I gave up reading that stuff a long time ago."

"Oh, I'm sorry you feel that way. I think the Bible has some amazing drama and adventure stories. But the life of Jesus—well, now, that's the greatest story ever told."

"You mean you believe it? Virgin birth, healings, 'coming back to life' stuff?" she asked with a hint of disgust in her voice.

"I do," Coop said. "And believing it changed my life. I once was lost but now I'm found, was blind but now I see. Believing in Jesus and the forgiveness of sins has given me an eternal purpose and a heavenly home."

Misty was beginning to feel uncomfortable. This wasn't going in the direction she had anticipated. She needed to change the subject fast.

"You said we were going to the lake. Do you mean Dooley Lake? I remember going there for senior skip day, back in high school. We had a blast. Were you there?"

"Yes, Dooley Lake. There's some picnic tables over on the west end of the lake. I thought we'd go there first, and then maybe hike around the lake some. If that's all right with you." He glanced down at her feet and saw that she was wearing sandals, not the best shoes for rough hiking. Oh well, maybe the hike idea wasn't going to work out. "And yes, I went on senior skip. What I remember most about that day was a volleyball game down on the beach, and then everyone went swimming. What do you remember?"

"I remember watching the volleyball game for a while, then sneaking off with Ricky Coleman and smoking in the woods. We never got caught either!"

"Oh, I remember Ricky. He was in my shop class, and industrial arts too. I wonder what ever happened to him. I haven't heard anything about him since school got out."

"I don't know," she said. "I haven't kept up with any of those kids. I just knew I wanted out of this boring small town, and I left it all behind. California is awesome. Have you ever been there?"

Cooper turned into the parking lot on the west side of the lake. "No, I've never been to California. The furthest west I've gone was to Denver for a teen youth conference. I liked Denver. But I really prefer Kansas small towns. I need space, fresh air, and wide-open skies. You can't beat the Kansas sky for studying the stars."

"Yeah, you hardly ever see the stars in California. Too much smog most of the time, and then there's all the city lights that dim out the starlight. But there's so much to do in California. You've got ocean, mountains, skiing, swimming, the cities, and tourist trap villages. It's got it all. I'd go back in a heartbeat, if I could find a job, and afford to live there. It's even worse there than in New York City."

"So you'd never settle down here?" Coop asked as he parked the truck.

"Hell no," she exclaimed. "There's no work for me here. I'd only land here if I had a very good reason." She got out of the truck and carried the picnic things Cooper had packed and the drink cooler she had brought along. Cooper took a blanket out of the back of the truck. He threw it over a picnic table in the shade and started to unpack the food. Misty sat on the bench across from him so they could share the food and talk comfortably. "I brought root beer," she said as she unpacked the cans from her cooler. I haven't had any for years. When you mentioned it the other day I thought, *That sounds good.*"

"Before we eat, I'd like to say a blessing. Would you pray with me?" Cooper asked.

"Um, okay. Yeah, sure." Misty shyly lowered her eyes. She didn't know what to do with her hands, so she just let them lay on her lap.

"We thank you, Lord, for this beautiful day and this beautiful place. We ask that you bless this food and our conversation. Thank you for Misty and our new friendship. Give her wisdom as she makes decisions for her future. In Jesus name we pray, Amen."

"That was nice. Do you do that before every meal? I noticed your sister prayed at the diner the other day."

"Yes, I talk to Jesus a lot throughout the day. But at mealtime especially, I take the time to thank him for all he has blessed me with. Like these sandwiches, and watermelon and root beer, and a new friend."

As they ate their food, the conversation covered many topics. Coop learned that he didn't know most of the people she called her school homies. She didn't know most of his friends either, just by name. Winslow High School had students from all over the county and was a fairly big school, so it was no surprise that they hadn't really known each other. He learned that she lived with her dad, when she was here in Kansas, but that she was unhappy with the living situation and wished she could move out. He was surprised to learn that she remembered when his brother Patrick had died in the sledding accident.

"Yes, it was sure a hard time for our family. We couldn't have made it without the help of our pastor, and the community. And believing that we'll see Patrick again in Heaven, well, that really helped." He paused and noticed that there was a blank, almost uninterested look on Misty's face. Then he went on to explain further. "Knowing that there's a Heaven can really help lessen pain. And now we're facing the end of Dad's life, so we're dealing with death once again."

Misty was paying attention now. "What's wrong with your Dad?" She reached across the table and touched his hand. He looked into her eyes and saw a compassion that rather surprised him. Maybe she wasn't as tough as she tried to portray.

"He has cancer. He's been through chemo and radiation, and it worked for a while. But then it came back, and Dad has decided to let it run its course. The doctors said it will probably be only months." He looked down and paused.

Misty noticed that he hadn't pulled his hand away, so she started making little circles on the back of it with her thumb. Cooper thought the motion was comforting. Misty thought it was sexy, and hoped it would lead to touching of a different kind.

"I'm so sorry you're going through this," she said softly. "I know it's hard. My mom didn't die, but she just packed up and left. Never heard from her again. So it's practically like she's dead. She might even be, for all I know."

"I'm sorry too. When did that happen?" Coop was watching her thumb moving in hypnotizing circles.

"Right after I got to California. She did write me a letter, telling me she was leaving dad. No reasons given. Just goodbye. Oh, and she did tell me to stay in school and get my degree and get out of Kansas! And find myself a decent man."

"Well, she'll be happy to know that you're finished with school." He started packing up the picnic things. "If we're going to take a walk, we better get going. We don't want to be halfway around when it starts to get dark."

Misty took the empty drink cans to the recycling trash can and came back in time to help Coop fold up the blanket. They put the things into the truck and started off on a trail that would wind around the lake. They went slow, and stayed on the trail, because of Misty's footwear. "If you had boots on," Coop said, "I'd take you off the trail. There's this hidden path that leads to a meadow that's closed off from the rest of the trail. I've seen lots of wildlife there. Rabbits and deer, of course, and foxes too. Raccoons, possums, even a skunk family one time. I like to go and just sit there sometimes. Just sit and wait for something to come out of the woods. It's really neat."

"Ever see a bear?"

"Nope. No bear. I did see an elk once though. He was huge!"

Just then Misty lost her footing on the loose gravel and slipped sideways. Coop caught her by the elbow and pulled her tightly to his side. "Careful there. Don't want you to fall. Are you all right? Maybe we should turn back."

Misty moved in close to his side and said, "I'm okay. Just slipped. Maybe if you hold my hand, I'll be safer."

So they walked on, holding hands and talking the whole way around the lake. The sun was slipping behind the trees when they got back to the parking lot. Coop unlocked the truck and opened the door for Misty. Before she climbed in, Misty put her arms around Coop's neck and pulled him close. She gave him a quick kiss on the lips. "Thank you for keeping me safe."

She hopped into the truck, and Coop took a step back. The kiss had surprised him. And it was a nice surprise. He closed her door and went around to his side. He was surprised again when he saw that Misty was sitting in the middle of the bench seat, not on the passenger side. When he slammed his door shut, she leaned in to him and put her head on his shoulder. "Let's just sit here awhile, okay? We should be able to see the sunset over the lake."

"Well, okay, if you want." Coop put his arm around Misty's shoulder and she snuggled into him, laying her head on his chest and wrapping her right arm around his waist. "Mmmm, you smell good."

Coop didn't know what to say, so he said nothing. He looked down at the tattoo on her arm and said, "That's pretty neat. Did it hurt?"

"There was a little bit of pain involved, but it was worth it. I really love it. Sometimes pain leads to pleasure." She pinched Cooper's hip and he yelped. Then she turned her head and kissed Cooper gently on his cheek. "See, pain leads to pleasure."

Coop chuckled slightly.

"I'm thinking about getting another one on my left arm. Only this time I want a snake. What do you think?"

"I think it's your decision. But I also think that God created man, and woman, and said it was good. So if he was satisfied, why would we need to add anything?"

"For the same reason women wear eye makeup or dye our hair, or paint our fingernails. It makes us feel good.

It gets us attention. Sometimes it's to attract a mate. It's beautiful."

"Hmmm, well, I still think natural is beautiful."

"So you don't like it?" She sounded hurt.

"No, I don't mean that. It's very pretty, in an artsy sort of way. I'm just saying that I would be just as attracted to a woman who demonstrated the beauty of God's natural creation without having to feel she needed to change it or improve it. But that's just me. I also think you can do whatever you want, if it makes you happy and doesn't hurt anyone else."

"Oh, believe me, this didn't hurt anyone else. In fact, it made Mic the artist very happy. I paid him handsomely. With cash and personal favors, and I became his personal free walking advertisement. I got the art and he got lucky."

They fell into a silence as the sun's beams hit the water. Streaks of red, pink, and purple lit up the horizon and colors reflected in the water. "Talk about art," said Coop. "Just look at that gorgeous sunset. God is the most amazing artist I know. I'm glad we stayed to watch this."

"Me too," Misty sighed. "I'll never forget it." She stroked her hand over Cooper's long muscular thigh. She felt him quiver involuntarily. She smiled and thought, *Baby, if you like that, there's lots more to come.*

"So, Coop, tell me about your old girlfriends." Misty chuckled. "I bet none of them had tattoos!"

"Well, I haven't really had many girlfriends. I dated a bit in college, and as I think about it now, one of those girls did have a tattoo. It was a flower, a rose I think, and it was right here on her collarbone." He touched her and tickled her with his finger. She giggled and squirmed a little, and as she did so, the shoulder of her T-shirt slipped down. If he hadn't noticed before, it was now obvious that she wasn't wearing a bra. She smiled, wondering if hers were the first breasts he'd ever gotten a glimpse of. Hopefully he'll get more than just a glimpse. Maybe not tonight, but soon.

She shifted in the seat and moved so that she was facing him. They sat closely, face-to-face, chest to chest. Her nipples were hard and pointed through the thin T-shirt material. She reached up with both hands, pulled his face down to hers, and kissed him deeply. He was hesitant, but he responded. With her eyes locked on his, she found his hand and lifted it to her breast. It was an open invitation, and she made it clear with her intense gaze what she wanted him to do.

They were interrupted by the ringing of Coop's cell phone. He started to reach for it on the dash, but Misty caught his hand. "No, baby, don't stop," she pleaded. But Cooper had come out of his trance, and he said, "I have to get it. It might be important. Maybe about dad."

Misty sighed and sat upright, moving away from him and straightening her shirt. He answered the phone. It was Doc Larson. "I'm sorry to bother you, Coop, but I thought you'd want to know. Riley had a seizure just now. It didn't last long, and he's sleeping now, which is normal. It was probably a reaction to the anesthesia I had to give him for the X-rays. I'm going to sleep here on a mat near him, so I can be close if he needs me in the night. Can you come in about seven in the morning? We can talk more then."

Coop was visibly shaken. Riley had never had a seizure before. "You sure he's okay? He'll be all right?"

Misty paid attention. Coop was quite upset. Was it his dad?"

"Sure, I can be there at seven. And thanks, Doc. I'm really glad you called."

When Coop slipped the phone into his pocket, he turned to Misty and said, "I think we better be getting home. I'll have to get up early in the morning."

"Why? Was that about your dad? Did something happen? Is he okay?"

"Oh, no, it wasn't Dad. It was about Riley, our dog. He's at the vet's for some tests, and he had a seizure tonight. Doc wanted me to know."

"Oh well, thank goodness it was just your dog. I was really worried. But a dog, well, that's not so bad."

Cooper started up the truck. "Better buckle your seatbelt," he said, and he fastened his own. Misty slid over near the passenger door and clicked her belt.

"Riley's been a part of our family for twelve years. If anything happens to him, it will be like losing a best friend. Our family is dealing with so much right now. We don't need one more bit of sadness."

"I'm sorry. I just have never been attached to a pet, so I can't imagine how it would feel to worry about one. My dad always said dogs were not worth the trouble, always barking and peeing in the house. And expensive. We had one once when I was in maybe first grade. I don't know what ever happened to him. One day he was just gone. I don't even remember its name."

Cooper drove on in silence until they got to town. "Where should I drop you off? Want me to take you to your dad's house?"

"No, actually, just drop me at the diner. I'll go in and get some coffee and see what's going on. Then I'll walk home."

"You sure? It's gonna be real dark soon. I could drive you."

"I'm a big girl, Coop. I walk home after work every night. Don't you worry about me." As they approached the diner and parked in front, she turned to Cooper and said, "I had a good time tonight. It was fun. Next time I'll wear better shoes, and you can take me to that magical meadow. And maybe we can get to know each other even better." She winked at him and got out of the truck. "Call me," she said, slammed the door, and walked into the diner.

When Coop pulled away, he noticed that her little cooler was still on the floor of the truck. Well, he'd have to get that back to her later. He really wanted to get home. He glanced down at the floor once more and saw Dana's paper lying there, and he recalled the verse she had written out for him. As he thought about how his evening had progressed, he was overcome with emotion. Had he been overtaken by temptation? Well, yes, it did seem to be headed in that direction. It had happened so suddenly, so easily. Misty may have initiated it, but he had followed blindly. Like falling off a cliff, once he started falling, there wasn't much he could do to stop it. Thank goodness the phone call had interrupted them.

That phone call! Oh thank you, God, for that phone call! It was all so clear to him now. That phone call was obviously of God. He had really made a way to escape. Just like the verse said! Praise God! Thank you, Jesus! "Oh Lord, you are my shield and my protector. Thank you for getting me out of a situation I may not have managed so well on my own. Help me to lean on you more, to follow your leading more closely. Help me to be a better witness to Misty. I thought we were making progress, with talking about Scripture and prayer. But I fell right into the trap of the devil. Please, God, forgive my weaknesses, and help me to stand strong in the face of temptation in the future."

He drove down the long driveway to the farmhouse. He wondered if Dana was still awake. He had a lot to tell her. She would be so worried about Riley.

Misty walked behind the counter, poured herself a coffee to go, and headed out the door. She wasn't going home, though. She was going to visit Patch. He would know how to take care of her.

CHAPTER 15

———— ✺ ————

Difficult Decisions

Coop parked his truck near the entrance to the vet's office. There were no other cars in the parking lot, being early on Saturday morning. He could see lights on in the office, and he knew that Doc was there. He had promised to sleep near Riley all night. The door was unlocked, and Coop walked right in. Doc came out from the back-office area. His clothes were rumpled, and his hair had obviously been smoothed down, not combed. He looked tired and worried. He welcomed Coop and asked him to have a seat in the lobby. "I was just about to pour myself a cup of coffee. Do you want some?"

"Sure, thanks." Coop sat back in his chair to wait for Doc. It was unsettlingly quiet in the waiting room. From somewhere in the back came the high-pitched meowing of a cat. He strained to hear but caught no indication that Riley was awake.

Doc returned with two steaming cups of coffee. He sat them on an end table beside Coop and took a seat nearby. "How's your dad doing this morning?" he asked.

"He was still asleep when I left," Coop answered. "So how's Riley? Is he ready to go home? Does he need a different medicine for his arthritis?"

"Coop, I'm sorry to tell you this, but the X-rays showed that Riley has a bigger problem than arthritis. He has some tumors along the bones of his legs. It's bone cancer."

Doc paused for a minute, to let the diagnosis sink in. "There are a few things we can do, but none of our options give him much time."

"What do you do for bone cancer in a dog? Is it like with people, you start chemo and radiation? What do you think is best?"

"We don't recommend either chemo or radiation for bone cancer. What's usually done is amputation of the affected limb. Riley's left front leg is most affected, but there is a small tumor on his left hind leg as well. And honestly, the prognosis after amputation isn't very good. It usually just buys a little time, like six months or so."

"Oh man, that's not very long."

"Now, I've seen many dogs do well with just three legs. Most can compensate quite easily. And there's always wheeled carts that can be fitted, to help him get around. But we would still be talking about just months." Doc Larson took a long drink of his coffee. "I know it's a lot to think about."

"If we did nothing, how long do we have?" Coop didn't want to think about this at all.

"It's hard to say. I could give you a prescription for pain, but he will still have difficulty getting up off the ground and walking. There's a big chance that the bone would break, if he fell or jumped. He would be very limited as to activities. It might come to a point where you would have to lift him up to take him to the bathroom. And then there's the likelihood that the cancer will spread to other parts of his body. I would say that, without amputation, he has less than three months. Amputation would give him another six months. Either way it's not long. You need to prepare for the next step."

Coop gulped, "You mean we need to put him to sleep?"

"I'm afraid it's going to come to that. It's up to you to decide when, and what we do in the meantime."

Coop thought a moment, then asked, "If I took him home, would you give us some prescriptions for pain or something to keep him more comfortable? I'm thinking I'd want to take him home for a while, before we put him down. To give us some time with him, you know. I mean, I need to talk to the rest of the family too. This is going to be hard on everyone. Riley's been in our family a long time." He couldn't keep the emotion out of his voice.

Doc Larson put his hand on Coop's shoulder. "I sure understand what you're feeling. It's never easy to make a decision like this. Yes, he could go home and take some pain medications. It won't cure anything, of course, but it can make the next weeks more comfortable. Then, when you all are ready, we could do the euthanasia. It's a simple procedure, just an injection. We can do it here in the office, or I can come out to your place do to it. Many people choose to do it at home, where there's less stress on everyone."

"This is going to kill Dana."

"Let her spend some time with Riley, say her goodbyes. She needs to be part of this decision too."

"Well, I think I can positively say that we won't be doing the amputation. It wouldn't give us that much more time, and besides that, I don't think Riley would like it. And there's the expense too. We also have a lot of other doctor bills to deal with." Cooper was thinking about his dad, and the stack of hospital bills that was slowly getting chiseled down.

"I understand, and I agree that under the circumstances, that's a good choice. Well, I'll get you some pain medication, and then get Riley ready to go home." Doc stood up, shook Coop's hand, and patted him on the shoulder. "It's hard, I know. But you have given Riley a great home, a life on the farm that he loved, and now you're going to do the best you can to give him love in his last days. He will appreciate it." Doc left the lobby to go in the back to get some medications. When he came back, he found Cooper sitting with his head bowed in prayer.

CHAPTER 16

No Condemnation

Becky was looking through her closet, trying to decide what to wear Sunday. Normally she wore some dress pants and a pretty blouse, but she was thinking that this Sunday she might want to wear a skirt. She realized that she was trying to look extra nice, and she was slightly bothered by the fact. Shouldn't she just be satisfied to be herself? Why was she trying to make a good impression? In fact, who was she trying to impress? And why did she feel the need to impress anyone anyway?

When Becky thought back on the last five years, she did have to marvel at how much she had changed. Her opinion of herself used to be so wrapped up in what she thought other people thought of her. She entered college her freshman year, eager to fit in, be accepted by the popular kids, make friends, and be invited to all the best parties. She did her hair and makeup, carefully selected her clothing, even changed the way she talked. All to impress her classmates. And it worked. For a while anyway.

Derek was older, very popular, very sure of himself, and drop-dead gorgeous. When he paid attention to her, Becky melted. He made her feel so confident, so accepted, and so included in the college crowd.

When they first got intimately involved, Becky had felt very special. She told her mom about him, but she kept the sex privately to herself. Deep down, she knew that her mother would not approve of sex before marriage, and she knew that she probably should not be doing it anyway, with or without her mother's okay. There was an element of guilt and cheapness when she made love with Derek. But the excitement, the pure thrill of being chosen by him, well, she just couldn't resist. And to be honest, she did enjoy the sex. Being with Derek opened up a whole new part of herself that she had only read about in paperback romances. This was far better than a novel, she thought. It was real.

But Derek didn't think it was real. He tossed her aside like a rotten apple. He was even angry, telling her she had gotten pregnant on purpose, and he wasn't going to let this ruin his life. He didn't offer to help in any way. He didn't even suggest she get an abortion. He just walked away, leaving her totally deserted. Becky was devastated.

She didn't tell her mother about the pregnancy until it got to the point where she had to. Overcome with fear, she finally admitted to her mother that she was pregnant, and that Derek was no longer interested.

Talking with Dr. Whitefield had done her worlds of good. The guilt and self-loathing had pushed Becky to the point of depression. She felt worthless and was withdrawing from things that used to bring her happiness. It was a good thing that Dr. Whitefield had been recommended.

Who knows where she would be now if she hadn't had Dr. Whitefield to show her the way out of her depression?

She had explained, in a very gentle way, that Jesus did not condemn her, and that the pregnancy was not a punishment for her sin. It was a consequence of her choice, but not God's way of wagging his finger at her in displeasure. He wouldn't do that. God is love. He could grieve over her choices, and care about how the consequences could make her life more difficult, and how they didn't fit with the perfect plan he had for her. He had allowed her free will, the freedom to choose her own actions. But now she would be living with her choices. He did not condemn her. He loved her unconditionally.

She went on to say that the same consequences that Becky had been considering to be utterly unacceptable evidence of sin could, in fact, be priceless growth opportunities. Repentance would lead to forgiveness, and forgiveness leads to the outpouring of God's grace. "Our consequences can be priceless growth opportunities that mature us and point us back to the infallibility of Scripture," she said. "Draw close to Christ, Becky. He offers you forgiveness and unconditional love. He will bless you in unexpected ways."

It took a few weeks of self-reflection and prayer, but Becky did accept the forgiveness Jesus offered her. She prayed in her room, with her hand resting on her unborn child. "Jesus, thank you for loving me anyway. Thank you for dying for my sins, all of them. The sin of immorality, the sin of doubt, the sin of self-condemnation. I ask your forgiveness for them all, and others that I ask you to reveal to me. I trust you. With your help, I can be a good mother to this little girl. I ask you to guide me as I raise her, and teach her about you."

At her next session with Dr. Whitefield, Becky told her about her decision to pray for forgiveness and accept Christ. The older woman was pleased, and gave Becky a long hug. "Now, you know you will never be alone. There's no need to fear what the future holds for you, and your baby, because God will be with you. Deuteronomy 31:8 says, 'The Lord himself goes before you and will be with you. He will never leave you nor forsake you. Do not be afraid; do not be discouraged.'"

"Thank you, Dr. Whitefield. I finally realized that if God can love me no matter what, then I should accept myself. I can't worry about what other people think, because the only opinion that matters is God's, and he loves me and accepts me. I'm sure I'll slip back into old thought patterns sometimes, but knowing that Jesus is with me will help me to not be afraid."

Becky thought back on that conversation, from four years ago. She remembered how she had called upon the Lord for courage to walk into her mom's church for the first time, with an infant Jenny in her arms. She remembered fearing raised eyebrows and maybe outright condemnation, yet finding neither. She was welcomed with acceptance and open arms. She was supported as a new mother, befriended by many, and encouraged as a new follower of Christ. Just a year ago, she had been invited to join a group of single moms for Wednesday-night Bible study.

The leaders of the single-moms' group had provided instruction in Scripture applications for her life. She had grown in her faith, and she felt closer to God than ever.

Her new job with Doc Larson was certainly an answer to prayer. She felt that God himself had led her to apply at the vet's office, and that being offered the job was one more affirmation that she was under his wing.

Not that everything was always sunshine and rainbows. Doubts and fears did creep into her thinking from time to time. Like right now. Why was she worried about how she would be accepted in the Sunday school class? The opinion of others was not that important. As long as she was doing her best to follow Christ, live by his example, and trust him, that's all that mattered. Physical appearance and first impressions were not a top priority. She would just be herself.

And that ridiculous moment of jealousy, when she saw Coop with that woman outside the diner, she would put that behind her. "Oh, Lord, remind me that you are working all things for my good. I trust you. I don't want to do anything on my own, without your leading and directing. I know you have a plan for me, a plan that is good. Reveal it to me, in your timing, Lord. Help me be patient."

So Becky decided to wear some lavender dress pants with a pretty flowered blouse. She ironed out some creases, hung the blouse back in her closet, and headed for the shower. Jenny was already asleep, excited about seeing her friends at Sunday school the next morning.

CHAPTER 17

——— ❧ ———

Joys and Sorrows

Coop was getting into the shower too. It had been a long day. The news about Riley had been hard to take. It wasn't what he had been expecting. He wasn't ready to think about having to put him down. Talking with Dana had been difficult, too. She cried and questioned if there was anything else they could do. They decided that they wanted to give Riley the best last days that they could, and that they wanted to be with him at the end. They did not want him to suffer, or be in pain. If the meds didn't seem to be making him comfortable, they would know it was time.

Marla Jean sat near Walter, holding hands, as Coop and Dana talked about Riley. Marla Jean tried not to let the tears slide down her cheeks. Walter squeezed her hand and pulled her close. He spoke, softly, "I wish I was a dog." She didn't ask for an explanation.

Cooper had carried Riley from Doc's office to his truck and laid him on the back seat. Riley had looked up at him with his trusting big brown eyes. His tail thumped on the back of the seat, and he raised his head slightly to see out

99

the window. Riley had always loved hanging his head out of the window, and he loved the wind blowing through his hair. But today, he was satisfied to rest on the seat and let the wind circulate around him.

He spent most of the rest of the day sleeping on the mat near Walter's chair. When he got up to go outside, his movements were slow and deliberate. But he was able to walk, seemingly without pain, and did his business outside, then walked around the yard a bit. When Coop called him, he came right to the door. He was almost acting normal by evening. Coop gave him his bedtime medication, made sure his water bowl was filled, and went to his room to get ready for bed. After his shower, he pulled his Bible from the shelf and looked in the concordance. He wanted to find the verse about Jesus being the same yesterday, today, and tomorrow.

"Ah, here it is. Hebrews 13:8." He copied it into his journal and began to meditate on the words. After a few minutes, he wrote down his thoughts: *There have been joys in my life, and there have been sorrows. I know I'm going to have some more sorrows before long. (Hopefully, I'll have more joys too.) The one thing that never changes is that Jesus is with me through it all.*

Never one to dwell on the sorrows, Cooper let his mind wander to some joys. Tomorrow was Sunday. That was always a day to rejoice. He always looked forward to fellowship with his friends at Sunday school, and tomorrow he would introduce them to Becky. He was looking forward to seeing her again. It would be nice to get to know her better. Then he would go into the sanctuary to worship. Coop always got so much out of the praise team's songs, and he often felt the Spirit of God moving through the music. The familiar words of the old hymns brought him reassurance and comfort.

He wondered if Becky would feel comfortable sitting with him during the service. Well, he'd ask her and see.

CHAPTER 18

Getting to Know You

Coop was waiting in the church worship center near the door. He was drinking a cup of coffee, chatting with some friends, and watching for Becky. Right on time, he saw her walking up the sidewalk, holding hands with Jenny. He immediately noticed her brown hair, shining in the sunlight. She was laughing at something Jenny had said, and her face was glowing with a big smile. He excused himself from his friends, set his coffee cup in the sink, and went to hold the door open for Becky and Jenny.

"Hi, Becky! Right on time. Good morning, Jenny. Are you ready to go to your Sunday school class?"

Jenny still held Becky's hand but nodded. Coop led the way to the children's area, where they got Jenny registered. Becky hugged Jenny goodbye, promised to pick her up after church, and turned to walk with Coop down the hall toward the adult classrooms.

"I'm so glad to see you, Becky. Glad you could come today. I think you'll like this class. Romans is an amazing book, and this study has really helped me a lot."

"I know Romans a little. Some of my favorite verses come from Romans." Becky looked up at him and smiled. *Man, he's really, really tall*, she thought. He must have been reading her mind, because he laughed and said, "Jeez, I didn't know you were so short."

"It's just because your boots have heels, and I'm only wearing flats!" She gave him a friendly punch in the arm. "How tall are you, anyway?"

"Well, in these boots, probably six foot two. How short are you?"

"I'm a perfect five feet tall. Wouldn't have it any other way!"

"Jenny looks pretty tall for a five-year-old. Did she get her height from her father?" he asked, and then wished that he hadn't. Maybe he was prying, or bringing up a subject she didn't want to talk about.

Becky didn't look uncomfortable, though. "Yes, I think she did. He was pretty tall. Not over six feet, though."

Coop ushered her into the classroom, where several young people were gathered in small groups, chatting before the class got started. Many turned and looked at them as they entered the room. A couple came over and introduced themselves as Greg and Nancy Martin, and they welcomed Becky to the class. When they heard Becky's last name, Nancy asked, "Emerson? Do you have a daughter named Jenny?"

"Why, yes I do. How did you know?"

"We have a daughter who's in Jenny's class on Wednesday nights. We volunteer as helpers in the classroom once a month or so. Jenny is a really sweet little girl. She'll be in kindergarten this fall, right? So will Hannah. Maybe we should get them together sometime before school starts. Maybe at the park, or our pool."

They took their seats as the teacher moved to the front of the classroom. Becky sat between Coop and Nancy. "We'll talk more later," Nancy said and Becky nodded.

The class started with prayer and as Becky bowed her head, she noticed that Greg and Nancy were holding hands. She felt Coop's arm pressed lightly along her arm, and his leg touching hers. She took a deep breath and sighed quietly. Coop noticed.

After prayer, Coop stood and introduced Becky to the class. The teacher invited her to stand also, and tell something about herself. She stood beside Coop and said, "I'm Becky Emerson. Oh I guess Coop already said that!" She chuckled a little nervously. The rest of the class smiled reassuringly. "I am a vet tech working with Doc Larson. I have a daughter named Jenny who is almost five." She smiled down at Nancy. "I've been going to the single-moms' group for a couple of years and really get a lot out of it. When Coop invited me to come to this class, I thought I'd give it a try. It's interesting that you are studying Romans, because it was a verse in Romans that led me to accept Christ as my Savior. So I'm looking forward to learning more. Thanks." She sat down and only then realized that she was shaking a little. Coop reached over and patted her knee.

The teacher, David Cole, asked her, "If you don't mind, Becky, could you tell us which verse you're talking about? And maybe what the verse means to you?"

"It was Romans 8:1, the verse that says there's no condemnation for those who are in Christ Jesus. It's special to me because, well, because I have done a lot of things that

I felt condemned for. I even condemned myself. But when I realized that Jesus forgave me, died for me, and loves me no matter what I had done, then I thought, if he doesn't condemn me, then why should I condemn myself? I had a life-changing conversation with myself, accepted Christ as my Savior, and here I am."

"Thank you, Becky," said Mr. Cole. "Would anyone else like to discuss this verse? We covered it a couple of weeks ago, and maybe you have had a chance to think about it and apply it to your own life. Anyone?"

A discussion followed, in which almost everyone participated. The time flew by, and before long it was time to leave. Before class was dismissed, Mr. Cole asked them all to stand, take hands, and close with a prayer of benediction. He asked Coop to pray, and with Becky's hand in his, Coop prayed and then led the class in the Lord's Prayer. His voice was strong and confident, and as Becky recited the prayer beside him, she felt a stirring in her soul. Coop might have felt it too, because when they said "Amen," he gave her hand a little squeeze. She felt warm all over.

As they filed out of the classroom, several people spoke to Becky and said it was nice to have her in class. Mr. Cole said he hoped she would be back the next week, and Becky thanked him and said she'd like that very much.

Coop took her by the elbow and led her out of the room. "Well, I'd say they like you! Did you enjoy the class?"

"I did. Everyone is so nice and welcoming. The discussion was good too. Lots of new insights. Thanks for inviting me. I don't know why I didn't get involved long before this. I've always been kinda shy about doing new things."

"Shy? I sure wouldn't say that you were shy today. You had some great things to say, and you said them very confidently. I think you added a lot to the class discussion. It was great to have you there." They were almost to the sanctuary, and Coop asked her, "Would you like to sit with me during the service? Or do you have other people to sit with?"

"Oh, I usually sit by myself. I'd be glad to sit with you. I usually sit in the middle on the choir side. I like to listen to Mom sing. Where do you like to sit?"

"I'm usually on the opposite side. Which explains why I haven't run into you here before. But I'd be glad to sit near the choir with you. You pick the row."

Becky led the way, and they were seated just as the opening music began. Coop's mom was playing a beautiful prelude on the organ. The congregation quieted and settled into their seats for worship. Becky looked up into the choir loft and saw her mother smiling at her. Mrs. Emerson gave a wink, and Becky smiled back.

Coop sang the hymns with a strong bass voice. Becky's soprano was soft but note perfect on the melody. They shared a hymnal as they stood to sing and the fingers on Coop's large hand touched Becky's, giving her a pleasant shock. When it was time for the Scripture reading, Coop opened his Bible and quickly found the passage, then leaned close to Becky so she could read along. During the sermon, Becky wrote some notes on the back of her bulletin. Coop noticed and nodded to himself.

When the service was over, Coop walked with Becky to pick up Jenny from the children's area. There they ran into Greg and Nancy, who were also picking up their daughter

Hannah. Greg said, "Hey, I've got an idea. Why don't we all go out for lunch?"

"Gee, that sounds great, Greg, but I don't think I can today. I need to get Mom home, and I have some things I have to do." Coop looked at Becky and said, "But maybe next week? Maybe the four of us could go out somewhere after church?"

Two little girls came through the door laughing at some little girl humor. Nancy looked at Coop and said, "I think you mean the six of us!"

"Oh, well, yes, I guess I do. I'm sorry. I'm just not used to having littles around."

Greg smacked him on the back and said, "Better get used to it, Coop."

Becky laughed and said, "I think we would like that. As long as we go somewhere that is kid friendly!"

"Oh yeah, that's definitely a priority for us too," Nancy said. "How about the diner? It's decent food, and a good place for kids."

Becky looked at Coop, wondering how he would feel about being there with her and Jenny. After all, he was somehow involved with a woman who was somehow connected to the diner. But he was nodding his head, and he agreed that the food there was good. So it was settled. Next Sunday, after church, party of six.

Coop walked Becky and Jenny to their car and as they walked along, Becky said, "I've been meaning to tell you, I was so sorry about Riley. I saw the X-rays and Doc Larson told me about the options. What did you decide?"

"I brought him home, with some pain meds. We are not going to do amputation. We just want him to be home with us, where he's happy and comfortable. We'll know when it's time to let him go. He was a little groggy yesterday, and didn't eat much. But he drank a good amount of water, and went to the bathroom. That's another reason I need to get home now. Besides checking on Dad, I want to make sure Riley's okay. But thanks for asking about him."

"I've been thinking about him all yesterday and even this morning. This has got to be hard. How is your sister taking it?"

"As to be expected. She's upset, but she wants what will be best for Riley. Well, thanks again for coming to Sunday school with me. I'll see you soon. Bye, Jenny. Be good!"

Jenny giggled, Becky smiled, and Coop moved away from the car. Becky started the engine and drove away with a wave.

Back in the church, Marla Jean and Elizabeth were deep in conversation. Both agreed that their children made a very cute couple.

CHAPTER 19

Under His Wings

Coop was surprised to see Riley lying in the sun on the front porch as he drove up the driveway. "Hey, look at that, Mom. Riley is waiting for us, just like he always used to. Maybe he's feeling better." As they got out of the truck, Riley stood wagging his tail and came over to Marla Jean for an ear rub. It was a very good sign. Marla Jean stood, looked up to the bright blue summer sky, and thanked the Lord.

Dana had stayed behind today, missing church, so she could be home if her dad needed her. Someone needed to stay with him almost all the time now. He was stubborn, and didn't think he needed to be hovered over, but he was unsteady on his feet, especially when he first tried to stand up. So someone needed to help him get his balance and walk beside him as he made his way into the bathroom. So far, he had been able to manage getting on and off the toilet on his own. It helped that they had handicapped rails around the seat. Dana knew she would feel a little odd if she had to help him in there. And she figured he would feel more than a little uncomfortable. But so far, they hadn't had to worry about that.

Dana was in the kitchen taking a chicken pot pie out of the oven. It was bubbling hot, and she sat it down on the table quickly. Even with hot pads on her hands, she could feel the warmth. Marla Jean dropped her choir folder on the piano and went to change out of her Sunday dress. Cooper also changed from his good clothes into jeans and a T-shirt.

They usually had a large dinner on Sundays after church, and then just snacked in the evening. They tried to make it a day of rest, as much as they could. In the tradition of his father, Coop didn't plow or harvest on Sundays. Some chores couldn't be put off, though. He needed to milk Bessie and check on Lolly's twins. It might be a good day to ride his horse around the pastures and check on the fences. That would be relaxing, as well as productive. Maybe Dana would like to ride with him.

Walter sat at the table with the family but only ate a few bites. He listened as Coop and his mother talked about the church service. He smiled when Marla Jean said, "You and Becky looked so cute together. She is so short, and that makes you look so much taller."

"Oh right, I forgot you were meeting her for Sunday school," said Dana. "How did that go? Did she like it?"

"Oh yes, I think she did. She said she'll go back next week. People were nice to her, of course, and she felt welcomed. She met Greg and Nancy, who have a daughter about the same age as her Jenny. So that was good. In fact, we're all going out to lunch next Sunday after church."

"Hey, next Sunday was supposed to be your turn to stay home with Dad." Dana smiled and said, "But that's okay. You go and have fun with your friends. Really. You work so hard around here you deserve to have a nice time once in a while. And I don't mind staying home, really. This morning I watched *Turning Point* on TV, and it was as good as being in church."

"I'm glad you watched something. I wouldn't want you to miss out on Sunday teachings completely." Marla Jean served herself seconds on the pot pie and passed the bowl to Coop, who also took more. He sat it down near Dana and asked her, "I think I'll ride Slick today, out to check the fences. Want to come along?"

"Okay, that sounds like fun. I'll even help you with the milking first, so we can go sooner."

"You sure are a good sister!" Coop joked. "You must want something. You're being awfully nice. There's got to be a reason."

"No reason," she answered. "Just being nice for the sake of being nice. Take it while you can. It might not always be this way!"

Walt got their attention by tapping his fork on the table. Everyone looked at him and he asked Dana, "How's Riley?"

"He seems pretty good today. He got up on his own this morning, came to me and pawed at me, then walked to the door. I let him out, and he stayed out all morning until Mom and Coop came home. I think the pain medicine is making him more comfortable."

"That's good. Don't want him to be in pain."

Marla Jean asked him, "Can you eat a little more, Walt? Or do you want something else? Maybe some applesauce? Or some soup?"

He waved his hand and said, "No, I'm fine. Not really hungry. Nothing sounds good." He looked at Dana. "But I'm sure it *is* good, I'm just not hungry. Sorry."

Dana touched his arm and said, "Don't worry, Dad. You can eat some whenever you get hungry. It's okay. We just want you to try and keep up your strength."

He lifted her hand to his lips and kissed it lightly. "You're a good girl."

Sunday dinner dishes done, Marla Jean went to the piano in the living room and thumbed through her hymnal collection. She was singing softly as Coop and Dana headed outside. Riley followed them out, but lay down in the shade of the big walnut tree in the front yard.

Marla Jean played "We'll Understand It Better by and By." From his recliner across the room, Walter listened. He had always loved hearing his wife play and sing. It was good to hear today; it brought a spirit of peace and comfort into the house. When she was finished, he called her over to sit near him.

"Get the Bible please. Read to me."

"What do you want me to read?" she asked as she reached for Walt's Bible.

"Psalms 91," he said, and settled back into his chair. "It's a good one." She found the place and started to read. "Whoever dwells in the shelter of the Most High will rest in the shadow of the Almighty. I will say of the Lord, 'He is my refuge and my fortress, my God, in whom I trust.'" Marla Jean looked over to her husband. His eyes were closed; his hands were clasped over his chest. He was breathing shallowly, but he was not struggling for breath. He looked peaceful. She read on.

Verse four said, 'under his wings you will find refuge.' When she read that, Walter opened his eyes and asked, "Isn't there a song about that? Being under the wings of Jesus?"

"Yes, it's called "Under His Wings". I have it in one of my books. Would you like me to play it for you?"

"Finish the Psalm, then play it. I would like that."

Marla Jean read on. She particularly liked verse eleven, *For He will command His angels concerning you, to guard you in all your ways.* She set the Bible aside and went back to the piano. Looking through the table of contents in her hymnals, she finally found the song Walter was waiting for. She sang, "Under his wings I am safely abiding, though the night deepens and tempests are wild. Still I can trust him, I know he will keep me, he has redeemed me and I am his child." Her voice was strong and did not falter as she sang the chorus. Walter mouthed the words with her. "Under his wings, my soul shall abide. Safely abide forever."

"I'm not scared, you know," he said, as Marla Jean left the piano to sit near him again. She held his hand and whispered, "I know. And I'm not afraid, either. I just don't want you to be in pain. And I don't want you to worry about me, or the children. We wish you didn't have to go, but we know we'll see you again. And we know Jesus will come quickly to comfort us. He is our safe harbor, our rock of ages. You have been a good and faithful servant, and God will be well pleased with you. When he sees it's time to call you home, we will rejoice through our tears, because we will know you are with Jesus. And we will join you someday. Then we'll have eternity together, praising the Lord and worshiping him."

"I think I've been to church!" he chuckled. "Now I know where Coop gets his preaching style." Talking so much had taken his breath away, and he started to cough. Marla Jean put her hands on his shoulders and massaged him gently with circular motions. It calmed him enough that he was able to relax and catch his breath. They sat together there for several minutes, just enjoying the companionship. The only sound was the ticking of the cuckoo clock in the hall.

"I don't want to sleep in this recliner anymore. I want to sleep with you."

Marla Jean widened her eyes and sat up straight. "Do you think that's wise? Don't you need to be elevated in order to breathe better? I would like nothing better than to sleep near you again, but I don't think it's a good idea, for you."

"Check into getting a hospital bed. Put it next to your bed. Then I can be elevated, and still be near you." He ran out of breath again and had to stop talking. "Please," he said after a minute.

"Walt, you just stop talking now, ya hear? I want you to rest. I'll call somebody about a hospital bed tomorrow. You rest now." She took off Walt's shoes and rubbed his feet. He smiled and relaxed a bit, then he drifted off to sleep. Then she pulled a chair up beside his, and she curled up with her head leaning toward him. It was a good time for a nap. She was wearing thin emotionally. A nap would help.

CHAPTER 20

Hero

Dana stood at the edge of the pond, looking down. She found the stone she was looking for and pulled her arm back to skip the rock over the surface of the water. One, two, three. Not bad, but she could do better. She searched for another flat stone.

Over her shoulder, she heard a slight whizzing sound, and Coop skipped his stone. He counted the skips. "Seven! Beat that!"

Dana's stone skipped five times and dropped into the water. "You win," she said. "Like usual."

Coop walked out on the short dock and sat down. His feet dangled above the water, and he let them swing. Dana sat beside him, reached into her shirt pocket, and brought out a bag filled with mixed nuts. She picked out a couple of cashews and passed the bag to Coop. He also selected cashews and said, "Should have brought all cashews. They're my favorites." Far out in the water, a fish jumped. Ripples gently circled out toward them.

An old flat bottom boat was tied to one leg of the dock, and it bounced and swayed when the ripples hit it. "Remember when we were kids, and Dad took us out fishing? Remember how you never wanted to wear a life jacket, but Dad made you? You were so mad at him, until you caught that big crappie, and he nearly pulled you overboard. I grabbed a hold of the back of your life jacket to keep you in. Otherwise you would have gone swimming. Or drowning, in your case, because you didn't know how to swim yet."

She laughed and handed him the bag of nuts. "Yes, I remember. You have always been my hero. I rely on you for a lot, you know. Especially now."

Dana looked up at the sky and sighed. "It's a beautiful day. I love it out here. Sometimes being out here helps me forget everything bad or scary or uncertain that's going on all around us. Dad's getting worse, isn't he? So fast."

Coop put his arm around her and they sat. Without words, they shared a time of silent prayer. It was comforting just to be together, just to know that they were not facing the future alone. They sat in silence a long while, then both of them stiffened and sat slowly upright. At the far edge of the pond, stepping cautiously out of the trees, came a doe and her two fawns. "Oh look, that's so sweet," whispered Dana. The young deer drank from the pond while mother stood watch. Always on alert, she bent her neck and drank briefly, then stood tall to look around before drinking again. She seemed to lock eyes with Dana, and stood motionless, while deciding if they were in danger. Then she lowered her head again and took a long drink.

The deer family walked calmly along the tree line and was almost out of sight when Coop stood. "Seeing those twins reminds me, we need to go look for Lolly and check on her calves. They were near here the other day when I first saw them, but who knows where they might be now? Let's go." They walked together to their horses, which were tied to brush nearby, happily munching on grass near the pond's edge.

They found Lolly standing in the shade of a big tree in the middle of the pasture. The calves were resting in the grass near her. Other cows in the herd were nearby on the hillside. It was a peaceful scene, and Coop thought once again how fortunate he felt to be part of this environment. It was a good life. Yes, it was hard work, but at times like this, he couldn't imagine anything he'd rather be doing or anywhere else he'd rather live.

They turned their horses toward the fence line and walked them slowly home, checking to be sure the fence was tight and unbroken. A few times, Coop dismounted and did some adjusting. Dana handed him tools when necessary. An hour later, they were unsaddling the horses and brushing them down. They put everything away in the tack room and turned the horses out to the pasture.

Riley met them as they neared the house. He was limping slightly, which reminded Coop that it was time for his medication. He washed up, then went to the pantry to find the peanut butter. Riley always took his pills best when they were disguised in peanut butter.

Dana was standing in the doorway to the living room, and when Coop walked near her, she turned to him with a finger to her lips. "Look," she whispered. Coop looked over her head and saw his parents, napping together. His dad was reclined back nearly flat, and his mom was in a chair beside him, with her head resting on his chest. He put his hands on Dana's shoulders and felt her slump back into him. "That's beautiful," he said, and she nodded. She couldn't speak.

CHAPTER 21

❦

Money Troubles

Misty took a shower and got ready for her afternoon shift at the diner. She and Patch had stayed in bed until almost noon. Sleeping in on Sundays was always a pleasure, especially after a late shift on Saturday. And she always loved groggy, early-morning lovemaking followed by more sleep and then a wide-awake, full-of-sensation second round. This morning was no exception. She felt alive and ready to take on whatever came at her today or even the rest of the week.

She let her mind wander to what might happen the rest of the week. Would Coop call her? She had felt like she was making a little progress with him. He seemed to be getting into her, until that damned phone call ruined everything. All because of a stupid dog.

Ya, I'm going to call him later. Maybe tomorrow, if he hasn't called me first, She thought. *I'll ask about the dog. He'll like that. I'll ask about his dad too. Then I'll ask him if he liked feeling me Friday night. That ought to get his attention.*

She had to admit, Coop wasn't really her type. He was clean and settled and steady. He was not like Patch or the rest of his biker buddies. Oh, they were decent people, but not all that clean, and definitely not settled. Life was free and easy for them. Coop was more set into a routine and responsibilities. And my god, he was a farmer. That's about the farthest thing possible from a biker!

Misty opened the door of the diner, still thinking about Coop. How was she going to break him down? How was she going to get him to want her, to yield to her, to come under her bewitching spell? She laughed at herself and thought, *Just wait, Cooper Smith, you are going to be mine in no time.*

"You're late again," grumbled Al from his spot behind the cash register.

"Just a few minutes, Al. Give me a break. I was here real late last night." She went to the back, got her apron, and slipped a notepad into the pocket. She said hi to Matt the cook and washed her hands before going out onto the floor. Time to make some money.

Sunday afternoons were sometimes busy, with people coming in for dinner after church. Then there would be a lull, because everyone would be home napping and resting. That was what most of these farmers did, Al had told her. It's how they kept the Sabbath. Whatever that means. All it meant to Missy was that for a couple hours on Sunday afternoon, she wouldn't be busy. So she wouldn't be making much in tips until Sunday evening.

Money troubles—how she hated them. There must be something she could do to get that school loan paid off. Maybe if she could get Coop in bed, he'd love her so much he'd give her some money to pay off the bills. After all, he was a farmer. He owned land. She wondered how much cash she could get if he sold off a few acres. Or a cow or something. There must be money to be had.

Patch had suggested a way to make some money, but she was not ready to go that way unless things got really bad. She liked sex a lot, but didn't feel right risking her health, even though she could pay off the bills. She'd watched too many movies. She knew the *Pretty Woman* story was not likely to repeat in her own life. She wasn't stupid.

But so far, she hadn't thought of any logical way to get extra money. Short of robbing a bank or something, which, let's admit it, wasn't a really good idea. She'd have to keep working on a plan. Meanwhile, she had Patch to rely on, somewhat. He could be counted on for a place to crash, food once in a while, and beer. Throw in her hourly minimum wage plus tips, and she could get by. For now.

CHAPTER 22

Reading Too Much?

Becky and Jenny cuddled into the couch with pillows, throw blankets, and a book. *Winnie-the-Pooh* was Jenny's new favorite, and Becky loved reading it to her. She found the characters endearing, and Jenny loved it when Becky tried out different voices for Tigger and Eeyore. Sometimes Jenny tried to do voices too, which always led to rolling on the couch in a heap of giggles. It was one of Becky's favorite times of the whole week.

If she was lucky, and today she was, Jenny would eventually relax enough to drift off to sleep while Becky stroked her hair and hummed softly. Becky closed her eyes and tried to take in the sheer bliss of the moment. Snuggled together, Becky enjoyed being with her daughter in a few minutes of unhurried quiet. No rushing to get ready for day care or Grandma's, no pressure to get laundry done or supper fixed. Just time to be together with no distractions. Even when Jenny was sound asleep, Becky held her and enjoyed the peace.

She let her mind replay the morning at church. She was really glad she had gone to Sunday school. The people were nice, she felt comfortable with them, and she even surprised herself about speaking up in the group. *Thank you, Dr. Whitefield,* she thought, not for the first time. That woman had been a blessing in Becky's life, on many levels.

She liked being with Coop too. He was so sure of himself, so strong in his character, and so knowledgeable about Scripture. When he had prayed at the end of the class, Becky felt the sincerity of his words. He wasn't praying for show. He was just talking to his friend Jesus. And that little hand squeeze at the end, now that was a pleasant surprise.

Becky wondered if she was really ready to think about having a relationship with Coop, or with any man. So far, her impression of Coop was that he was a real prize. A man of integrity and honesty. A man who would be a godly leader for his family. A man who would be dependable and faithful. Just the kind of man Becky needed. But was she really ready?

She had made errors in judgment before. The characteristics she thought she had seen in Derek were not genuine. When it came to hard times, he turned and ran. When she needed him the most, he was gone. What she thought she saw in him turned out to be just what she wanted to see in him. Big difference. Had she matured enough now to know the difference, to spot an impostor? She thought so, but she wasn't sure.

"Dear Lord Jesus, thank you for opening up the possibility of a new relationship. Guide me carefully. Give me wisdom, patience, and self-control. I place this new friendship in your hands. You alone will lead me in, or out, of this relationship. I trust you to know what is best for me and Jenny. Amen."

Relationship! she thought. *How can I call this a relationship? He was just being a Christian friend, inviting me to a church meeting. That's not like a date or anything; that's a friendship, not a romantic relationship. Even lunch next week can't be called an actual date. It wasn't his idea. He didn't invite me, Greg and Nancy did. It's a big group date, if anything. I can't read too much into it. Even the little hand squeeze could be just something he does every time after he prays. Oh God, I don't want to read too much into any of this. Make it clear to me, please.*

CHAPTER 23

Be Still and Know

The day the hospital bed arrived, Coop helped his mother rearrange furniture in the bedroom to make everything fit. They had also requested a bedside commode, and sat it near Walter's side of the bed. Dana put a plastic mattress cover, sheets, and blankets on the new bed. There was just barely room for a bedside table, where Dana arranged a large cup with a lid and a straw, filled to the top with nice, cold ice water. He needed to stay hydrated, the hospice care team had told her. She also placed her dad's well-worn Bible on the table, in case he felt like reading.

They had spoken with the hospice intake nurse, to get things in place for the day they would eventually need actual hospice care. But for now, they were able to manage his daily needs by taking turns. Marla Jean did most of the care, but both of the children pitched in as they could. Because it was summer, and Dana was only taking one class at the community college, she was available to help a lot. Her mom appreciated the break. Giving care full-time to someone she loves, someone she saw slipping away before her very eyes, was putting her on an emotional roller coaster. She was grateful for every day and every hour she had to spend with this man she loved so very much. She was relieved that, to this point, he hadn't been in much pain. Or maybe he was just good at hiding it. But she was also aware that every day he became a little weaker, he ate a little less, he had less energy, and he had more frequent coughing spells.

So Walt settled into the hospital bed and played with the remote control until he was arranged comfortably. His head was elevated, his knees were bent, and he smiled at his family. "This is perfect," he said. "Thank you all."

Coop and his mother left the room. Dana stayed behind and pulled the blinds to darken the room. She pulled the sheet up around her dad's shoulders and fluffed his pillow.

"Anything else I can get for you, Dad?" asked Dana. "There's water here in this cup, and your Bible is here. Do you want anything else? A snack? The radio turned on? Do you want to take a nap?"

Walt patted a space on the side of his bed. "Just sit with me for a while." Dana took a seat, being careful not to crowd him. There was plenty of room, though; even his legs seemed to have shriveled to half their normal size. *Probably because he doesn't use those muscles much anymore,* she thought. She reached for his hand. "I love you, Daddy."

Walter squeezed her hand back, but she barely felt it. She was saddened by his lack of muscle tone. He used to be so strong. He used to throw bales of straw around like he was flipping pancakes. Now he could barely lift a cup to drink a sip of water. Although he did not seem to be in pain, Dana knew that it must be difficult for him to admit he needed help.

He must have been reading her mind, because Walter said, "This isn't how I imagined my life to end. For some reason, I always thought I'd die in a farming accident. Fast and sudden." He struggled to take a deep breath. "Not slow like this. Getting tired, weaker every day."

"It's okay, Dad. We're here to help you. We want to help, however you need. Don't you worry."

"I'm sorry," he said. "Don't want to be a burden."

"Oh, Dad, don't be silly. We'd do anything for you and be happy about it. In fact, I really love taking care of you. After all, you did an awful lot to take care of me in my younger years. It's only right that I take care of you in your older years."

"Shouldn't be now. I'm not old. Just my body is, I guess."

"Whatever, whenever, I'm here, Dad." They sat in silence for several minutes. Then Dana asked, "What are you thinking about, Dad?"

"Psalm 46:10."

"Do I know that verse? I can't think what it is." Dana reached for his Bible, to look it up, but before she could, Walter quoted the verse. "Be still, and know that I am God."

"I lie here, still, and think about that. A lot."

"That's a good thing to do, I would think," said Dana.

"I know he is God. I know he is good." Walter paused, then added, "I know he is my Savior."

"And I believe, with all my heart, that there's a Heaven, and we'll all be there together forever." Dana looked directly at her dad and said, "What seems like the end, here on earth, is just the beginning of eternity. Revelation says all things will be made new. No suffering, pain, or death. No fear, no heartache, and no sadness. The end is going to be much better than the beginning."

Walter's eyes were closed. "It'll be good. I want to see Jesus." His breathing slowed as he fell asleep. Dana leaned up, kissed him on the forehead, and said, "Sleep now, Dad. Get some rest. I love you."

Dana went into the kitchen and poured herself a glass of iced tea. She took it out to the porch and sat watching squirrels play in the tree branches overhead. Riley lay at her feet, watching the squirrels with his eyes, but making no attempt to chase them. He was content to be still and rest. *Just like Dad's verse,* Dana thought. "Be still, and know that I am God." She said the words out loud, and they brought her comfort.

Riley's ears perked up, and he raised his head slightly. In the kitchen, someone was popping popcorn. The smell drifted through the screen door and made Dana's mouth water. Cooper brought a large bowl of buttered popcorn and sat beside her. They ate in silence for a bit, and every once in a while, one of them tossed a kernel to Riley. Popcorn was one of his favorite treats. He used to beg for pieces, but now he was content to accept what was offered to him.

The sun was setting, and the sky was ablaze with red and pink colors. "Weather should be good tomorrow. I got the tractor and combine tuned up today, so I'll start mowing the wheat tomorrow. I hired a couple of guys to help, and hopefully we'll be done in a couple of days, if the weather holds."

"You are doing great, running this place. Dad must be really proud of you."

Coop shrugged his shoulders. "You know, a few years ago I would never have thought I could be content staying on the farm. I had other plans. I even believed that God had put me on the path toward the ministry, and I was excited about it. Now things have changed, and God has given me a different purpose. I'm sure this is where he wants me. He has given me contentment, and I'm able to rest in his presence here on the farm. There's a verse about God leading us with his strong right hand. When I remember that I'm his child and he is guiding me, teaching me, leading me, well, then I feel safe and protected. There's nothing too hard for God, and I'm not in this alone."

"Don't you ever worry about the future? I mean, what's really going to happen when Dad's gone? Will we stay here? Will we sell the farm? Where would we go? What if you get married? Would you move away? If you stayed here, where would Mom go? There's so much to think about."

"The thing is," said Coop, "there's a difference between thinking about things and worrying about things. When I think about options, I try to let God show me which direction I should go. If I make the decisions on my own, I'm always thinking that I'm in charge. Turning the decision-making over to the Lord takes a lot of pressure off me. I just have to listen, and obey."

"Easier said than done," said Dana. "I'm not sure I have ever heard God telling me what to do." She sighed and said, "There's so much I don't understand." Dana gathered the popcorn bowl and turned toward the kitchen. "What do you want me to do tomorrow while you're working the fields? What is the best way I can help you?"

"Well, Mom used to fix a pretty big lunch for the workers. If you could do that, or at least help her, that would be great. She can focus on taking care of Dad, and you can be in charge of the food. Ask her, of course. You don't want to just get in there and take over. Ask her how you can help. She'd probably really appreciate your help in the kitchen."

"No problem, I'd be happy to. Well, I'm just going to clean up this bowl and then head to bed. Good night, Coop."

"Good night, little sis. See you in the morning."

Coop took Riley outside to do his business for the night. He was glad to see Riley head off to the chicken yard, to gather the hens safely into the chicken house.

Once back in the house, Riley went to his mat near Walter's recliner. He saw that the chair was empty and tilted his head up toward Coop with a questioning look. "You're looking for Dad, aren't you? Well, he's sleeping in the bedroom now. Do you want to be with him?" Riley walked down the hall toward Walter and Marla Jean's bedroom. The door was shut, so Coop knocked softly. His mom responded with a glance toward her sleeping husband. "Yes?"

"I think Riley wants to sleep in here with Dad. Is that okay?"

"Sure. Just put his mat at the foot of the bed, so he's not in the way if Dad needs to get up in the night."

Coop placed Riley's mat on the floor and said, "I've always heard that dogs, especially collies, have a sense about when someone needs extra help or comforting. Like if someone is sick, or upset about something, the dogs just know."

"I've heard that too. That's why they make good therapy dogs. And have you noticed how often Riley has been lying close to your dad? Even when Riley himself is sick, he wants to comfort your dad. He's been a wonderful family member. It will be hard to lose him." Marla Jean was in bed and turned to face Walter. "Good night, Cooper."

"Night, Mom. I love you. I hope you get some good sleep tonight." Cooper bent to tell Riley good night, then he left the room. He left the door slightly ajar, in case Riley needed to go out to get a drink or something.

Coop locked up the house and turned out the lights. When he walked into his bedroom, he noticed that his cell phone on the nightstand was lit up, indicating he had messages. He looked down and saw that there were three text messages from Misty. He'd been planning to call her for days. He still had the cooler in his truck and needed to return it to her.

Even though he had a reason to call her, and also a reason to see her again, Coop had been hesitant to get in contact with her. He felt uncomfortable, thinking about the time they had spent together last week. It was bothering him that he had come so close to giving in to temptation. If that phone call from Doc Larson hadn't come in at just the right time, would he have been able to resist? She was beautiful, seductive, and intense. Not characteristics he was usually drawn to. But could he stand strong if there were a next time? Only with God's help.

He took a deep breath and started to punch in her number. Then he cancelled that, and he decided to text her instead. *It might be the chicken way out,* he thought, *but I can't deal with talking to her right now.*

It's late. I can't talk now. I do need to see you. I have your cooler. When can we get together?

He sent the message, then he took a quick shower. When he got back to his room, he saw that he already had a reply from Misty. *Oh baby, I need to see you too. It felt so good when we were together. I loved the feel of your hands on my body. My breasts long for your touch. My nipples are hard just thinking about you. Call me. I want to be with you again. Really BE with you.*

"Oh, dear God. That wasn't the reaction I expected. Help me, please." But as he got into bed, he realized that his body had already begun to respond to the suggestive tone of her words. He turned out his light and lay there, trying not to think of her body. It was not easy. Just the mention of breasts and nipples had created a picture in his mind.

Coop sat up quickly in bed and turned on his light. He reached for his Bible and just let it fall open on his lap. He started reading in John, "I am the true grapevine, and my Father is the gardener. Remain in me, and I will remain in you. For a branch cannot produce fruit if it is severed from the vine, and you cannot be fruitful unless you remain in me." He read the verse again and let the words sink into his heart.

"I want to be fruitful, Lord. I want to remain in you, close to you, completely submerged in your word and filled with your spirit. I have been tempted to wander away from you. I have forgotten that I can't be fruitful unless I dwell close to you, and you fill me. Don't just live in me, Lord. Fill me, top to bottom. I'm all yours."

He thought about the word *fruitful*. He thought about his witness to Misty. He prayed that God would help him find the words to lead her to the cross. He asked God to help him be a witness in word and in action. "I want to abide in you, Jesus, the vine, so I can be fruitful and useful, bringing life to all those around me."

Sleep came easily. He dreamed about a gardener, pulling weeds, staking up weaker plants, watering and tending the crop. He dreamed about grapevines loaded with plump purple grapes. He dreamed about a table laden with plates of fruits and vegetables of all sorts. Jesus sat at the head of the table, smiling at all the fruit. At the other end of the table, Coop saw his father, also smiling as he popped a grape into his mouth.

CHAPTER 24

All in a Day's Work

The hired work crew arrived early the next morning. They worked in the wheat field until almost noon and then took a break for lunch. Dana and Marla Jean had outdone themselves with the meal. There was fried chicken, mashed potatoes with gravy, cooked carrots and broccoli, sliced tomatoes and cucumbers from the garden, and rolls with blackberry jam. As the men sat around the table enjoying the abundance of food, they thanked Dana and her mother over and over.

The youngest worker, Marco, laughed as he reached for another roll. "If I knew you would feed me this good, I wouldn't have needed to eat breakfast." His Mexican accent was thick, but he was quite understandable. "You ever need help, you call me," he said to Coop. He looked at Dana and smiled. "I like the way you cook. Is very good."

"Thank you," she responded. "Will you be here tomorrow? I think I'll make a meatloaf. Would that be okay?"

"Si! Meatloaf is good. You put in onions and peppers?"

"If that's the way you like it, I will." The men had finished eating and were starting to push back from the table. "I have brownies too. Anybody want one?"

Each man carried his dirty dishes to the kitchen sink, picked up a brownie, and walked outside to stand in the shade of the walnut tree. They made their plan for the rest of the work to be done that afternoon. Marco walked alongside Coop as they went toward the tractors. "Your sister, she is a good cook. And cute too."

They made an odd-looking crew as they walked across the lot. Coop was tall, in his blue jeans, plaid shirt, and black cowboy hat. Marco was short, wearing jeans and a gray T-shirt. Coop easily reached over to tussle Marco's dark hair and said, "Watch yourself, kid. I'm a very protective big brother." Marco pulled a baseball cap out of his back pocket and pushed it down on his head. They laughed and climbed aboard the machinery, ready to get back to work.

Dana watched from the porch. She saw the interchange between Coop and Marco and smiled. *I wonder what that was all about,* she thought. Then she went to the pantry to see if they had onions and peppers to put in the meatloaf for tomorrow. "Onions yes, but peppers no. I better run into town and get some."

She hurried out of the house and waved her arms over her head as she ran toward the tractor that Coop had just started up. He turned off the motor and called down, "What's the matter?"

"I need to go in to town for a few things for tomorrow. Can I drive your truck?"

"Sure. The keys are in it. Hey, while you're in town, could you do me a favor? There's a little cooler on the floor of the front seat of the truck. It's Misty's. Could you run over to the diner and drop it off to her? And just tell her I'll call her later."

"Okay. I'll see you later. Stay safe out there." Dana walked back to the house, unaware of a set of dark brown eyes watching her as she crossed the yard.

CHAPTER 25

Learning to Share

Dana placed a bag of groceries on the truck seat and reluctantly remembered the cooler she promised to take back to Misty. She started up the truck, pulled away from the grocery store, and drove a couple of blocks to the diner. The street parking in front of the diner was filled with a few cars and a motorcycle. There was a small parking lot on a side street, and there were no cars there. *Good,* she thought. *I don't like parking this big truck in small spaces. There's plenty of room here.*

She picked up the cooler, locked the doors, and headed down the alley to the diner. Like the parking lot, the diner was empty. There were no customers at the tables, and only a couple of people were on barstools at the counter. Dana recognized Misty, but not the two men she was deep in conversation with. One was a large man, heavyset, with arms covered with tattoos. He had a scruffy beard, greasy-looking hair under a ball cap, and a patch over one eye. He sat up straighter when Dana approached. She didn't like the way he looked her over, up and down.

The other man had his back to her but turned around to see what or who his buddy was looking at. He had an unlit cigarette sticking out of his mouth, a graying beard, and a piercing in his eyebrow. He looked at her like the first guy had, and Dana felt her skin crawl. She turned her attention to Misty and held out the cooler toward her.

"Hi, Misty. Remember me? I'm Dana, Cooper's sister. He's busy getting the wheat in, and he asked me to bring this cooler back to you."

Misty looked annoyed and took the cooler from Dana. "Oh shit. Oh, sorry, I mean oh shoot. I was hoping he'd bring it back himself. I wanted to talk to him some more."

"He said to tell you that he will call you tomorrow." Dana was anxious to get out of the diner. She made a move toward the door, but Patch stood quickly too close to her and blocked her way. "What's your hurry, sweetheart? Sit a spell. I'll buy you a drink."

The man with the pierced eyebrow stood up from his stool at the counter, but he didn't make a move toward her. He was watching her very closely, though, and it made Dana nervous.

Dana backed away a bit. She didn't want to be rude, but this big man was making her uncomfortable. He was still so close she could smell him. Beer, cigarette smoke, greasy food and onions, mixed with his unclean body and another smell she couldn't identify but didn't like.

She knew lying was a sin, but she did it anyway. "Oh thanks, but no, I can't. I've just been to the grocery store, and I have some ice cream in the truck. I need to get right home to put it in the freezer." She maneuvered away from him and said quickly, "Bye, Misty." She wanted to run, but managed to walk through the door with as much composure as she could. She could feel his eyes following her every step. It was creepy. The truck keys were in her hand, ready to use as a weapon if needed. *That's silly,* she admitted to herself. *It's the middle of the day. And he's not even following me.* But she unlocked the truck, got in, and quickly locked it again. It would be good to get home. She felt like she needed a shower. She could still smell his overpowering odor on her clothes.

"Sorry about the lie about the ice cream," she said out loud. "But I think you can understand and forgive me. I had to get out of there."

Misty laughed and said, "You guys sure did scare off that little girl. You had her shaking in her cowboy boots. You should be ashamed of yourselves!"

Patch smacked his buddy on the back. "What do you say, Billy? Want to share her? We could take turns. Teach her a few things!"

Billy said, "Hell no. I'm not the sharing type. I'd want that all to myself."

"Fat chance, guys. She's not your type." Misty looked at the clock. "Now you need to get out of here. You know Al doesn't like you guys hanging around, even when we're not busy. And he's gonna be coming in to work soon. So get going. I do not need to get in trouble because you are scaring off business."

Patch grabbed Misty by the arm and kissed her before he left. Billy reached out for her as he passed by and tried to kiss her too. Patch pushed him away and said, "I thought you weren't the sharing type. Get your hands off my girl."

Misty said, "Who says I'm your girl? I'm my own girl, and I'll kiss whoever I want." She sauntered over to Billy and kissed him. Billy's hands reached to her rear and pulled her close. She laughed and teased Patch. "Maybe you boys will learn to share after all.

CHAPTER 26

Peace

By the time Dana returned home, the workers were about to call it a day. They weren't finished, but the heat index had climbed into the upper nineties, and Coop decided that they could finish it up tomorrow. He didn't want to push too hard and have someone collapse with heat stroke.

All the hired help piled into an old truck, ready to head for their homes. Marco leaned out of his window and hollered to Dana. "Adios, Dana. See you tomorrow!" He waved as they drove past her. Dana smiled and returned his wave.

She was taking the groceries out of the bag when Coop came into the kitchen. He was hot and dirty, and she held her nose to tease him. "Get your stinky self out of my kitchen! Don't come back till you're clean."

"I know, I know. But I need a drink. It's hot out there, if you hadn't noticed." Coop went to the refrigerator and got out the iced-tea pitcher. He poured himself a tall glass and drank it down thirstily. Then he poured a second glass and took it with him to his room.

He felt much better after his shower. Supper was leftovers from their huge lunch, so Dana had everything almost ready when he came back into the kitchen.

"Thank you. You smell better now. Look better too!" Dana joked.

"It's hot work, that's for sure. But before long it will be winter, and we'll be complaining about the cold temperatures." He looked approvingly at the food Dana was setting on the table. "You sure made us a great lunch. The guys really appreciated it."

"Glad I could help. And I'm really glad there were leftovers."

"Marco thinks you're a good cook. He's already talking about your meatloaf. You better not disappoint him!"

"I'll do my best. Had to go into town to get the peppers he wanted cooked in the meatloaf. But I got some other stuff too, so it wasn't really a special trip. Oh, I took that cooler to Misty. She seemed a little ticked off that you didn't deliver it yourself."

"Oh well, I have a lot going on right now. Thanks for dropping it off. Was the diner busy?"

"Not at all. There were just two guys there, talking to Misty at the counter. They were creepy. Made me very uncomfortable." She gave a little shudder.

"What do you mean? Did they bother you?"

"No, not really. One of them just smelled bad and stood a little too close to me. He gave me the creeps. The other one just looked at me. But I left fast, so that was that." She heard her mother walking through the living room and put her finger up to her lips to keep Coop from talking about it anymore. She didn't want her mother to have one more thing to worry about.

Marla Jean came in and said, "Dad's going to eat in his bed tonight. He just wants some soup. And he asked for beet pickles, of all things!"

They bowed their heads for the blessing, this time led by Marla Jean. "We thank you, Lord Jesus, for your goodness and your mercies. We thank you for the abundance you have once again bestowed upon us. We thank you for being our peace. Amen."

As they began to eat, Dana asked her mom, "What did you mean by that, Mom, when you said Jesus is our peace?"

"It's from Ephesians chapter two. I was reading it to your dad this afternoon. We decided that because Jesus is in us, we can have peace, no matter what comes our way. Bad news? We have peace anyway. Fear? We have peace anyway. Illness? We have peace anyway. One disaster after another? We have peace anyway. If we have Jesus, we have peace. No matter what."

All three of them pondered these words. Each had a different set of disasters to be dealing with, but each could say that the peace of Jesus would never leave them. Loss of a husband, loss of a father, and change of plans for the future: whatever they were going through now or would go through in the future, Jesus would be with them. And they would have peace.

Alone in his hospital bed, propped up so he could sit comfortably, Walt also pondered these words. He thought about his life, how he had tried to faithfully follow Christ for nearly four decades. It was a lifetime of service, and now it was drawing to an end. And he was overcome with a sense of peace. "Because Jesus is my peace. No matter what."

CHAPTER 27

Sounds in the Night

By late afternoon of the next day, the wheat was harvested and on its way to the grain elevator. The hired workers were paid and piled into the old truck. Marco held a plate of leftover meatloaf, covered with plastic wrap. He waved to Dana, motioning for her to come near the truck. For at least the tenth time, he told her it was the best meatloaf he had ever tasted.

"I'm so glad you liked it. And I hope your mother and little sister enjoy it for your supper tonight." Marco had told her at lunch that his mother was a good cook, but she didn't make meatloaf as good as this.

Marco leaned further out the window and said, "Hey, you want to come to my casa sometime? My mama can make very good enchiladas. You come. Eat with us. She even teach you enchiladas. You teach her meatloaf."

Dana nodded and said, "Yes, I'd like that. It would be fun."

Marco smiled a big smile and said, "I call you." The truck roared off in a cloud of dust. Dana walked back to the house, where both Marla Jean and Coop were looking at her. Coop sang out, "Dana's got a boyfriend," in a teasing, singsong voice."

"Not hardly," retorted Dana. "It's just a cooking lesson from his mother."

"Yeah, right!" Coop laughed and said, "I will say, he's a nice kid. Real hard worker. And he thinks you're cute. But I think he needs to get glasses!"

Dana punched him playfully on his arm and said, "Thanks. Now go get cleaned up. We're having pork chops for supper, since I don't have any leftover meatloaf tonight. It'll be ready by the time you get out of the shower."

Riley followed them slowly up to the house. When they got to the back-porch steps, he stood at the bottom. Coop held the door open for Dana and Marla Jean, then turned to wait for Riley. Riley looked up at him sadly and did not climb the two steps to the porch. Coop went down and sat on the steps, petting Riley and talking to him. "Is it hard for you to do the steps now, buddy? Does it hurt you? I'm sorry. I'm so sorry it hurts. I can carry you up. Will that be okay?" Riley looked at Coop trustingly and leaned against his legs.

Coop stood, leaned down, and picked up Riley as he would a young calf. Wrapping all four legs in his arms, Coop carried Riley up the steps and to the door. Inside, he gently sat him down on the floor and got him some water and his evening medicine. It was a little early for his pill, but obviously Riley needed it. He was showing he was in pain.

Dana watched as Coop attended to Riley. She went to the refrigerator and took out a hard-boiled egg. Riley usually loved this treat, and it was good for him. She peeled the egg, broke it into several pieces, and placed it in his food dish. He did not move toward the dish, so Dana brought it over close to where he lay on the floor and put it in front of him. Riley lifted his head, sniffed at the bowl, and took a few bites.

"Normally he would gobble that right up," she said to Coop, who stood watching from the doorway. "He's really hurting."

"I know. Well, let's see if the pain pill helps. Doc said I could give it to him every six hours or as often as he needs it, if he's in pain. I don't like to see him hurting like this. And he looks so sad."

"Do you think it's time?"

Coop took a deep breath. "We'll see how he responds to the medicine. Don't worry. We'll know when it's time." He turned down the hall to his bedroom. First, he stopped into his parents' room to talk with his dad.

"Got the wheat done, Dad. It's a good harvest."

Walter raised his hand in an "okay" sign. He smiled at Coop and said, "At the elevator?"

"It's on the way. I paid the guys I hired, and we talked about having them back when the soybeans are ready. They are a good crew. They work hard and don't waste time. And they love Mom and Dana's cooking!"

"That's good. They're smart!"

Coop turned to leave, but Walt called him. "Coop."

"Yes? Do you need something?"

"Just thank you. You're doing good work. Hard work. I appreciate it."

Coop shrugged and said, "I really do like working the farm, Dad. I really do. Now I need a shower before supper. Talk to you later." He walked on down the hall with his head held a little higher. It was good to know that his dad was proud of him.

After supper, Coop called Misty.

"It's about time," she said as soon as she picked up her phone. "I was beginning to think you were ignoring me. Sending your sister to the diner instead of coming yourself, then not calling when you said you would. It could give a girl a complex."

"I said I'd call today, and I did. I've been really busy getting the wheat crop in. It's a busy time of year for farmers. And it's not going to lighten up much for months."

"You know what they say about all work and no play. You need to have some playtime, Coop. When can we get together and play some more?"

"Well, that's something I'd like to talk to you about. I've been thinking about what happened the other night, and I think we need to talk."

"You've been thinking about it? So have I! And I want more. I know we can have a lot of fun together. We can do a lot more than just talk about it."

Coop was getting frustrated. This conversation was already headed in a direction he had not anticipated. How did she always do that?

"Well, tomorrow is Friday. Are you off again?"

"I work until three tomorrow. Can you meet me after work?"

"Yes, I can do that. At the diner again?"

"Sure, baby. That works. Where shall we go?"

Coop had already been thinking about it, but he hadn't come up with a place yet. It needed to be somewhere they could be alone. He wanted time to talk with her without interruption. "I don't know yet. I'll think of something," he said. Before she could say any more, he ended the call with, "Well, I'll see you tomorrow a little after three."

He lay in bed that night, staring up at the ceiling. He was praying that God would give him the right words. He wanted to be a witness to Misty, to explain to her about salvation, and how he had dedicated his life to Jesus. He knew he was going to need courage to talk with her. And he also feared he would need courage to resist her temptations.

Through the bedroom wall, he could hear the quiet murmurings of his parents. He heard his mother get out of her bed and walk around to his dad's, to help him get to the porta-potty. His dad was weakening still, and he was struggling more and more to make basic movements. Even moving from a prone position to sitting up on the side of the bed was difficult.

A minute later there was a crash and a loud thump, then Marla Jean was calling, "Coop! Coop! Come quick!"

Coop was already out of bed and halfway to his parents' room. He met Dana coming out of her room. Together they hurried down the hall.

Walter was on the floor, struggling to get up on his knees. There was blood coming from a gash on his forehead. The bedside lamp was in shattered pieces on the floor. "He fell," Marla Jean said. "Help me get him up."

Despite his bare feet, Coop hurried over to his dad, put his arms under his dad's armpits, and lifted him to the side of the bed. Dana already had a wet washcloth to wipe the blood off Walter's face. Marla Jean was checking him over for any other injuries.

Little shards of glass were embedded in the ball of Cooper's left foot, but he didn't concern himself over it. He noticed that his feet were both damp, and he looked to see if the pot might have been spilled in the fall. But no, the floor was wet with urine, he could smell it, but the por-ta-potty was upright. Then he looked at his dad, sitting for-lornly on the side of the bed, and Cooper realized that his dad had wet himself. He pulled Dana aside and asked her to get clean sheets for the bed. Marla Jean was also aware of what had happened, and she was getting fresh underclothes and pajamas for her husband.

Cooper helped his dad stand at the side of the bed while Dana stripped off the wet sheets and put on clean ones. He held his dad steady as Marla Jean undressed him and put the clean clothes on him. Walter looked embar-rassed and kept saying, "I'm sorry. I'm sorry." They all reas-sured him that it was okay; he wasn't to worry.

When Walter was tucked safely back into bed, Coop swept up the broken glass on the floor. Dana covered Walt's open wound with gauze and secured it with fabric tape. It wasn't a deep cut, wouldn't need stitches. He had hit it on the corner of the nightstand and he fell, knocking the lamp over to the floor. It might have been a lot worse.

"Sit down," she said to Coop. "Let me look at your feet."

"Oh, I'm fine. It's nothing."

"It might be nothing, but you're tracking little droplets of blood all over the place. Now sit down, and let's at least get you cleaned up." She proceeded to wash his feet and check for pieces of glass. "There, you're good to go. Now I'll just wipe up the floor and make sure we get all the glass up." She busied herself with the cleanup.

Coop took his mother out in the hallway. "What happened?" he asked her. She was visibly shaken, and he led her to the living room to sit down. Her body slumped into a chair, and she held her face in her hands. Silent sobs shook her body.

"It was so fast. I just couldn't do anything. He needed to go to the bathroom, and he tried to get out of bed himself. I went around to help him, but he's so stubborn. He doesn't want to be a burden. He lost his balance when he stood up, and I was too far away to catch him. He fell, hit his head on the nightstand, and knocked over the lamp. And then he wet himself. He's so embarrassed. I feel so bad for him. Oh, Coop, what are we going to do?" Tears were flowing now, and she reached for a tissue to blow her nose.

"Well, the first thing is, we need to call the hospice nurse. She said she wants to know if there's a change in his abilities, or any falls." He located the folder with hospice information and called the nurse's number. He left a message and a phone number and then went back to sit with his mother. Dana came into the room and sat on the couch nearby.

"Dad's asleep," she said. "I cleaned up all the glass. Should we get another lamp to put beside his bed?"

Marla Jean answered, "Don't worry about it tonight, honey. We won't need it anyway. We can use the light on my side of the bed."

The phone rang and startled them. Coop looked at his mother to see if she wanted to answer, and she nodded.

"Hello? Yes, this is Mrs. Smith." She told the nurse on call about Walter's fall, the cut on his head, and that he was sleeping now. The nurse explained that it was their policy to go check on their patients after a fall, so she would be out to see him in about half an hour. Marla Jean said good-bye and told the kids. Both of them said they wanted to be there when the nurse came, so they went to get properly dressed before she arrived. Marla Jean put on a robe over her nightgown. She looked down at her husband in the bed and watched his chest slowly rise with his breathing.

The nurse introduced herself as Wanda. She calmly greeted the family, spoke with them about Walter's general condition and the fall, and then went to the bedroom to do an exam. Walter stirred when Marla Jean touched him and asked him to wake up. He opened his eyes to look at the nurse, but to everyone in the room it seemed like maybe he didn't really see her at all. He stared blankly forward until Marla Jean reached for his hand. Then he focused his eyes on her and answered the nurse's questions. She asked him when his birthday was, if he knew what day it was, and who was the president of the United States. He answered all the questions correctly, even joking a little about the day of the week. He said it was Thursday when he lay down, but he didn't really know if it was Friday yet or not. Marla Jean squeezed his hand and said, "It's still Thursday, dear, but not for much longer."

Wanda took his vitals, listened to his breathing, checked the cut on his head, and agreed that it did not need stitches. She rebandaged the wound and left some gauze and tape with Dana, asking that the bandage be changed in the morning. Dana said she'd take care of it.

"It was nice to meet you, Walter," she said as she gathered her things to leave. He smiled slightly at her. "I'll be back in a day or two, and we'll talk some more then. Right now, I want you to get some sleep. And if you need to get out of bed, you wait until someone is here to help, you hear? Your family loves you, and no one wants to see you fall again." Walter nodded slightly, and Wanda said good night. They left the room and went to the kitchen. Wanda sat at the table, pulled some papers out of her satchel, and wrote some notes.

Marla Jean asked, "Would you like something to drink? Coffee? Tea?"

Wanda said, "A glass of water would be nice." Marla Jean filled a glass with ice and added water. She put the glass in front of Wanda and asked, "Well, what do we do now?"

"For tonight, I want you to monitor him. Every couple of hours, try to rouse him from sleep. With a head injury, no matter how slight, we want to make sure he doesn't have a concussion. It's not likely, with this minor of an injury, but just check on him through the night.

I'll notify Walter's doctor about this fall. I can't say for sure, but I would suppose he might request that one of our nurses come out to see Walter every day or two. As we see his condition decline, we'll have a nurse here every day, and even several times a day. Eventually, we'll talk about medications that will make him more comfortable. There is no reason for him to be in any pain at all. We'll give him morphine, and show you how to administer it as well. He'll sleep a lot, but someone will need to be here with him at all times. Marla Jean, I know you're a strong woman, but are you able to lift Walter, should he fall again?"

"No, I don't think I could. Not if he was dead weight on the floor." She cringed when she thought of that word. Dead. She did not like that word. "Cooper is usually here, but not always right here in the house. He's doing all the farming. Maybe Dana and I could do it. I'm not sure, though."

"You might want to think about adult diapers. If getting out of the bed to use the bathroom is a problem, the diapers would eliminate that need. I can make a note to have one of the nurses bring you some the next time they come out, if you'd like."

Marla Jean nodded silently. She knew Walter would be resistant to the idea, but she would have to convince him that it was best.

Before Wanda left, she spoke comfortingly to the Smiths. "I know this is a difficult time. It's hard to watch someone you love failing in health and struggling. But we're here to make it as easy for you as possible. You can call us anytime, even if you just need to talk. We have lots of ways we can help you through all this. We can assist with bathing and dressing, even eating. We can be here while you take a break from all the caregiving. You have to take care of yourselves too, you know. We want to be here for you, as well as for Walter. Our mission is to take care of the whole family." Wanda saw that three sets of eyes were on her, looking for words of hope. She couldn't always offer hope, but she was able to bring comfort and compassion.

"After the doctor looks over these notes, one of our hospice nurses will call you and set up a time for our next visit. That might be tomorrow morning, but probably after lunch. If you need us before then, just call." Wanda said her goodbyes. Coop locked up the house and turned out the lights.

In her bedroom, Dana let silent tears fall down her cheeks. She saw the end coming more clearly now. She could barely imagine life without her daddy. Ever since she could remember, she had dreamed about her father walking her down the aisle at her wedding. Now she knew that would never happen. "Oh God, I'm going to miss him so much."

Marla Jean lay in her bed, on the side near to Walter's hospital bed. She reached out to lay her hand on his arm. She listened to his breathing, slow and quiet. His chest was rising slightly with each breath, just barely noticeable. At least he wasn't coughing. She was thankful for that: he was resting peacefully. "Heavenly Father, thank you for giving him a quiet night's sleep. Lord, you know the desire of my heart. I don't ask you for the miracle of healing. Yes, I know it's within your power, but may not be within your plan. Instead, I plead with you to release him from all pain. Please, Lord, let his last days be pain-free." She closed her eyes, but sleep did not come easily.

Coop put his head on his pillow and closed his eyes. He repeated Psalm 4:8: "I will lie down and fall asleep in peace because you alone, Lord, let me live in safety." Coop slept.

CHAPTER 28

Planting Seeds

Chores done, Coop walked back to the house in a sweat. The temperatures were climbing higher and higher. Some rain would be helpful. The cornstalks were almost knee-high and needed rain in order to develop ears. He looked up to the sky hopefully, but no clouds were to be found. Riley lay on the porch, panting and listless. "You better get inside, where it's cooler," Coop said to him, and lifted him gently. Riley used to weigh seventy-five pounds, but he had lost quite a bit of weight since he got sick. Now he was easy to lift, which was a good thing because Coop found himself having to carry him up and down the steps every time he needed to go outside.

Marla Jean was hanging up the phone when Coop came in. He washed his hands at the kitchen sink while she told him about the conversation with Nurse Wanda. "The doctor authorized hospice visits three times a week, which can be increased when it's necessary. Their main focus is comfort and pain management. I told her we didn't need help with bathing or dressing—we can handle that ourselves. She'll be here Monday morning."

Coop dried his hands and asked, "You doing okay?"

"As well as I can, all things considered. I know having Wanda here to check on things will be a comfort. She'll be able to monitor his progress. Or I guess I should say his decline. Maybe we should call it something like 'Walking to the river' or 'On the road to glory.'" She chuckled. "I think I'll ask your dad what he likes."

"Good idea. I'm sure he'll have some good suggestions. And it's nice to think of walking toward Heaven. It's a more uplifting thought that walking toward the grave. Thank Jesus for the promise of Heaven. Right, Mom?"

"Right. And I have an assurance that your dad isn't going to suffer or be in pain. It came to me in a dream last night. I couldn't sleep at first, so I was praying that your dad wouldn't have pain. Then I fell asleep and had this amazing dream. Everything was covered with a bright light, and it was so bright I had to cover my eyes. When my hands were over my eyes, I saw Jesus. Just like the pictures or movies show him. He walked to me and put his hand out toward me and said, "Don't be afraid, I am here to help him." Then he faded away, and the light faded, and I took down my hands and looked at your dad, sleeping there so peacefully. And I just knew that Jesus was with him, and would help him through this, with no pain. I just knew it. I don't think I've ever had a dream where the meaning was so clear. It was wonderful."

"That's really special, Mom." He reached for his mom's Bible on the kitchen table, where she had been having her morning devotions. "I think there's a verse in Isaiah that says something like that. There's so many verses that say 'fear not.'" He looked in the concordance under *fear* and ran his finger down the list. "Maybe it's this one. Isaiah 41:13." He turned to the verse and read it aloud. "For I the Lord thy God will hold thy right hand, saying unto thee, fear not: I will help thee."

Coop closed the Bible, set it on the table, hugged his mother, and said, "Well, I'd say that's the perfect verse for the day. For all of us."

"I think you're right, Coop. We all need to let God hold our hand and help us."

"So, Mom, say a prayer for me today. I am meeting with Misty this afternoon, at the diner. I think the Lord wants me to be a witness to her. I want to show her the way of salvation, but I want her to listen and not be offended. So please pray that she will be receptive. I'm not really sure what I'm going to say to her."

"I'll pray that the Lord gives you the words, and the courage. And that she will have an open mind, to listen and understand." Marla Jean gave him a big hug. "Um, you might want to put on some clean clothes. You kinda smell like a barn. Not that I mind, but other people might!"

At three o'clock, Cooper parked his truck in front of the diner. He had barely gotten out of the truck when Misty came bounding out of the door. She met him at the front bumper with a hug and a kiss on the cheek. "I'm so happy to see you. I missed you so much. I can't wait to spend some more time with you."

Coop chuckled, opened the door for her, and said, "It's only been a week."

Misty reached up and kissed him again before she got into the front seat. "I know, but it's been such a long, boring week. I was thinking about you every minute."

Coop closed the door and walked around to his side. *Please, God, help me*, he thought as he climbed in and fastened his seatbelt. He checked to see if Misty was wearing her seatbelt, saw that she was, and started the engine.

"I thought we could go out to the football field and sit in the bleachers and talk," he said. "There ought to be some shade there this time of the day. And I brought water bottles."

"Okay. Will it be private?"

"Private enough." Coop turned the truck south of town, where the school had built a new sports complex for the Winslow Wildcats. Baseball, football, and track fields covered several acres of farmland that had been sold to the school several years ago. The football field was in the farthest corner, and required a bit of a drive down a gravel road. He parked the truck near the entrance to the bleachers. The field was not kept locked, and many times kids would be out there, playing catch or practicing plays with a football. Not today, though, probably because it was so hot. They searched out seats in the shade and sat down on the top row, where there was a back railing to lean against.

As soon as they sat down, Misty leaned into him. She snuggled her body as close to his as she possibly could and started kissing his lips. Coop put his hands on her shoulders and pushed her away gently. "Wait, please. We need to talk."

"I am talking. With my body. I have a lot I want to say to you. We can have a long, hot discussion." Misty was persistent, and wiggled free of his hands. She put her arms around his waist and locked her hands behind him. "You can't get rid of me that easily. I know what I want, and I intend to get it." She kissed him again, and this time he relaxed a little. She snaked her tongue into his mouth, and he responded by opening his mouth a little wider and joining his tongue with hers. He felt himself responding in other ways also.

Misty loosened her grip on Cooper and placed her hand on his thigh. She rubbed up and down on his leg, each upward movement climbing higher on his thigh. All the while she continued to probe his mouth with hers. She placed her hand high on his thigh and sighed. She pulled away from him a bit, moaning. "Oh, baby. I want you. And I know you want me too." She worked at his zipper and said, "Let me see it."

That snapped Cooper back to his senses. He pushed her hands away and slid apart from her. "Stop. Really, Misty. I don't want to do this."

She looked at his crotch and laughed. "Oh yes, you do. Anybody could see that you are enjoying this."

"Okay, listen," he said, still holding her hands away from him. "Yes, my body is responding to you. That's what God made it to do. It's natural, and I like it. But to do what you are suggesting goes against God's plan for me. I know he wants me to save myself for one woman, the one who he blesses me with as my wife. I will not defile myself or his best wishes for me by engaging in any activity that he does not sanction. I have things I wanted to talk with you about. Please sit still while I try to explain myself."

Misty pulled her hands away and wrapped them under her arms. In a huff she said, "Well, I've never been rejected before. You're sure an odd one."

"In a way, I think you're right. I'm an odd one. I'm not in the majority of men these days. I have been called by my Lord Jesus, set apart from the world and worldly pleasures. True, that makes me an oddity, but I know that God knows what is best for me. He has a plan, and I want to be in tune to his leading. I believe that physical involvement before marriage is not in my best interest. It's not God's plan." He stopped to think a minute, but Misty jumped right back with disgust in her eyes.

"That's crazy talk. God, Jesus, this 'plan,' that's all old-fashioned. Let go, Coop! Stop being so uptight. You're missing out on all the fun."

"But I'm not missing out on fellowship with Christ, which is the most important desire of my heart. When I stay close to him, I know that he's going to help me through any trial or trouble I might encounter. I trust him, I love him, and I know he loves me too. So much that he died on the cross for my sins. I've accepted that, and now I'm a child of God. The gift of eternal life is mine. And it's available to you too. All you have to do is repent of your sins, and accept Jesus's forgiveness. He's standing at the door, knocking. All you have to do is open the door of your heart and let Him in."

"Oh no you don't. I've known holy rollers like you before. Always pushing sin and hell and all kinds of fear tactics. Well, I'm not interested. No way, man. I'm not falling for that mumbo jumbo. I thought you were smarter than that. Just another country hick, I guess." She stood up and balanced herself on the bleacher seat. Facing him, she yelled angrily. "And don't you dare go acting like you're better than me. You're not. You're just a blind little boy who hasn't seen the world. You have no idea of what you're missing." She turned and started down. "Let's get out of here. I'm done with you," she called back to him. Cooper sighed and stood to follow her.

They walked in silence to the truck, Misty several steps ahead of him. In the truck, before he started the engine, Coop turned to her and said, "Look, Misty, I'm sorry. I didn't mean to offend you. I just wanted to share what was on my heart. I was trying to explain that I'm a Christian, and my lifestyle is different than many other people. I'm not criticizing you, or comparing you to me. I'm just explaining, and offering you a chance to learn more about it. I don't want to be pushy or anything like that. I just wanted you to know where I stand, and why."

"Yeah, well, let's just go. I mean it. Take me back to the diner. We have nothing else to talk about." Misty sat stiffly by the door, looking out the window. She was ticked off. She should have seen this coming. Farmers! How could she have imagined that he would be able to help her with her money problems? What a joke! A pathetic, stupid idea. She must have been desperate. And to think that he could treat her this way. Pushing her away, telling her no, that he didn't want her. Well, he'd regret it. *You'll be sorry, farmer boy*, she thought to herself. *Just you wait and see. You'll wish you had never treated me this way. You and your religious fanatic talk.*

The truck hadn't even stopped in front of the diner before Misty had her door open and her feet on the pavement. She slammed the door and stalked away without a word.

Cooper put his head down on the steering wheel and prayed. He felt like everything had gone wrong. He had probably made things worse. *Oh, God, I'm sorry. What went wrong? Did I push too hard? Can I fix this?*

An answer came, loud and clear. *It's not yours to fix. You planted the seed, as you were led. I will honor your efforts.*

Coop thought about seeds. He remembered the parable of the sower in Matthew. Some seeds landed on good soil, and some didn't. Some landed among weeds. Some landed on rocky soil. Maybe that's what happened. She isn't ready. The seed can't grow yet. *Give it time,* said a voice in his head. *Give it time.*

CHAPTER 29

Sing of Your Love

"So after church tomorrow, we're going to go out to lunch at the diner," Becky explained to Jenny. "Hannah and her parents will be there, and Cooper. Remember him?"

"Yes, Mommy, I remember him. He has cowboy boots. And he's tall. And he liked my memory-verse prize." Jenny was holding her favorite doll, brushing her hair with a tiny pink comb. She was sitting on the floor, and Becky was sitting behind her, with her legs wrapped around her. Becky was brushing Jenny's hair.

"What do you want to do today, sweetie? We could go to the lake and look for the ducks. We could go to Grandma's and play in the sprinkler. We could pick some berries at the blueberry farm. Whatever you want."

"Blueberries!" shouted Jenny jubilantly. "And then can we make some blueberry muffins?"

"Sure! Sounds like a great idea!" The tangles were out of Jenny's hair now, and Becky asked, "How would you like me to fix your hair?"

"French braid, please," said Jenny. "And can you do my Amanda doll too? I want her to look just like me."

"Hmmm, I can try. But her hair is pretty short. I'll see what I can do." She continued working on Jenny's hair, humming softly as she braided.

"What are you singing, Mommy?"

"It's called 'I Could Sing of Your Love Forever.' We learned it this week at the single-moms' group."

"I like it. I like to hear you sing, Mommy. Can you teach me?"

"I don't remember all the words, that's why I'm humming! I'll try to learn it all next week, and then I'll teach you. Here, look in the mirror. How does your hair look?"

"Perfect. Now it's Amanda's turn." Jenny carefully handed the doll to her mom. "I combed it out for you. Now you can braid it."

"Okay. Why don't you go get your shoes on? And go potty. Be sure to wash your hands. Sing the ABC song, okay?"

Jenny put her hands on her hips and looked at her mother indignantly. "I know, I know, Mommy. You don't have to tell me everything. I'm almost five, remember? I know stuff."

Becky hid a smile and watched Jenny skip down the hall. That girl! How dull life would be without Jennifer Hope Emerson! "Thank you, God, for my baby girl, who isn't such a baby anymore."

CHAPTER 30

— ❦ —

Muffins and Cobbler

Dana tiptoed out of her parents' room. Her dad was sleeping quietly, with Riley sleeping on the floor near him. It was a peaceful scene, but one that brought her to tears. A great sadness came over her. She walked to the kitchen and sat dejectedly at the table. "I don't know how I'm going to survive this. Dad, Riley, it's just too much to take all at once."

Marla Jean pulled up a chair and sat close to her daughter. "I know, honey. It's a lot to handle. But of course, we will survive it. We'll have each other, and Jesus, to lean on. And remember, from Christ's perspective, the death of someone who belongs to him is a beautiful and precious thing. Your dad will be united with his Savior. We have that assurance, and the promise of a heavenly home for ourselves as well. That brings me great joy."

Dana reached for her mom's hand. "I love you, Mom."

"I love you too, honey." They sat quietly, listening to the ticking of the cuckoo clock in the hall. They heard Cooper outside, parking the four-wheeler. Then his booted footsteps sounded on the gravel driveway, and he climbed the steps to the back porch. They expected to hear the screen door slam, but instead Coop caught it and closed it quietly. They heard him kick off his boots. He came into the kitchen, carrying something inside his black hat. "Look what I found." He held his hat across the table, to show them what was inside.

"Oh, blackberries! Are they ready already? These look great," Marla Jean cooed.

"There's lots more where these came from. I just picked all my hat could hold."

Dana jumped up and got a container from the cabinet. "I'll go pick some more. I need something to do anyway. If there's enough, I'll make some cobbler this afternoon."

"Oh, there's enough. Must be three hats full left. I think you'll need a bigger container."

Dana traded her plastic container for a gallon-sized ice-cream bucket. "Think this'll work?"

Coop poured the berries from his hat into the strainer in the sink and ran cold water over them. "Yeah, that should do. Blackberry cobbler sounds delicious. Do we have vanilla ice cream to go on it?"

Marla Jean checked the freezer and said, "Yes, we have plenty. Enough for the cobbler, then we'll need to buy more. I'll put it on the shopping list for next time."

Dana went outside to the blackberry patch. Marla Jean turned to Coop and said, "You've been quiet. Never said anything about how your talk with Misty went."

Coop dumped the berries out on a paper towel to dry. "I think I messed up, Mom. I mean, she was not the least bit receptive. Actually, she got mad and refused to talk with me about Christ at all. I might have just made matters worse. And I'm sure she never wants to talk to me again. Or even see me. She made that pretty clear."

"Oh dear. I'm sorry that didn't work out the way you hoped." Coop sat down at the table near her. "But at least you tried. You may never know how your conversation may come back to her sometime down the road. You just planted a seed. God will take care of the watering and nurturing. You did your part."

"Funny you should say that, Mom. I was praying about it afterward, and that's pretty much what God revealed to me. I did my part. Now God would use my efforts. I shouldn't beat myself up over her refusal to listen. I did what he asked of me."

"Only time will tell, I guess. Sometimes we don't get what we pray for right away. Sometimes we just have to wait. God knows the best timing. Meanwhile, we trust."

Coop looked at her closely. "Are we talking about Misty here, or are we talking about Dad now?"

She took a deep breath. "Could be both, don't you think?"

"Yes. True. How is Dad today?"

"Well, he said he wants to get up and sit on the porch for a while. I hope it's not too hot for him, but he's usually cold anyway, so it might be okay for a bit. Would you help me move him to the wheelchair? I don't think he could walk that far, even with his walker."

"Sure. It's a good thing we borrowed that wheelchair from the family at church. Dad didn't want us to, at first, but I'm glad we took them up on the offer. It's going to come in handy."

They went to the bedroom, where they found Walter sitting up on the side of the bed. Marla Jean wagged her finger at him and said, "Walter Smith! You know you are supposed to wait for one of us to help you get up. Don't be trying this on your own!"

He waved his hand in the air and said, "I can do it. You all don't need to hover over me."

"Tell me that again, next time we have to pick you up off the floor. Now, let's get you into this wheelchair, and then Coop will take you out to the porch."

"Bathroom first," he said, pointing to the porta-potty. Coop left the room to give them some privacy, and Marla Jean assisted Walter with his clothing.

Coop waited in the living room for them to get ready. This process took several minutes, he knew, and was taking longer and longer each time. Since he had a few minutes, he decided to make a phone call.

Becky and Jenny were carrying buckets of blueberries to their car when Becky heard her phone ring and felt the vibrations in her back pocket. She quickly unlocked the trunk and sat her berries inside. She grabbed the phone just before it went to voice mail. She didn't recognize the number but answered it anyway. "Hello?"

"Hi, Becky, it's Cooper. I'm just calling to say hi."

"Coop? Oh, hi! How did you get my number?"

"I asked Doc Larson for it a couple of days ago. I hope you don't mind."

"No, of course not. It's fine. Just surprised me, that's all." She helped Jenny lift her bucket into the trunk and slammed the lid. "How's Riley? Is everything okay?"

"Riley's doing okay. Really slowing down, and he can't do the steps anymore. I have to carry him up and down. He spends most of his time sleeping beside my dad."

"And how is your dad?"

"He seems pretty good today. Talking quite a bit, and he wants to go outside and sit on the porch. I'm just about to get him loaded into the wheelchair and take him out there."

"That's good. Some fresh air and a change of scenery can really perk up the spirits. Better than medicine sometimes." Jenny got in the car and closed the door. Becky also got in and sat in the driver's seat. She closed her door, started the engine, and put all the windows down, to get a little breeze blowing through the car. At least they had parked in the shade.

"Hey, are you busy? Did I hear car doors? Do you need to go? We can stop talking if you're driving. I don't want to bother you."

"It's no bother at all, Coop. Yes, we're in the car, but I don't need to drive right away. Jenny and I just picked at least two gallons of blueberries at the pick it yourself field. We're going to go home and freeze most of these, and make some blueberry muffins." From the back seat, Jenny popped in, "Yummy, yummy! Muffins in my tummy!"

Coop laughed. "Tell her that I'd love to try one of her muffins!"

Becky relayed the message and Jenny said, "We can take you one tomorrow at church."

"Great idea!" Coop said. "I picked some berries myself this morning. Blackberries. Dana is going to make a cobbler."

"Mmmm, that sounds good too," said Becky. "With ice cream?"

"Of course! That's the only way!" He heard his parents' bedroom door open and saw his mother peek out, looking for him. He waved at her, pointed to his phone, and held up his index finger to make a sign indicating he needed just one more minute. She nodded.

"Hey, Becky, I gotta go. Mom and Dad need me to help get him into the wheelchair. Listen, about lunch tomorrow. I just wanted to tell you that I'm buying. Lunch for you and Jenny is my treat."

Becky stumbled over the words. "Well…but…no, you don't need to do that. I can pay."

"Nope. My treat. But tell Jenny I want one of her muffins. See you at Sunday school." Coop clicked the button on his phone before Becky could protest further.

As he walked back down the hall, he realized that he was smiling. When he entered his parents' room, he saw that his mother was smiling too.

Sitting in her car at the pick it yourself field, Becky was also smiling. Jenny was swinging her feet, singing, "Yummy, yummy! Muffins in my tummy!"

CHAPTER 31

— ✑ —

Time Off

"You look really nice this morning," Marla Jean said to her son. "You don't need to drive me to church today, honey. I think I need to stay home with your dad. Dana's going to stay home too. She said she's falling behind a little with her classwork. She's only taking one class this summer, but with everything else going on, she hasn't spent enough time on her studies. So you're on your own today."

"I think I can handle that," Coop said. "Remember, I'll be going out for lunch today, so don't expect me until afternoon."

"That's right. Well, have a nice time, honey. You're going to the diner?" she asked with raised eyebrows.

"Yeah, I know. Maybe not the best choice, but it was Greg and Nancy's suggestion. It'll be okay."

"I already told Kaye that I won't be able to accompany the choir today, or play for the hymns during the service. She was real nice about it, of course. We're blessed to have a lot of people in our congregation who can play piano and fill in. I even told her that I would like to take some time off, until we get through this crisis at home. I don't know how long that will be, but I thought it would be the best thing. It'll all work out."

Coop crossed the room and hugged his mother. "Love you, Mom."

CHAPTER 32

Table Talk

The first thing he saw as he walked up to the church was Jenny standing near the glass entrance doors. Then she disappeared a second and returned holding a sandwich bag with a blueberry muffin inside. She began jumping up and down excitedly as he neared the door. As soon as he opened the door, she thrust the muffin at him. "Here's your muffin!" she said proudly. "I made it."

He noticed Becky standing a little ways off and waved to her. Then he examined the muffin and said, "Mmm. Mmm...this looks delicious. I bet it smells good too."

"Open it. You can smell it. You can eat it too. It's really good. I had two already at breakfast!" They walked over to the coffee bar in the foyer, and Becky joined them. She had two cups of coffee in her hands, and sat one down in front of Cooper. "I didn't really know if you drank coffee, but I brought you some."

"I do, thanks. And it will be perfect to drink while I eat this amazing-looking muffin." He took a bite and smacked his lips. He bent down a little to talk to Jenny face-to-face.

"This is the best blueberry muffin I have ever eaten. Did you really make this all by yourself?"

"Well, Mommy helped me of course. I can't do the mixer. But I put all the ingredients in. You like it?"

He took another bite, chewed as if taste testing, and nodded enthusiastically. "I do. I really do. You can make blueberry muffins for me anytime."

"We have lots more at home. Maybe you can come over and have some more. Okay, Mommy?"

Jenny looked up at her mom, who was looking a little embarrassed and she took another sip of coffee to hide her face behind the paper cup. "We'll see, honey. Now you need to get to class. Look, I see Hannah coming right now." The Martin family had just come through the doors.

Greg came over to chat with Cooper while the two moms took their daughters to class. When they returned, Greg had coffee cups ready for himself and Nancy. Cooper wiped the last of the muffin crumbs off his chin with a napkin and handed Becky her half-empty cup of coffee. "Did you want some more" he asked.

She shook her head and said, "No, this is fine. Thanks, though." Coffee cups in hand, the four of them walked to the adult classroom.

Friendly greetings were exchanged as they walked into the room. Becky felt welcomed, as if she had been a member of the class for years. The lesson was on Romans chapter 10, verses 1 and 2. They had a lively discussion about Paul's great desire to bring souls to salvation. Everyone participated, with Coop being especially vocal. Becky sat beside him and admired his ability to get points across. It seemed like he spoke from the heart.

During the church service, while they were singing, Coop leaned down and whispered, "You have a nice singing voice. You should be in the choir."

"Thank you," she whispered back. "You too."

Coop leaned a little closer. He liked the smell of her hair.

After church, they all went to the diner. They parked in the lot on the alley and were the only three vehicles there. Coop had driven alone, so that Becky didn't have to leave her car parked unattended at the church.

Inside, behind the counter, Misty saw Coop's red truck drive by and turn into the alley. *Humph. Some nerve, coming here after the way he treated me.*

As they entered, Coop held the door for everyone. First the couple holding hands, then two little girls, and then a short brown-haired woman, then Coop. As the short lady came through the door, Coop placed his hand comfortably on her back and ushered her in. Misty noticed that his hand stayed there until they reached the table. He slid out a chair for one of the little girls and pushed her up to the table. Then he held the chair for the short lady, who sat down, smiled up at him, and said, "Thank you."

Misty brought over six glasses of water and asked if they would like anything else to drink. She spoke to everyone at the table, but avoided eye contact with Coop. The women ordered milk for the little girls, but everyone else just drank water. *Cheap*, thought Misty as she turned to get the milk.

Looking over the menus, the adults talked with the children about their choices. It wasn't busy in the diner, so Misty was able to hear most of the conversation from her place behind the counter. Both little girls decided on macaroni and cheese, hot dogs, and green beans. One of the little girls turned up her nose at the idea of the green beans, but her mother said, "Hannah, you just have to eat a few. Give it a try. Remember, we're trying to eat something green at every meal."

The other little girl laughed and said, "I love green beans. Mommy makes them good. They have bacon."

Cooper laughed at the girl, then turned to the short woman. "You cook your green beans with a little bacon? My mom does that too. Makes them really delicious."

"Yes, my mom taught me that trick. It's especially good with beans just picked from the garden."

Misty took their orders, talked to the cook, and waited. She cleared another table, washed the counter, and made herself unnecessarily busy with filling salt-and-pepper shakers. All the while she eavesdropped on the conversation at the table. There was talk of Sunday school lessons and Bible verses memorized. They talked about the beautiful song sung by the choir and the inspirational message preached. Misty shuddered. *Are all these people lunatics?* she wondered.

Becky watched to see if there was any interaction between Coop and the waitress, whose name was Misty, according to her name tag. However, there was no hint of recognition from either one of them. It was like they didn't even know each other at all. That seemed odd. It made Becky curious. Did they have something to hide?

When their food arrived and everything was set, they all joined hands in a circle around the table. Greg said he would pray, but first he had an announcement. He looked at his daughter and said, "Hannah, will you tell everyone our news?"

Hannah nodded and said, "I'm going to be a big sister!" Amid cheers and smiles, Cooper and Becky congratulated their friends. They learned that the baby was due in December, Nancy was feeling fine with no morning sickness this time, and they were thinking about buying a minivan.

Greg prayed, thanking God for the food, friends, and their growing family. As he said amen, Cooper squeezed Becky's hand. She squeezed his back. Jenny said, "I wish I could be a big sister," and they all laughed a little nervously. Coop leaned over to her and said, "Maybe you will be, someday." She giggled and looked at her mommy, who acted like she hadn't heard his comment.

Misty had heard. She was seething mad. She told Al she needed a break, stalked out of the back door with an ice pick in her hand, walked over to a car parked in the alley parking lot, and slashed a tire. She didn't know whose car it was, and it didn't really matter; she was so mad. But she hoped it belonged to that bitch who was obviously Coop's new girlfriend.

CHAPTER 33

Big Plans

Conversation continued at the lunch table. "You have any plans for the fourth?" Greg asked.

"To tell you the truth, Greg, I've totally lost track of days and holidays. With everything going on at home, I just haven't focused on anything but Dad and farmwork. When is the fourth?"

"It's Thursday." Greg looked at Becky. "Will you be off that day?"

"Yes, Doc Larson has decided to close the office. He'll be available for emergencies, but I'll have the day off unless he really needs me. Why?"

"Why don't we have a cookout at our house?" He turned to Nancy. "Would that be all right with you, hun? I'll do all the cooking on the grill. You girls can make some sides. Hannah and Jenny can play in the pool. Then we can go over to the football field and watch the fireworks. What do ya say?"

Coop looked doubtful. "Sounds like fun, but I'm not sure what will be going on with Dad. I could say yes, but then have to back out at the last minute. All depends on how his day is going. He has some good days and some bad, but lately the bad days are coming more often."

Becky reached for his arm as a gesture of comfort. He looked at her with appreciation and said, "You go on, though. Have a fun day. I'll join you if I can."

"I'm so sorry to hear about your dad," Nancy said. "I hope you can come, but we'll understand if you don't. Anyway, it will give me a chance to get to know Becky better."

"I'd like that," Becky said. To Coop she said, "I hope you can make it. I love watching fireworks."

"Me too," piped in Jenny. "Except the loud ones. The pretty ones are good."

"I'll try real hard to make it. It would be fun to watch the fireworks with you two." Then he looked at Greg and Nancy and said, "Well, with you guys too!"

Greg laughed and said, "Guess we know where your priorities lie!"

Becky changed the subject. "Jenny and I are making plans too. Her birthday is on the twentieth. It's a Saturday. I'm not planning anything big, just cake and ice cream with a few of her friends. Hannah, of course, and some other girls from church. I'm planning a couple of games, but mostly it will be playtime for the girls. I like simple parties. Less stress!"

Nancy answered, "As far as I know, there's nothing going on that day. I'll check the calendar when we get home and let you know. Hey, you know, I don't have your phone number. And I'll give you mine too."

Becky looked at Nancy and said, "If you needed my number, you could always ask Doc Larson!" She gave Coop a sideways glance, and his face turned a light shade of red.

"Hey, it worked, didn't it?"

As they stood to leave, Becky noticed that Nancy was reaching into her purse. She took out a three-by-five index card and laid it on the table. "What's that?" Becky asked.

"Oh, it's just a little note I like to leave when I go places. It's got some basic Scriptures and shows easy steps for salvation. I typed up a bunch and always leave one at restaurants and other places I shop. Sometimes I leave them on the checkout counter, and a few times I've put them inside books at the library. Just a little quiet way to witness and spread the gospel."

"That's nice. And goes right along with our Sunday school lesson this morning. I should do that too. I'm not so good with face-to-face witnessing, but this would be a way of sharing without pressure. And if someone were interested, they could dig deeper. Kinda like sowing a seed," Becky said, and Coop looked at her with a sort of wonderment.

"My dad told me about tracts they used, back in the day. He said it was a just like this, a way to witness but without personal contact, which was confrontational sometimes, and also to 'plant seeds.' They were small professionally printed booklets. I think he said one of them was called 'The Roman Road' and used verses from Romans to explain sin and salvation. They could be used as a guide for one-on-one witnessing too, but were often just left in public places, with a prayer that God would open the heart of the reader. A pretty good idea, really," Coop said. "Are we ready to go?"

They left the diner, and Misty went to clear the table. She found Nancy's note on the table and slipped it into her apron pocket. She'd read it later.

CHAPTER 34

Fixing Things

"Mom," Coop said into his phone, "I'm going to be a little later than I thought. I'm helping Becky with a flat tire. Is everything okay there?"

Marla Jean answered, "Everything's okay with your dad. Riley isn't doing too well, though. Dana just gave him another pain pill, but I'm not so sure that's going to help. He's really breathing hard."

"Okay, I'll be home as soon as I can. Do we still have a lot of that blackberry cobbler left? I was thinking I'd ask Becky and Jenny if they wanted to come out to the farm for some."

"Sure, hon, that would be fine. We have plenty left, and enough ice cream too."

Coop said goodbye and reached into Becky's trunk to get the jack. As he raised the car and began to remove the flat, he asked Becky if she'd like to follow him out to the farm for cobbler. Trying not to look too eager, Becky said, "Are you sure? By the time you finish this tire change, you'll probably have had enough of us. I don't want to impose on your afternoon plans."

He was busy removing the lug nuts on the tire, so he didn't notice her watching him. He had removed his dress shirt and was wearing only a tight white undershirt. With every twist of the lug wrench, Becky could see the muscles in his arms ripple and strain. He was strong. And fit. Very nice to look at.

His words brought her back to reality and made her heart skip a beat. "I can't think of any way I'd rather spend a Sunday afternoon than with you and Jenny sitting at the table with me, eating blackberry cobbler."

"With ice cream," put in Jenny.

"Yes, with ice cream." Coop removed the tire and put it into the trunk. Then he put the spare on and tightened the lug nuts. He lowered the car, put the jack away, and closed the trunk. "That should last you till you get to the tire store. You must have run over a nail or something. Maybe it would have been better to have left your car at the church."

"Maybe. But then I wouldn't have gotten to see how masterfully you can change tires. I'd probably still be working on the first lug nut. You are really strong." She reached over and massaged his upper arm muscle. He flexed it, and she sighed with exaggerated admiration.

Sweat was dripping down his face, but he was smiling. "Let's get out of here. It's hot."

Coop led the way out of town, down country roads, and finally to the driveway to the farm. As they pulled into the parking area near the house, the screen door opened, and Dana came running down the porch steps.

"Coop! Come quick! Something's wrong with Riley."

Coop took off on the run, and Becky followed quickly behind him. They found Riley lying on the porch floor. His body was still, and he looked like he was sleeping, with a blank faraway look in his eye. "What happened?" Becky knelt on the floor beside Riley. She put her hand on Riley's back and spoke soothingly to him. "It's going to be okay, baby." She looked at Coop and said, "Keep talking to him. Pet him, but not near his head." Then she turned her attention to Dana.

Dana said, "It was weird. We were just sitting out here, and he started whining. He tried to get up, but he couldn't. He was looking all around, whining. I didn't know what he needed. I thought maybe he wanted to go outside, so I stood up, and he like collapsed. Just fell over on his side. And his legs were twitching, like he was trying to run."

"Sounds like he had a seizure. How long did the twitching last?"

"Not long, really. Maybe a couple of minutes. But it seemed like forever. I didn't know what to do."

"As long as he's someplace where he can't hurt himself, there's not much you can do," Becky said. "Do you have a fan we could cool him with? We don't want him to get overheated." Dana went to get a box fan from the hall closet.

Becky said to Coop, "I know he had one seizure before, at the office. Has he had others?"

"No, never."

"Well, fortunately this didn't last too long. Over five minutes, and we'd be taking him in. But for now, we keep him cool and comfortable. Call Doc Larson, and tell him what happened. But you know, Coop"—she looked sadly at the dog—"you know this is only going to get worse. The seizures will be more frequent, and probably last longer each time."

"Oh, buddy, is it time? Are you ready?" Coop stroked Riley lovingly. Dana came back with the fan and turned it on. She knelt beside her brother and cried quietly while she petted Riley's hip. Becky went to stand beside her daughter, who was waiting patiently beside the door. Marla Jean was standing beside her.

Suddenly, they became aware of a slow, shuffling noise coming from the house. Marla Jean went to investigate and found Walter, walking slowly from the living room, using his walker and moving cautiously. She went close to him and walked at his side to steady him. When they got to the porch, she helped him sit down on a chair near Riley, who was beginning to recover as he lay on the floor.

Riley lifted his head when Walter sat down. He looked up at him, then laid his chin down on Walter's slipper, covering the toes. Walter reached down and patted his head. "Good boy, Riley. Good boy."

Walter looked around at his family, eyes finally resting on Dana. "We have to let him go. Don't make him suffer. We love him too much to let him suffer."

It was a lot of words, and took all the strength he could muster. He sat back in the chair and rested, trying to catch his breath. Becky had never met Walter before, and she was struck at how small and frail he seemed, especially in comparison to Coop's strong, healthy body. But the kindness in Walter's eyes was reflected in his son's. Becky had seen similar facial expressions in the younger Smith.

Marla Jean rested her hand on Walter's shoulder, and he reached up to place his hand on top of hers. He looked up at is wife and smiled. His smile was so like Coop's.

Coop stood and cleared his throat. "I'll call Doc in the morning and arrange it." He turned to ask Becky, "Do you think he would come out to the farm? I think Riley would understand it better if we were all here with him."

She stood at his side and said, "I'm sure he would. I'll come too, if you want."

Coop took her hand in appreciation. "I'd like that a lot. Thank you."

Becky knelt down at Riley's side and petted him, running her hand gently from head to hip. "He's coming around now. Just let him rest as long as he needs. Sometimes they urinate when they have seizures, but I don't think Riley did. That's good."

She stood and looked at Walter, holding out her hand to shake his. "Hello, Mr. Smith. I'm Becky Emerson, and this is my daughter Jenny. We're friends of Coop's, from church. It's a pleasure to meet you, sir."

Walter had a little twinkle in his eye as he said, "Two pretty girls in my house! Good thing I don't have heart troubles! Might not be able to handle it!"

Everyone laughed, and Walter started coughing. The fit didn't last long, and Marla Jean said, "How about we let Riley rest out here, and we all go in the kitchen and have some blackberry cobbler?" They all moved inside, and Marla Jean noticed that Coop had taken Becky's hand again.

Over cobbler and ice cream, the family got to know Becky and Jenny. Marla Jean asked, "Coop told me you had a flat tire. How did that happen?"

"I don't know. We came out of the diner, and it was flat. Good thing Coop was there to help me. Those lug nuts were on tight. I probably couldn't have gotten them off myself."

"Be sure to take the doughnut into the tire shop as soon as you can. You shouldn't drive on it more than you have to. Call me if you need any help. I could pick you up if you need a ride anywhere," Coop offered.

"Thanks, I appreciate that." Becky ate the last bite of her cobbler and scooped some melted ice cream with her spoon. "This is really good. I'd love the recipe, if you share!"

"Oh sure, I'll write it out for you," said Dana. "We have lots of blackberry bushes here. It tastes best with freshly picked berries. Maybe you and Jenny could come out and pick some sometime."

Jenny sat up and licked her spoon. "We picked blueberries. I made muffins."

Coop added, "And they were delicious. Jenny is a good muffin maker. I bet blackberry muffins would be good too."

Jenny said, "Blueberries. Blackberries. Why aren't raspberries called redberries?"

"That's a good question, Jenny," said Marla Jean. "I wonder that too!"

Dana gathered up the dishes and set them into the sink. Becky offered to help, but Dana shooed her away. "You're company. Maybe next time, when you're family." She giggled, a little embarrassed by her brashness, and Becky blushed. "Seriously," said Dana, "He's a good guy. I can tell he likes you."

Marla Jean and Cooper were helping Walter get settled into his recliner. Coop came back to the kitchen and asked,

"Becky, do you and Jenny have time to take a walk with me around the farm?"

Jenny jumped up and down and said, "Can we, Mommy? Can we? I want to see the animals."

Walking to the barn, Coop again reached for Becky's hand. She willingly walked along with him, talking while Jenny ran ahead to the fence around the chicken yard. Coop opened the gate and let them all go through. He motioned to Jenny to follow him and took her to the hen-house. They went in, and Coop raised one of the hens up off her brood. There were several newborn chicks, just days old, fluffy and yellow. "Can I hold one?" Jenny asked in a whisper. He showed her how to carefully hold and protect the baby. From the doorway, Becky pulled out her cell phone and took a picture.

As Jenny cradled the chick, Coop said, "The hen protects her chicks by hiding them under her wings. She can get a lot of little chicks under her wings. She spreads her wings and covers them, so a fox or possum doesn't see them. She can keep them safe and dry in a rainstorm too. Whenever I see a hen with chicks under her wings, I remember the verses in the Bible that talk about how Jesus wants to cover his people with his wings, and keep us safe from danger." He took the chick back from Jenny and returned it to the nest. "Lots of things on the farm remind me how Jesus loves us and promises to protect us."

Jenny suddenly burst into song. "Jesus loves me, this I know. For the Bible tells me so." Coop and Becky joined her at the end. "Yes, Jesus loves me, the Bible tells me so."

Coop took them through the barn and into the barn-yard. He whistled, and two horses appeared. "This one is

Dana's horse, her name is Nell. And this is my buddy Slick. He's looking for a carrot, which I just happen to have in my pocket." He pulled two carrots out of his back pocket and offered one to Jenny. "Do you want to feed him?"

"Okay. How?"

"Just hold out your hand flat and put the carrot on your hand. He'll pull it off with his lips. Just keep your hand flat. Don't try to hold on to the carrot."

"Oh, his teeth are big!" She giggled. When Slick pulled the carrot free of her hand and gobbled it, she said, "I did it. Let me feed Nell too!"

Becky smiled and snapped another picture.

Horses satisfied, Jenny said, "Do you have cows?"

"Yes, we do. And baby calves too. They are out in the pasture eating grass and getting fat! They stay out there most all the time, except for one. Her name is Bessie, and she gives us fresh milk every day. I milked her in the barn this morning before church."

"Can I milk her too?"

"Well, she only gets milked once a day, so we'll have to do that some other time when you are here. Okay?"

"Let's come back again, Mommy. Then you can take my picture with a cow. Tomorrow, okay?"

Becky laughed and said, "Not tomorrow, honey. But yes, we will come back. If we're invited," she added looking at Coop.

He took both of her hands in his and, looking down, said, "Oh, you're invited. Definitely. Anytime."

Becky smiled up at him and said, "I'd like that. We'd like that."

Walking back to the house, one of the barn cats came across the yard and twined herself among Becky's legs. Jenny sat down on the grass, and the cat came over and plopped on her lap, purring and licking herself. "Listen, Mommy. She's purring. She likes me!" Becky took a picture.

Coop said, "I do believe Jenny has made a friend. This cat's name is Muffin, but she's not a blueberry!"

Jenny giggled, "You're silly, Coop. Muffin is a silly name. She's a cat, not a muffin."

"You'll have to talk to my sister about that. She's the one who named her."

Becky said, "Come on, Jenny, we need to get going. I'm sure Coop has plenty to do today, and we have Winnie the Pooh waiting at home."

Walking to the cars, Jenny squeezed herself in between the adults, grabbed one hand from each, and said, "Swing me, swing me." Over her head, Becky and Coop looked at each other, kept walking, and said together, "One. Two. Three," and lifted Jenny from the ground. They swung her back and forth as they walked to the car. Jenny giggled and said, "Again, again please."

From the kitchen window, Marla Jean and Dana watched and smiled at each other.

Becky opened the back door of her car, and Jenny climbed in. Becky shut the door and went up front to her own seat. Before she got in, she turned to Coop and said, "Thanks for lunch and everything. The tire, the cobbler, the time with your family. Thanks for showing Jenny the animals. We've had a nice day."

"I'm happy too. It's nice to spend time with you. And Jenny's a great little girl."

"Oh, you've just seen the good side of her! She can be a handful sometimes!"

"Really? I'd like to see that! In fact, I'd like to see a lot more of both of you. I hope I can make it to the picnic Thursday. I think I might need a diversion about then anyway. Besides that, I want to be with you watching fireworks. Does Jenny like them?"

"She's never seen them, actually. When she was little, I thought she was too young. I was going to take her last year, but it rained. We've watched them on television, and seen a few set off in our neighborhood. We just stayed in the house and watched from the window. So this will be her first time for a real fireworks display."

"Well, then, I'll really try to get there. I'd love to see her reactions."

"I'd like that too." Becky looked up at him, and he leaned down. She thought maybe he was going to kiss her, but instead he gave her a warm hug.

"Drive safe. And get that new tire." She got into the car, and he closed the door. She rolled down the window and said, "Good luck with Riley tonight."

"Thanks. And thanks for your help with him today. You'll be at work tomorrow at nine?"

She nodded and he said, "I'll call the office at nine or so. Talk to you then. Bye."

"Bye," she said and Jenny added, "Tell Muffin I love her.

"I will! Bye, Jenny!"

CHAPTER 35

ᴄ᷎ꝏ

See Ya Soon

When the phone rang at Doc Larson's office the next morning, Becky's heart skipped a beat, and she took a deep breath before she answered. She suspected it was Coop, but thanks to caller ID she knew. "Hi, Coop. How are you?"

"I'm okay. We all are. We know this is the right thing to do."

"I hope you don't mind, but I already told Doc to expect your call. We cleared some time off the schedule around eleven o'clock, if that works for you."

"Yes, that should be fine. Thanks for doing that."

"You're welcome. Do you want to talk to Doc first? He's with a patient right now, but I could have him call you back."

"No, that's okay. I know what to expect. I don't have any questions. Will you be coming with him?"

"If you still want me to."

"I do. I really do."

"Okay then, I'll be there." Coop heard someone come in and ask her a question. "Sorry, Coop, I have to go now. See you in a bit."

"Goodbye, Becky."

At shortly after eleven o'clock, Doc Larson's truck pulled into the driveway. He and Becky got out and walked to the porch, where the family had gathered. Even Walter was there, sitting on the lawn chair. Dana was sitting on the floor with Riley cradled in her lap. She and her mother were crying. Coop was trying to be strong. Walter was looking at something off in the distance, with a slight smile on his face.

Doc Larson brought a syringe out of his bag and looked around at his friends. "Are you ready?" he asked, and reluctantly they all nodded their heads. He knelt beside Dana and Riley and positioned the syringe in Riley's leg. To Dana he said, "It will be just like he's falling asleep." He patted Riley on the head and said, "You've been a good boy. Now cross the Rainbow Bridge, and run pain-free. Wait for us. We'll all see you soon." He inserted the needle and pushed down the plunger.

Riley took his last breaths, and it was done. Peaceful and calm. Done. Walter burst in to a big smile. "See ya soon, buddy. See ya real soon."

CHAPTER 36

Almost as Good

Wanda and Judy, another hospice nurse, arrived that afternoon to check on Walter and schedule future visits. Wanda noticed right away that something was wrong. There was an atmosphere of grief in the room, and it was obvious that Marla Jean and Dana had been crying. Red puffy eyes were a dead giveaway.

Wanda went right over to Marla Jean and grabbed her hands. "What's wrong? Is Walter okay?"

"Oh, yes, everything's all right. It's just that, well, we had to put our dog down this morning. It's been really hard." The tears welled up in Marla Jean's eyes again, and she dabbed them away with a tissue. "I'm sorry. Riley was a big part of our family, for over twelve years, and this is just so hard."

"Oh, honey, I understand. Our pets do become family. Is there anything I can do for you? Do you need to talk about it? How's Walter doing with the loss?"

"We'll be fine. It's just strange not having Riley around. And Walter, he's taking it great. In fact, he's dealing with it better than any of us."

"That's wonderful. It wouldn't do for him to be agitated or upset by this." Wanda motioned for the other nurse to come over, "Marla Jean, this is Judy. She'll be the nurse coming to help you in the weeks ahead. Judy will help with bathing, dressing, and other personal-care responsibilities, as you need them. And she will also be here for you to talk to, so any questions you have, or concerns, bring them to Judy."

Judy stretched out her hand to Marla Jean and said, "You might not need my help much at first, and that's fine. Some visits we might just sit and talk. It's often a good time to talk about memories, share funny stories, things like that. But as you need more assistance, I'll be here. And also, I'll be monitoring vitals and sending notes to the doctor. Together, all of us will work out the best care plan for your husband."

"Thank you," said Marla Jean. "This is our daughter Dana. She has been helping a lot with her dad. And our son Cooper is out in the field now, but he also is helping a lot. We're doing okay for now, but the time may come…" She drifted off and didn't finish the sentence, but everyone knew what she meant.

Judy said, "You've been carrying this burden for a while already. I'll be here to give you a break from time to time. I can stay with him if you need to run into town for something, or make phone calls, or visit with a friend or even take a nap. You just need to know you are not in this alone."

"Thank you," she said again. "I appreciate your kindness. Well, we all do."

Judy asked, "Could I meet Walter now?" and they moved down the hall to the bedroom. Walter was sitting up in bed, reading his Bible. His eyes brightened as he focused on the two nurses. "Wanda, I see you brought a friend! I must be a tough patient, if it takes two of you to take care of me." He sat back, out of breath already. But he was smiling at his little joke.

"I'm Judy. Nice to meet you, Walter. I'll be coming to see you Monday, Wednesday, and Friday. How are you feeling today?"

"Oh, pretty good. Better, now that I have a room full of pretty ladies!" That lightened the mood in the room slightly.

Judy went on to take Walter's vitals and record them. Before long, they were talking like old friends. After a few minutes, Judy said, "I'm sorry to hear that you lost your dog this morning. Want to talk about him?"

Walter told Judy some stories about Riley as a puppy, and how quickly he learned herding and tricks. He had to stop often, to get a deep breath, or to work through a coughing spell.

To give Walter a chance to rest, Wanda interrupted his storytelling to talk about her own dog and some tricks she could do. Walter rested against his pillows and listened, laughing when Wanda told some funny anecdote.

Then Judy asked, "And how are you feeling about Riley's passing?"

"Well, the thing is. I believe in Heaven," Walter said. "And I think dogs will be there. So I'll see him again. Soon. He won't have to wait long."

"That's a comfort to you, isn't it?" asked Judy.

Walter nodded. "Almost as good as seeing Jesus!"

CHAPTER 37

The Plans I Have for You

Cuddled up with Patch in his bed, Misty pitched her plan. Her head was lying on his chest, and she was twirling his chest hairs in her fingers. She seemed calm and confident, but inside she was excited and giddy. She'd show him. Benjamin Cooper Smith would regret the way he had treated her. She was about to make his life miserable. And she was going to get rich doing it too!

"It might work, but only if we have help. He's a big guy. I don't think the two of us could move his dead weight. How about I ask Billy?" Patch shifted onto his side and nibbled on her ear as he thought. "We'd have to pay him something."

"Well, something maybe, but not a three-way split. Just enough to keep him quiet." Misty shuddered as Patch's hand crept up her thigh. She opened her legs and welcomed his probing fingers.

"He might even do it for free, if we offered him a little of this," he said as he mounted her. "Then there'd be more cash for the two of us."

Misty squirmed and settled herself comfortably under him. "Mmmm. Good idea. Good, baby. Don't stop."

On Wednesday, Becky called Coop to say that Riley's ashes were ready and could be picked up anytime. "Or I could drive out to your place and bring them," she offered.

"Dana has class this afternoon, so she should be able to get the ashes on the way home," Coop said. "Although I'd like the chance to see you again. But I'd hate to have you drive all the way out here, if Dana's right there for class anyway. Hey, did you get your tire fixed?"

"I did. Actually, I had to buy a new one. The hole in the old tire was huge. The guy at the tire store said he didn't think it was a nail, but he didn't know what caused it. Anyway, he took the doughnut off and put it back in the trunk. Hopefully I won't need it again for a long, long time!"

"Good, I'm glad you took care of it. Now I feel better. You'll be safer driving on good tires, not that doughnut."

Becky was touched by his comment. "And how are you doing, Coop? And Dana? About Riley, I mean."

"It's funny how much we miss him. I go out to the chicken house and expect to see him follow me to bring the chickens in. Or Dana starts to feed him, and then remembers. I saw Dad sitting in his recliner, with his hand over the arm of the chair, like he always used to do to pet Riley while he was sleeping there. It's going to take a while to get used to, I guess."

"What time do you think Dana will be here? The office closes at four today."

"Her class is over at three, I think. So she should have plenty of time to get there by four." Coop didn't want to hang up, but he also didn't want to bother her while she was at work. "Hey, are you busy? Do you have a minute to talk?"

"Not very busy. It's nearly lunch, and we don't have any patients scheduled until afternoon. What's up?"

"I just like talking to you, that's all." He paused a minute and could picture her smiling. "Um, I was wondering."

"Wondering what?"

"Wondering if you would like to go out with me. On a real date. Just the two of us."

"Sure, I'd like that! Where?" She hoped she didn't seem too overly eager. But then again, maybe that would be okay. It would be real, at least.

"I haven't thought that far ahead yet. I just wanted to see if you would want to. I'll work that out and get back to you."

"I'll need time to figure out someone to watch Jenny, of course. Mom is usually available, except for Wednesday evenings because of choir. Do you know yet if you can go to Greg and Nancy's tomorrow for the picnic and the fireworks?"

"I hope to. Dad has had a couple of really good days, so maybe tomorrow will be good too. Did they say what time?"

"Nancy said anytime after three. She said we'd eat about five. She gave me directions, and I think I can find it easy. Did you know they have a pool?"

"I do remember Greg talking about that when they were doing some landscaping around it. Do you plan to go swimming?"

"Oh no, not me. I don't know how to swim. But Nancy says there's a shallow end, so I might let Jenny play in it."

"You can't swim?"

"Nope. Years of lessons during summer camp, and I still never learned."

"Maybe I'll have to teach you."

She laughed. "Maybe not. I'm a hopeless case."

"We'll see about that. Well, I better let you get back to work. Sure hope I can get over there tomorrow. It'll be fun." He really wanted to say something about how being close to her made him happy, but he thought better of it. It was too soon. It was the truth, but too soon.

They said goodbye, and Becky smiled as she put down the phone. This was beginning to feel nice. Real nice.

Just before closing time, Dana arrived to pick up Riley's ashes. Doc Larson was in the lobby when she arrived, and he looked at her compassionately. "How are you doing, Dana? You okay?" He handed her a small wooden box with a paw print engraved on the top. He also gave her Riley's collar and tags. "I thought you might want these too."

"Yes, I do. Thanks. I'm all right. It's just different, empty, without him around." She looked at Becky and said, "I saw this idea for a project I can do. I'll take Riley's food dish, put the collar around it, and plant something in it, maybe hens and chicks since Riley took care of the chickens at our place. It'll be a little memorial to him."

"That sounds like a nice idea," Becky said. "Collies are so special. I grew up with them. I think they're the best dogs ever. I know you're going to miss him for a long time to come."

"It's funny, though. Dad seems to be almost happy these last couple of days. He keeps looking far off and smiling. I thought he'd be really upset about Riley, but it's like he is happy he's gone."

"I don't think he's happy that Riley is gone," said Doc. "He's happy that Riley is pain-free and waiting at the Rainbow Bridge for him. And knowing that his own time is coming soon, he is thinking that they will be reunited soon. It's a very comforting thought for him right now."

"You may be right," Dana said, and tears came to her eyes. "It's comforting to me too."

Becky came out from behind the counter and gave Dana a hug. "Hey, if you need to talk, I'm right here. I know we don't know each other really well, but I'm a good listener. In fact, if you're not doing anything tomorrow, why don't you come over to the Martins for a picnic? I'm sure they won't mind having you. Coop said he would try to make it, unless your Dad needs him. So if you want, come along with him. I'd like to get to know you better too."

"Well, if you're sure it would be okay with the Martins. I don't want to spoil your party."

"Don't be silly! You are most welcome. I'll call them and let them know, but I'm sure it's just fine. I'm making potato salad and some Rice Krispies treats. You can bring something if you want, but you don't have to. Nancy has baked beans and watermelon."

"How about some deviled eggs? I can bring that."

"That's perfect. I hope you can come. And Coop too."

"I'll tell you one thing," said Dana. "I haven't seen Coop so happy in a long time. You are having a good effect on him!"

Becky chuckled. "I think it's actually Jenny who makes him laugh. She can be a real character!"

Dana looked at her and said, "Jenny might make him laugh. But you make him smile." Becky blushed and cast her eyes down. "I better get going. You need to close up and get on to church for Wednesday-night services."

Becky glanced at the clock. "I guess you're right. I usually have supper at Mom's on Wednesday nights. She and Jenny will be waiting for me."

Dana left, carefully carrying her mementos. Becky closed up, said goodbye to Doc Larson, and headed to her mom's. She made a quick stop at the grocery store to pick up marshmallows and ten pounds of potatoes. She'd get going on the potato salad after church. Tomorrow morning she'd let Jenny help her with the Rice Krispies treats.

Driving along, Becky found herself humming the song she was learning at the single-moms' group. She wanted to find all the words, so she could teach Jenny. Her heart danced a bit at the thought of being with Cooper tomorrow. She smiled as she remembered walking with him at the farm, swinging Jenny between them. Her giggles made the day complete. Well, Coop's big hug did too.

CHAPTER 38

———— ❧ ————

Getting to Know All About You

Becky carried the potato salad and had a bag of swimming things thrown over her shoulder. Jenny proudly brought the dessert. They walked up the sidewalk, and Becky was about to ring the doorbell when suddenly the door was opened, and Hannah called out, "Mommy! Jenny is here!"

Nancy appeared around the corner of the kitchen, wiping her hands on a dish towel. "Hi, Jenny. Hi, Becky. Welcome! Come on in. The kitchen's right this way."

They put their food dishes down on the counter, and Hannah took Jenny off to see her room. Nancy offered Becky a seat at the island and said, "I'm almost finished with everything, but I need to cut the watermelon slices." When Becky offered to help, Nancy brought her the watermelon and a big knife. As Becky sliced watermelon, Nancy placed condiments, paper plates, and plastic silverware on a tray.

Becky looked around the kitchen. It was cheerfully decorated with sunflowers on the towels and curtains. A fresh bouquet of sunflowers stood in the corner between the refrigerator and the farm sink. "You have a beautiful home, Nancy," she said. "How long have you lived here?"

"We moved in just before Hannah's first birthday. We were in an apartment before that, but when this house came on the market, we knew it was a great deal. And we were ready to buy instead of rent. Where do you live?"

"I rent a little two-bedroom house over on Garth. It's fine for us. I like that I don't have to worry about mainte-nance or lawn care. The landlord does it for us. As a single mom, I think it's better not to have those heavy responsi-bilities. I have enough to do without mowing a lawn!"

"I'm sure you're right. Do you like your job with Doc Larson?"

"Oh, I sure do. I think God provided that job for me, at just the right time. I feel like he wants me there. That might be kinda odd to say, but I think I'm there for a rea-son. Just a feeling I've had from the beginning." She looked around the kitchen and noticed a pet food dish on the floor in the corner. "What kind of pet do you have?"

"We have a cat named Marmalade. She's probably with the girls in the bedroom. She loves Hannah to pieces."

Becky chuckled. "That's funny. Coop has a cat named Muffin! Muffin and Marmalade. Too cute."

"Actually, Muffin is Marmalade's mother. When Muffin had kittens a couple of years ago, the Smiths were giving them away, and Hannah started begging for a kitten as soon as she heard. We went out to the farm, and Hannah got to choose. She wanted two, but we had to say no! If not, we probably would have ended up with six or seven!"

"Jenny hasn't been around animals much, but she fell in love with Muffin."

"So you've been out to the farm?"

"Yes, we went out after Coop changed my tire Sunday. Dana made blackberry cobbler. Really good. Oh, by the way, I invited Dana to come over with Coop. Hope that's okay. She's going to bring deviled eggs. That is, if they come."

"Sure, it's fine. The more the merrier. I hope they can come. Have you heard from Coop today? I wonder how his dad is doing."

"We talked yesterday, but I haven't heard anything today. His dad is looking frail, but hanging in there. At least on Monday when I saw him last."

"You were out to the farm Sunday and Monday too? That's nice. You're spending a lot of time with Coop. He's a great guy, I'm glad he's found a girl."

"We're just friends, Nancy. Nothing serious. I do agree, he's a great guy. But we barely know each other. And I'm not about to rush into things. Did that once, and learned my lesson."

"Care to talk about it? I don't want to pry." Before Becky could answer, Greg came in from the deck and said, "Hi, Becky. Hey, if the girls are going to get into the pool, they better come out now. Everything's ready out there. I'll start grilling in about an hour, but that will give them time to play before we eat. Coop's not here yet?"

Nancy went to Hannah's room to get the girls, and Becky answered, "Not yet. I really don't know if he's going to make it or not."

Greg laughed. "There's food. He'll be here!" He looked at her and smiled. "And you're here. That's extra incentive." Becky blushed and turned to wash the cutting board and knife in the sink. "I've seen that boy put away some burgers. He can eat four or five, no problem."

"Really? That's crazy! Well, I guess he's a hardworking man, needs lots of protein!"

Jenny came into the kitchen with a big orange cat draped over her arm. The cat was so heavy Jenny could hardly carry her. "Look, Mommy. This is Marmalade."

Becky laughed and patted the cat's head. "Goodness, she's a big one!"

"Yeah, we figure Marmalade's daddy was a mountain lion," Greg joked. "This is a mighty big cat. We never imagined she'd grow this big!"

"We see a lot of cats at the vet's office, but I've never seen one so big." Becky went to her swim bag and said to Jenny, "Put the kitty down, honey, and let's get you ready for the pool." Jenny had her swimming suit on under her clothes, and as Becky helped her get out of her shorts and shirt, she reminded her about staying in the shallow end and being careful. Once outside by the pool, Becky covered Jenny with sunscreen. As she adjusted Jenny's water wings, she said, "Now remember, stay at the shallow part." They walked to the pool's edge and were splashed when Hannah jumped into the four-foot water.

"Hannah's quite a good swimmer already," she said to Nancy, who was standing beside her. "This is Jenny's first time." Becky kicked off her sandals and walked down the steps in the shallow end, holding Jenny's hand. Hannah swam over to her friend and encouraged her to walk in. Jenny ventured out, with water about chest deep. Becky sat on the edge of the pool, with her feet dangling in the warm water and watched her daughter, amazed at her courage to try new things. *My baby's growing up*, she thought. *She'll be fine in kindergarten.*

Just then, a big beach ball flew over Becky's head and landed with a splash right in front of her. She leaned back in surprise, sputtering, shaking her head, and rubbing water off her shirt. Coop leaned down behind her, put his hands on her shoulders and his face close to hers, and said, "Surprise!"

Becky laughed and said, "You!" He stood and Becky looked up at him, shielding her eyes with her hand. "I'm glad you could make it. Is Dana here too?"

"Yes, she took the eggs into the house. I wanted to sneak up on you." He turned to Jenny and said, "How's the water, Jenny?" He was walking toward the deep end, and Becky noticed that he was wearing cutoff shorts and a T-shirt. She'd never seen him in anything but long pants, and noted that his legs were pale in comparison to his arms. *Makes sense, I guess. He probably wears jeans around the farm all the time, even in summer. That's practical.*

Coop stood at the edge of the six-foot end, reached for the bottom of his T-shirt, and raised his hands over his head. He peeled off the shirt, tossed it aside, and said to Jenny, "Here I come, ready or not." Becky noticed his chest muscles and tight abs. She sighed and hoped that no one noticed. Coop winked at her and jumped.

Water splashed everywhere, little girls squealed in delight, and Coop swam swiftly underwater to Jenny. He surfaced right in front of her, and she burst into laughter. "You want to go out deeper?" Coop asked.

"Can I go with Coop, Mommy? Please? I'm not scared."

Becky said, "As long as you hold on tight." To Coop, she said, "You know this is her first time in a pool. Watch her carefully."

"Fear not. I know what I'm doing. I taught Dana how to swim." He looked up to see that Dana was just coming to the pool's edge. "Didn't I, Dana?"

"That he did," she said, as she lowered herself to sit beside Becky. Coop carried Jenny to the deeper water and showed her that her water wings would keep her afloat. "Of course, he didn't tell you that he pushed me into the pond, so it was basically sink or swim. And I swam. I was five, he was twelve. He thought he was pretty funny."

"Oh my goodness. Think I can trust him to take care of Jenny?"

Dana kicked her feet in the water. "Sure. He's grown up since then. A little." She laughed as Hannah swam over to Coop and splashed him. He splashed her back, and Jenny smacked her hand onto the water to make splashes too. Soon water was flying everywhere. The girls were giggling, and Coop seemed to be having as much fun as they were.

Nancy came and sat with Becky and Dana. "I'm so glad you guys could come," she said to Dana. "I didn't know Coop would be such a good babysitter. I'll have to remember that! How is he with changing diapers?"

"I have no clue." Dana laughed. "He has no trouble dealing with cow pies and manure in the barns, so I imagine he'd be fine with a baby diaper!"

"I never had problems with poopy diapers," Becky said. "But it was the vomit that could turn my stomach."

"Oh right, vomit is the worst," Nancy said. "But let's not talk about that now, just before we eat!"

"How've you been feeling? Are you having morning sickness?" Becky asked while keeping her eyes on Jenny and Coop. He was letting her float on her own, but staying close enough to reach her easily if she needed him. Becky began to relax but stayed watchful. She was enjoying watching them play. It was also nice to sit back and have some girl time.

Nancy shook her head. "So far, so good. I just get tired easy. And there's a lot to do. I need to get the nursery set up. We are going to turn the office into the baby's room. We can put the computer and files pretty much anywhere."

"If there's anything I can do to help, just let me know. Decorating a baby's room would be fun. When Jenny was born, I lived with my mom, and Jenny just shared my room. We didn't do anything other than buy a crib."

Greg called from near the grill, "Hey, Nancy, I think I'd better start cooking the burgers. Better get the girls out and dried off."

Coop walked with the girls to the steps and made sure they got out safely. Becky stood up and got a towel for Jenny. "Did you have fun?" she asked, as she removed the water wings.

"Yes, Mommy, I did have fun." Becky wrapped the towel around Jenny's shoulders and squeezed some water out of her ponytail. Jenny put her arms around her mother's neck and pulled her close, so she could whisper in Becky's ear. "I like Coop, Mommy."

Becky whispered back, "I think he likes you too. It looked like you were both having fun." She watched Coop as he climbed out of the pool. He whipped his head around to splatter droplets of water from his hair. He picked up a towel from a lawn chair and draped it across his shoulder.

Coop walked to Becky and said, "Next time, you're getting in too. I promise I won't let you drown. I took good care of Jenny, didn't I? You're safe with me!"

"I'm not so sure about that. Dana told how you nearly drowned her when she was little."

"Nah, I wouldn't do that to you. Trust me. I'll take good care of you." He leaned down and kissed her lightly on the top of her head. His touch was so gentle Becky wasn't even sure he had kissed her. Maybe it was just her imagination.

Greg called, "Coop, if you can tear yourself away, get your shirt on and come help me with these burgers. I need a hand."

"Sure," Coop said as he searched for his shirt. "I hope you're making lots of burgers. I'm starved. Bet I could eat four. Maybe five."

Greg caught Becky's eye and winked. "Told ya!"

Dana and Nancy came from the house carrying the sides. Nancy asked Becky to bring out the plates and condiments. Soon the group was seated around a long, wooden picnic table. Before they ate, Greg asked them all to join hands, and he offered a prayer. Once again, Becky felt Coop squeeze her hand at the Amen. But instead of dropping hands, Coop held Becky's a few seconds longer than necessary. He only loosened his grip when Becky needed two hands to help Jenny pass a heavy bowl of baked beans.

The meal continued with eating, laughing, talking, laughing, and more eating. Then more eating. "Who made the potato salad?" Coop asked as he reached for his third helping. He looked around at the table and said, "Greg, pass me the plate of hamburgers please. I'm ready for number four."

"Four? Why don't you just take two this time? You know you're going to want the fifth one."

"Good idea," he said as he placed two burgers on his plate. "So who did make the potato salad?" he repeated.

"I did," said Becky. "I take it you like it?" She chuckled as she pointed to the heap on his plate."

"Very good," Coop said, and he lifted another forkful to his mouth. "Best I've ever had."

Dana said, "I won't tell Mom you said that."

"Oh, she'd understand. Mom knows how to recognize a good cook, and this potato salad tells me that Becky is a good cook." He looked past Becky to Jenny sitting on the other side. "And Jenny makes delicious blueberry muffins." Jenny smiled and took another big bite of her hamburger.

When everyone had eaten all they possibly could, they worked together to clear the table and put away leftovers. There weren't many! Coop polished off the last deviled egg as the tray was carried past him. Jenny and Hannah were in charge of finding the paper plates and cups and putting them in the trash bag. The women wrapped leftovers and put them in the refrigerator. Greg and Coop cleaned the grill and closed it up. Soon Jenny and Hannah went off to Hannah's room, Marmalade following close on their heels. The adults all retired to sit around the pool. The sun was starting to go down, but it would be hours yet until the fireworks at the football field began.

Conversation flowed easily among the group. College classes, work, farm crops, kids, and pregnancy: they covered it all. Nancy talked about a new outreach she had been invited to join, a group of people from church who would go visit people in the hospital in Atkins. Pastor Green had created this Compassion Care Team, and they went to visit people from the church, and anyone else that the hospital Chaplin requested. Nancy said that sometimes there was a patient who had no family nearby to visit, so it was important for the Care Team to offer support. She was excited about this new way to witness and bring comfort.

Coop and Dana talked about their dad and his failing health. Nancy was concerned with how Marla Jean was coping. She wanted to know if there was anything she could do to help. Greg asked, "What are your plans, Coop? After he's gone, I mean. Will you sell the farm? Maybe go back to seminary?"

"Honestly, I've thought about it. But I think God wants me right here. I have a peace about it, believing that God can use me right where I am."

Dana put in, "Coop once said the best sermons don't come from behind a pulpit, but by watching the way godly people live in the world."

"Well, that's not exactly what I said, but yes, I guess you have the gist of it. But I'll stay on the farm, and try to be the hardworking, honest, godly type of farmer my dad has always been. I've been practically running the farm for the last couple of years, so I know I can do it. And I don't think Mom would like to move. She's lived in that house for over thirty years."

Nancy turned to Becky and asked, "What about you, Becky? What plans do you have for the future? What are you long-range goals?"

"Jenny is my priority right now, of course. And getting by day to day, which can sometimes be a challenge. I'm taking classes online, trying to get my bachelor's degree. It's taking a while, but I'm not going to give up. I used to think I wanted to be a veterinarian, but that would be a long way down the road. I'm really happy working as a tech for now. I get to do a lot of hands-on stuff with Doc Larson, and he's a great teacher."

"Didn't Doc tell me you had a year of college already?" Coop asked.

"I do. I finished one year at State, but then I had to quit because I had Jenny. We lived with Mom awhile, I had a variety of jobs, then Doc hired me. Now I'm renting a little place, making car payments, holding down a job, and carrying a light load of college classes. Plus raising Jenny. But I wouldn't change a thing."

"So you've always been a single parent?" Dana asked. "You've never been married?"

Coop gave her an evil look, the one brothers are so good at giving their sisters who ask inappropriate questions. Dana stared at him with annoyance and said, "Don't look at me that way. I want to know. We probably all want to know."

The others looked at each other and didn't know what to say. Then Nancy said, "We only want to know if Becky feels comfortable sharing." She looked at Becky reassuringly.

"It's okay, you guys, I don't mind. Yes, I got pregnant my freshman year. No, I've never been married. I was on my own with Jenny from the time I first told her father that he was going to *be* a father. It's been hard, and there have been times, especially at the beginning, when I was embarrassed and depressed and angry and even wished I could die. But by the grace of God, I was led to a wonderful Christian counselor, who showed me that God knew all my sins and yet loved me anyway. Once I accepted that love, my whole life changed. That sounds melodramatic, but it's true. Satan tries to throw all his evil darts at me, darts like fear and condemnation and hopelessness. But I know that I'm not fighting him alone, and the God of Abraham and Moses and Joshua can lead me through whatever wilderness I find myself wandering in. I'm so thankful for that.

Coop looked at her with admiration. "And I'm so glad you shared that, Becky. I think we all need to remember what you just said there at the end. God will lead us through whatever wilderness we are wandering in. We all find ourselves in situations from time to time, situations that make us fear or doubt or want to give up. But just grab hold of God's right hand. He will lead us and hold us and keep us safe."

They all sat quietly and thought about those words. Greg broke the silence by saying, "Coop, I think you and Becky can both preach sermons from in front of the pulpit, instead of behind it."

Twilight settled over the backyard. Little specks of twinkling lights appeared, and Becky said, "Look, fireflies."

"We call them lightening bugs," said Dana.

In the distance they could hear the first muted explosions of firecrackers and other noisy things that were being set off in neighborhoods around town. "We better get going," said Nancy. "We want to get there early enough to get some good seats."

CHAPTER 39

Fireworks

The parking lot was beginning to fill up when they arrived. The sheriff's cruiser was parked near the entrance, and Sheriff Bert Bertell was directing traffic. As they made their way toward the bleachers, Dana scanned the crowd to see if she saw anyone she knew. A crowd of Spanish-speaking young men passed by them, and one stopped, turned around, and came over to her. "Hola, Dana. Happy Fourth of July!"

"Hola, Marco! How are you? Happy Fourth to you too! Enjoy the fireworks!"

"You want to sit with us to watch?" Marco asked.

"No, thanks, I'm here with my family. But you have a good time. See ya later!"

Coop said to her, "You could have gone to sit with them, if you wanted."

"It's okay. I'd rather be with you and Becky and Jenny tonight. It's a family thing. Besides, I don't really know them."

"Yeah, you're probably right. Okay. Let's get some good seats."

Fortunately, there were still seats available on the top row of the bleachers. As the group stepped carefully on the bleacher rows and climbed higher and higher, Becky held Jenny's hand, and Coop walked right behind them, ready to catch Jenny if she slipped. They settled into their seats, with Becky in the middle. The others gathered around and got comfortable. Coop pointed to the goal line to their right. "The fireworks will be right down there. See them setting things up? We'll have a great view from up here."

Patriotic music blasted from the loudspeakers. Greg passed out American flags to everyone in the group. Coop stuck his into the band of his cowboy hat. Hannah and Jenny waved theirs enthusiastically to the beat of the music.

There was a roar of loud engines as a dozen or more motorcycles raced to the opposite end of the field. Sheriff Bertell watched as the riders parked in the grass, got off, and began spreading blankets in the end zone. He'd had some run-ins with these motorcycle guys in the past couple of months. Mostly driving erratically, sometimes on the sidewalks, running stop signs, just being a general nuisance. Most of them were men, but a few women accompanied them. Standing tall above the rest was Misty, with her black-and-purple hair shining in the floodlights around the field. She had already seen Coop's truck in the parking lot as they rode through, so she knew he was here somewhere. Her eyes scanned the bleachers until she found him.

It wasn't easy to miss him. With that flag stuck in his hat, he was pretty easy to spot. He sat taller than most of those around him, which included some kids, his sister "what was her name?" and that other woman again. They were looking at each other, laughing and talking, and Misty saw Coop reach up to the woman's forehead and push some hair off her face. *Nice move, Coop,* she thought. *Well, enjoy your fun tonight, honey, 'coz your fun is about to end.*

Misty grabbed Patch's arm, and they walked over to where Billy was standing near his bike. She pointed to the top of the bleachers, told Patch and Billy where to look, and waited for them to locate Coop. "Oh yeah, him. I've seen him around. So when are we gonna do this?" Billy looked at Misty and licked his lips. "I'm getting hungry," he said with a leer.

"I'm workin' on it." Misty said, looking up at the bleachers again. "Just gotta work out some details. We want this to be perfect, no mess ups. I'll let ya know." She watched as Coop put his arms around the woman's shoulders, pulled her close, and they laughed with their heads nearly touching. Misty never took her eyes off the scene but said to Patch, "Get on it. I want this done."

The seats were filled, and darkness fell. The lights on the field were turned off. An announcement came over the loudspeaker, asking everyone to stand. The local Boy Scout troop marched onto the field proudly lifting the American flag high. Music rose, and the whole crowd sang "The Star-Spangled Banner." As they took their seats, the fireworks began.

It was a very nice display, considering it was put on by a small town. Jenny loved every burst of color and didn't even seem to mind the loud explosions. Becky enjoyed it too, but she especially enjoyed the comfort of Coop's arm around her shoulders. A few times, when the explosions seemed especially close and caused Becky to jump in her seat, Coop pulled her closer and whispered, "I got you. I'm right here." It made Becky feel safe.

When the grand finale was finished and people started leaving, Coop suggested that they stay seated a bit longer, to let the crowd thin out some. Otherwise they'd be stuck sitting in traffic anyway. He tossed the truck keys to Dana and said, "You go ahead. I'm going to sit here with Becky and Jenny awhile. I'll meet you at the car in a bit."

Greg and Nancy stood to leave, saying their goodbyes. Greg picked up Hannah, who was acting quite sleepy, and carried her carefully down the bleachers. Jenny was sleepy too and had her head resting on Becky's lap. It wouldn't be long until she was asleep. It had been a long and very busy day. Becky ran her hands through Jenny's sweaty hair. Showers would have to wait till morning. This little girl needed her bed.

"Greg and Nancy are really nice," Becky said. "I enjoyed myself today."

"Yeah, it was a great day. Lots of fun. I liked playing with Jenny. And I liked sitting close to you." He pulled her a little closer, being careful not to disturb the sleeping Jenny.

"I liked it too," Becky said with a little sigh. Then she added, "I think you're pretty good with kids. The girls loved swimming with you."

"Next time, you get in with us. I'll teach you how to swim."

"Like I said before, we'll see. I'm actually kinda scared. Drowning and fires, that's my two fears."

"Don't worry. You don't need to be scared as long as I'm with you. I'll take care of you."

They settled into a comfortable silence. Becky listened to the beat of his heart. Before long she realized that the thumping of her own was matching the rhythm of his. She wondered if he felt it too.

Soon the crowds had cleared, and they were the only people left in the stands. Becky said, "Maybe we better be going. Dana will wonder what happened to you."

"In a minute. Before we go, I want to ask you something."

"What's that?"

"Can I kiss you?"

"I think I might like that."

"Well let's see if you do." Coop leaned to her face and she lifted her lips up to meet his. The kiss did not linger long, but was sweet and comfortable.

Becky smiled and said, "I did like that. But I think we better try it again, to see if maybe I like it even better this time."

"Oh, I think you will," Coop said and kissed her longer and harder. Becky moaned softly and relaxed her jaw. His tongue made quick contact with hers, and he pulled away reluctantly. "Better?" he asked.

"Yes, indeed. Very nice." Becky laid her head against his shoulder. "Very nice," she repeated with a sigh.

After a minute, Coop said, "I don't want this night to end, but I guess we better leave." He stood, lifted Jenny from Becky's lap, and they walked down the bleachers and across the parking lot. Most cars were gone. Coop's truck sat parked next to Becky's car. Dana had the truck running and was listening to the radio. They could hear the music as they approached.

Becky unlocked the car and opened the back door for Coop to put Jenny into her booster seat. He buckled her in, closed the door, and turned to Becky. He walked toward her, and she backed up until she was pressed against the car door. Coop lowered his head to hers once more, and their kiss was long, probing, and wet. Becky felt tingles in the pit of her stomach. Coop felt a surge of energy flow through him, and he didn't want the kiss to end. He pulled back for air and kissed her again. Becky's arms were around his neck, and she felt the full length of his body alongside hers.

Dana was trying not to watch, but she was. "Good," she said out loud. "Very good."

Just then a group of motorcycles roared through the parking lot. Misty rode on the back of one of the bikes. She pointed the driver to the couple kissing at the car in the middle of the parking lot. *That's the car, all right,* she thought. *The one I stabbed with the ice pick! Ha! I got the right one!*

The bikes, led by Patch and Misty, approached the two vehicles parked side by side and circled them twice, throwing rocks and dust on the vehicles and the couple standing there clinging to each other. The riders were wearing helmets, but Coop noticed the woman sitting on the back of one of the bikes. She had long black hair.

Sheriff Bertell was watching from his cruiser parked near the entrance. He was about to drive over and intervene, but the bikes roared off in a burst of dust and laughter.

Coop turned to Becky and said, "I'm going to follow you home. I want to be sure you get there safely."

"Oh, Coop, you don't have to do that. I'll be fine. You guys just go on home."

"Nope. I insist. I told you I'd take care of you, and I meant it. I'll follow you and wait until you get into your house. Now get going," he said, and turned her around toward her car. He opened the driver's door, and she took her seat. Before he shut the door, he kissed her one more time.

A few blocks away, a lone motorcycle sat in the dark. As the car and then the pickup pulled out of the parking lot and went down the road, the bike followed at a distance. The riders watched as the car pulled into a carport; the driver got out, took a child from the back seat, and entered the house. The pickup truck drove away, but the motorcycle circled the block before leaving.

CHAPTER 40

Details

The skies opened up, and rain poured solidly for hours. The cornstalks, over knee-high, swayed wildly in the wind. Trees near the farmhouse were dancing and twisting. It was quite a storm.

Dana sat at her desk in her room, trying to concentrate on her classwork. It was hard to study when there was so much racket outside. The rain blew hard against her window, and lightening shattered the dark sky. She closed her textbook and moved her chair over to the window, so she could watch the storm.

Her thoughts drifted to the Fourth of July festivities from the night before. She liked Becky, and really liked that Coop seemed so happy. There was a lot of sadness lately, with Riley's death, and Dad's situation. Becky seemed to make Coop smile. That was good. Coop deserved some happiness.

Dana didn't want to jump ahead too quickly, but she did wonder what the future held. What would happen after Dad died? She didn't want to think about it, but she knew it was going to happen sooner rather than later. Would Coop want to stay on the farm? What if he and Becky got married? Where would they live? If they lived on the farm, would they still let her live there too? And what about Mom? There were so many unanswered questions flying around in her head. It was impossible to concentrate on school stuff. Maybe she better talk to Coop. There were things they needed to work out. Plans to be made.

Coop sat by his dad's bedside, making plans. The storm was raging outside, and there wasn't much he could do out in this rain. His mind wandered to Becky and Jenny. Yesterday was such a good day. He felt so comfortable with Becky, and he was growing quite fond of Jenny too. It was fun playing with her in the pool. She was a good kid, and Becky had apparently been a good mother. Raised her right.

He wanted to see Becky again. He needed to plan a real date with her. Just the two of them, with lots of time to talk. Lots of time to really get to know each other. Hopes, dreams, fears, and wishes. He wanted to know the desires of her heart. He wanted to know everything about her. They had lots to talk about. And he wanted to kiss her again.

It was early in the day, and Becky would be at work. Otherwise he would call her, just to say hi and hear her voice. How was it possible that he missed her so much? *I'll call her tonight*, he thought. *Maybe by then I can have a plan about what we can do. I wonder if she's ever ridden a horse?*

Becky and Jenny had been making plans of their own. Jenny's birthday party was just a couple of weeks away, and there were lots of things to do. Becky put her to-do list on the counter at the vet's office. At the top of the list was "CAKE." She was going to call Janice Thomas as soon as she got a break. Becky was going to ask her to make a special birthday cake for the party. Janice was a substitute teacher, a single mom, and a cake-baker extraordinaire. Decorating cakes helped to supplement her income, and Becky was happy to help her out in this way. Janice, whose husband had been killed in a tragic car accident last year, had two teenaged children. She had been coming to the Wednesday-night single-mom's group for several months.

Jenny was suddenly obsessed with cats. Ever since visiting Coop's farm and meeting Muffin, Jenny had talked of nothing else. Meeting Marmalade at the Martins' house had sealed the deal—she wanted cats on her birthday cake. *Janice, I hope you can come up with a cat cake! And I hope it doesn't cost me too much!*

Thoughts of the birthday party should take priority right now, Becky knew, but yet her mind had been wandering a lot lately. She could close her eyes and feel Coop's arms around her. Feel his lips on hers. Being with him felt so natural, so safe.

He'd said he would take care of her. He had followed her home, to make sure she got in safely. That was really nice of him. *Did he know those motorcycles had spooked me?* she wondered. It was nice to feel like someone cared about her.

I wonder if I should invite Coop to the party. She thought about it and decided not to. It might seem a little presumptuous. No, this was Jenny's day. Jenny should be the focus. She'd have other times to be with Coop. Or at least she hoped so.

Misty, Patch, and Billy sat around the little table in Billy's trailer. Cigarette smoke circled above their heads as they made their plans.

"That was a damn lucky break," said Patch. "Now we know where she lives, and we didn't even have to hunt her down. They led us right to the front door."

"We'll have to be extra careful about the kid, though," said Misty. "We don't want to traumatize the sweet little thing."

Patch grunted and shrugged. "Ever heard of collateral damage?"

"I know, but I don't want to be responsible for hurting a kid. I really don't."

"Just don't worry," Billy said. "I know what I'm doing." He stubbed out his cigarette and took a long drink of his beer. "It'll take me a couple of days to get the cameras and tripods I need." He looked at Patch. "You gonna get the roofies?"

"Get off my case. Yeah, I'll get the roofies. I told you I would, and I will." He was cutting his fingernails with his pocketknife, and little bits of nail were piled in a heap on the wooden table. "You worry too much."

Misty said, "Get plenty. He's a big guy. We want him out. Don't want him coming to in the middle of the fun."

Billy looked at her with a sneer. "Fun? You think it's gonna be fun? Oh no, bitch, the real fun starts after. I'll show you fun." He reached across the table and grabbed Misty's hand. "Can't wait to collect my reward."

Suddenly Patch stabbed his pocketknife forcefully into the table just inches from Billy's hand. "What the hell?" Billy yelled.

Misty jerked her hand back and stared at Patch. "Hey, cool it. This was your idea, don't forget."

He pulled his knife out of the table, folded it, and stood up. He slipped the knife into his pants pocket. "Yeah, but you better not make a habit of it." He pulled her by the hair until she was standing beside him. He yanked her head back, kissed her hard, and released her slightly. He leered at her, then he leaned close and bit her lip.

Misty reared back and slapped his face. Blood was trickling from the side of her lip, and she wiped it with the back of her hand. Patch grabbed her wrists and pulled her away from the table. With one quick movement, he threw her onto the couch and climbed on top of her. She was kicking and squirming, trying to get away, but his weight was too much for her.

Billy lit a cigarette and watched.

CHAPTER 41

***

Love Song

Becky and Jenny had enjoyed their Friday-night girl time. When the movie was over, Becky sent Jenny off to get ready for her bath and bedtime. She took the DVD out of the player and put it back into its case. She'd return it to the Redbox tomorrow when she went to the grocery store.

She sat on the couch, scrolling through her phone options for ringtones. Becky set the ringtone on her phone to play "How Great Thou Art" whenever Coop called her. She thought it was cute. Because after all, he was pretty great! Not to be sacrilegious or anything. Of course, she knew that the song really was about how great God is. It just seemed fitting somehow.

When the song played later that night, Jenny was in the bathtub. Becky was sitting on the stool next to her, with the shampoo and conditioner bottles lined up on the sink. Becky fished the phone out of her pocket and was already smiling by the time she said hello.

"Hi, Becky. What'cha doing?"

"Getting ready to wash Jenny's hair. She can play in the tub a few minutes while we talk, though."

"Or I could call you back. Or you could call me."

"Well, no, this is okay. Her hair can wait a minute. What's up?"

"Nothing really. I was just thinking about you."

Something warmed inside Becky. She smiled bigger and said, "That's nice. As a matter of fact, I've been thinking about you a lot today."

"Really? Good stuff, I hope."

"Mostly," she teased.

"Just mostly?" Coop pretended to be hurt. "What did I do wrong? I'll fix it!"

"Well, Jenny's been talking and talking about you and the swimming pool. It's like I don't exist anymore. It's 'Coop this' and 'Coop that.' She keeps saying she wants you to teach her to really swim."

From the bathtub, Jenny piped up and said, "Like this, Coop." She put her face in the water and blew bubbles.

"Wait, honey. Let me put it on FaceTime." Becky reset the phone camera, so it could show Coop what Jenny was doing. He laughed and said, "That's terrific, Jenny. You'll be swimming in no time!"

Becky adjusted the phone, so she and Coop could see each other. "You've created a monster," she said to Coop. "Or at least a little fish."

Coop took a few seconds to look at her. She had pulled her hair up onto the top of her head. Her brown eyes looked really big and beautiful. His heart beat a little faster, seeing her face so close like this. "You look beautiful."

Becky was a little surprised and looked into the mirror quickly. Thankful that she looked at least halfway decent, she chuckled and said, "Thanks. You look pretty good too."

"I like this FaceTime idea. It's almost like I'm right there with you."

"Yeah. Technology. Pretty cool." Becky paused a second before going on. "Hey, thanks for driving behind me to the house last night. I did feel better, knowing you were back there. Those motorcycles kinda scared me."

"It was pretty rude of them, circling us like that. So you were okay, once you got into the house?"

"I was. I locked the door as soon as I got inside. I did hear a motorcycle go by a little later though. A couple of times, really. But it was probably nothing."

"Probably. Hey, I've got a question."

"What's that?"

"Do you know how to ride a horse?"

"I do," said Becky, "but it's been several years since I've ridden. I suppose it's like a bike, though, right? If you can do it, you never forget how. Why?"

"Because I want to see you again. And I thought horseback riding would be fun. If you'd like to, that is."

"Sure, I'll try it again. You might have to take it slow, though. When did you have in mind? I'll need to ask Mom to watch Jenny."

Jenny stood up in the tub and started to get out. "No, honey, we still have to wash your hair. Sit back down, and we'll get to it." Becky turned back to Coop and said, "I'll have to talk to you about this later. Jenny's getting restless."

"Okay, well, have a good night. Can I call you tomorrow?"

"I'd like that. Good night."

"Goodnight, Becky."

Becky washed and rinsed Jenny's hair, towel dried it, and combed through it to take out the tangles. Then she braided it and sent her off to bed. Jenny always liked to play with her stuffed animals for a while before climbing into her bed for the night.

Becky went into her own room and got ready for a quick shower before she went to tuck Jenny into bed. As she was drying off, she studied her body in the mirror. She thought she looked all right, considering she had had a child and was a little thick around the middle. *Probably could stand to do some sit-ups and leg lifts*, she thought to herself. She had only a few pale stretch marks. Her breasts were firm, and her leg muscles were strong and tight. She slipped a nightgown over her head, ran a comb through her hair, and walked to Jenny's room humming "How Great Thou Art" as she went.

Jenny was already in bed, snuggled in with three stuffed animals. "Sing me that song," she asked.

"Is there room for me in that bed with you?" Becky asked and began to move some of the animals around. When there was space on the side of the bed, Becky slid in beside her daughter. She sang a few verses of the song, and Jenny drifted off to sleep. Becky tried to sneak quietly out of the room without waking her daughter, but just as she got to the door, Jenny mumbled sleepily, "Mommy, you forgot to teach me the love song."

"Love song?" Becky asked, trying to remember what song Jenny was talking about. "What love song?"

"You know, Mommy. From the moms' group. 'I Could Sing of Your Love Forever.'"

"Oh, I remember now. I only remember part of the words."

"Sing what you know," Jenny said and patted on the bed.

Becky went back to sit on the edge of the bed. She stroked Jenny's head and sang, "I Could Sing of Your Love Forever," over and over until she fell asleep. Each time she repeated the phrase, Becky was thanking God for his many blessings. Her daughter. Her mom. Her job. Their home. Their church. Her friends. Salvation. Protection. Coop. So much to be thankful for.

She tiptoed out of Jenny's bedroom and closed the door. She opened the Bible app on her phone, looking for a verse that she had in mind. She didn't know where it was, so she tried to find it by using the search icon. She looked up the words "good and perfect gift" and found James 1:17. "Every good gift and every perfect gift is from above, and cometh down from the Father of lights, with whom is no variableness, neither shadow of turning."

She closed her phone and prayed, "Thank you, God, for all these good gifts you have given me. You have blessed me with so much, and I love you for it. Help me, Lord, to live a life worthy of your love and blessings. May I be a witness to Jenny and teach her about the greatest gift of all, your son, Jesus Christ. And now, Lord, about Coop. I put this relationship in your hands. I ask for your leading and direction. I want to remain true to you, most of all, and remember that you are the source of my joy and happiness. Even my peace and safety come from my relationship with you. I ask that you keep me in your care. That you make me strong. That you give me clear direction. And patience." She paused and sang the chorus of "How Great Thou Art" and said, "Thank you, Jesus," and she turned off the light.

CHAPTER 42

—— ⌒♊⌒ ——

Shutting Down

Marla Jean walked with Judy down the hall and into the living room. "How's he doing?" she asked, but she already knew the answer. He was getting weaker with each passing day. She was grateful for every day he could stay here, but she realized that each day was more difficult than the last.

Judy packed her supplies into her satchel and looked at Marla Jean with compassion. "His body is starting to shut down. His organ function is declining, and he is weakening."

"Are we getting close then?" Marla Jean asked, swallowing hard. She had known this day would come, but facing it head-on like this was difficult. Even though she knew he would soon be out of his pain and fellowshipping with Jesus, it was so hard to imagine life without him here. How could she go on? She already felt empty and incomplete. Just thinking about it brought her to tears.

Judy hugged her and said, "It's always hard to predict exactly, but I would say within the next couple of weeks. Is there anyone you need to call? Maybe someone who he would like to see before he's gone? Maybe someone who needs to find closure? Or someone who would want to see him one more time?"

"I'll call Michael. He needs to come. Before it's too late." It would be good to see Michael again, and hopefully he would bring Stacy. Unfortunate that it would be under these circumstances. But still, she needed her firstborn. The Smith family was strong, and they would find added strength in just being together.

Marla Jean wiped the tears from her eyes and took a deep breath. She wanted to be composed when she talked to Michael. She wanted to be strong. But she felt so tired, so weary. Weary of the care of her beloved, weary of the fear of loneliness, and weary of the weight of the future without her life partner.

Before she picked up the phone, she reached for her Bible, and as had happened so many times in the past, she prayed for God to bring her a verse of comfort. She looked at the open Bible lying on her lap. It had opened to Revelation chapter twenty-one. She began to read. "He will wipe every tear from their eyes, and there will be no more death, or sorrow, or crying or pain. All these things are gone forever. And the One sitting on the throne said, 'Look, I am making everything new!'"

"Thank you, Lord God. I will trust you to make everything new," she said, and reached for the phone.

CHAPTER 43

Back in the Saddle Again

Coop had the horses saddled and tied to the fence in the barnyard. When Becky arrived, he met her in the driveway. He was carrying a knapsack and had a blanket rolled up under his arm. It was a little awkward, but he managed to give her a little hug as she got out of the car.

Becky was wearing blue jeans, a pink tank top, and her cowboy boots. Her hair was pulled into a short ponytail that hung down the back of her neck. She had covered her arms and neck with sunscreen, as well as her face and the backs of her ears.

"You look great!" Coop said. "I've got something for you, though. You're just missing one thing."

As they walked toward the horses, Becky said, "Here, let me help carry something." Coop handed her the blanket roll. Then she asked, "What do you mean I'm missing something. What?"

"You'll see," Coop said playfully. "Just be patient." He busied himself putting the knapsack on the back of Slick's saddle and securing the blanket on Nell's back.

While Becky gently stroked Nell's soft nose and talked to her quietly, Coop went into the barn. He came back with a white cowboy hat, which he sat on top of Becky's head with a flourish. "Now you look perfect!" he said, and he kissed the tip of her nose.

She giggled and Coop pulled back, licking his lips. "Mmm, that's an interesting taste."

"Oh, that's my sunscreen. Sorry! Does it taste bad?"

"It's okay. Maybe not my favorite flavor. Did you put sunscreen on your lips?"

Becky smiled and said, "No, I didn't."

"Good," he said, and kissed her on the lips. "Oh, that's definitely better."

As they moved apart, Becky said, "Nell and I are becoming friends. She told me she would go slow, and she promised not to throw me off. I hope she's trustworthy."

"She's a good ride," Coop said. "Dana's never had any problem with her. Course, she's been riding all her life."

"Oh, gee, thanks, that's reassuring!" Becky laughed and approached Nell's side. "Let's see if I remember how to do this." She put her left foot into the stirrup and threw her other leg up over Nell's back. Once seated she adjusted herself slightly and said, "That wasn't bad!"

Coop mounted Slick and said, "You look like a pro." He turned Slick and said, "We'll just walk around in the barnyard a little, so you can get comfortable. Then I thought we'd go out in the pasture. How fast we go is up to you. If you're ready to trot, we will. If not, that's okay. But before we head out, I always pray. Is that all right with you?"

"Of course," Becky said, looking him in the eye. "I think that's a great plan."

As Coop prayed, a feeling of peace fell over Becky. Here was a man who honored God in everything he did. Even riding a horse into a pasture was reason to call upon God.

"Lord Jesus, go with us now. Keep us safe on the journey. Guide our conversation. Bless our time together. We thank you for this beautiful day, and I thank you for bringing Becky into my life. We are your children, in need of your protection and guidance. Thank you. Amen."

Becky hadn't taken her eyes off him. When he finished praying and opened his eyes, he found her looking at him. He smiled in embarrassment, but Becky spoke up and said, "I'm thankful you are in my life too."

Coop tipped his hat to Becky, clucked to Slick, and they started walking around in the barnyard. It took Becky a while to get comfortable with the movement and the feel of Nell beneath her, but soon she was feeling pretty confident. Coop asked her if she was ready to go out into the pasture, and she agreed that she was. He dismounted near the gate, opened it, and Becky and Nell went through. He led Slick through, turned to close the gate, and got back into the saddle.

Riding side by side, Coop said, "You're doing great. It looks like you really know how to handle a horse."

"Well, Nell is pretty calm. That helps. But yes, I'm surprised, but it feels pretty good to be in the saddle again." She looked around at the pasture, with its tall grasses and wildflowers. There were a few cows and their calves grazing on a nearby hill. A large bird was circling high overhead. From the trees, she could hear the cooing of mourning doves and the twitter of songbirds. "It sure is peaceful here," she said to Coop, who was riding beside her. "I bet you spend a lot of time out here."

"I don't have as much free time as I'd like, but every chance I get I do try to sit back and take in the beauty. It's a good place to come out and think."

They rode on a bit further, and Coop asked, "How ya doin'? Do you think you're ready to go faster? There's a more open space up ahead, not so many trees or bushes. It would be a good place to try a trot. If you want."

Becky took a deep breath and let it out slowly. "Okay, yes, I'd like to try it. You know first aid, I hope!"

"I do, but you'll be fine. Just let Nell's rhythm show you how to relax your body. But don't relax so much you fall off!"

"That's a big help!" Becky laughed.

"You go first, we'll follow a little behind."

Becky urged Nell into a trot and settled in to a good rhythm with the horse. From a few paces behind, Coop watched her bounce up and down on Nell's back gracefully. She looked at ease and very confident. They trotted around the open pasture for a few minutes, and then Becky slowed Nell to a stop. Coop came up behind her and said, "You are absolutely terrific on a horse. It's fun to watch you. Did you like it?"

She laughed with exhilaration. "That was so fun. I can't believe I've wasted so many years when I could have been riding more. Thank you for getting me on a horse again." She patted Nell's sweaty neck and said, "You're a good girl. But you sure look thirsty."

"Follow me," said Coop, and they walked their horses to the pond. They dismounted and let the horses drink from the pond and graze on the grasses. Coop took the knapsack from Slick's back, and Becky got the blanket. Coop led her to a shady area along the shore of the pond. She spread out the blanket, and he unpacked water bottles and a covered container of fruit slices.

They sat on the blanket and enjoyed a cool breeze that was blowing across the water. Becky took off her hat and loosened the ponytail from the back of her head. She shook her head, and the air blew through her hair. Coop watched her with pleasure.

Becky took a big swallow of water and sighed. "I'm so glad you thought about bringing water. It's really hot. This helps." She held up the bottle in appreciation.

"I brought some fruit too. Apple slices, grapes, some melon chunks, and oranges. Just thought I should feed you something!" He passed the bowl to Becky, and she picked out an apple slice. He placed the bowl between them and ate an orange slice. They sat in contented silence for a while, enjoying the peace and each other's company.

The silence was interrupted when they heard a splash in the pond. Looking over, they saw three turtles sunning themselves on a log and one more swimming in the water.

"I've always loved turtles," said Becky. "Had one as a pet when I was a kid. We bought him at a little dime store. I named him Julius." She chuckled. "I would play with him in my bedroom and then forget to put him back in his bowl. I would find him days later, crawling around under my bed and covered in dust."

Coop leaned close to her and took her hand. "Becky," he said, "I want to learn everything about you. Your pet turtle, what you like for breakfast, if you sing in the shower, what's your favorite color, movies, everything. Your hopes and dreams, your fears and failures. I want to know it all." He lifted her chin so she was looking directly at him. "Becky, I'm finding myself wanting to be with you all the time. I count minutes until we can be together. I think you are beautiful and a good mother. You're a godly woman, and I think we could be a great team. I feel like the Lord has put us together at this time in our lives for a reason. Maybe we need each other. I mean, I guess I can only speak for myself, but I need you. I need to see you and talk to you and play with you and ride horses with you and eat with you and pray with you and share Scriptures with you and, well, you get it. I want to be with you through everything.

Becky twined her fingers with his. She looked at him with apprehension. "I could tell you about my favorite movies and colors and stuff like that, but there isn't much risk in sharing that sort of thing. It's when we talk about fears and failures and even hopes and dreams that I get worried. I have a past, and although I've gotten right with the Lord and I know he's forgiven the things I have done, it's still hard to think that people, especially a man, would respect me and accept me for the person I am now. It's like they say, I have baggage. My baggage happens to be almost five years old, and is evidence of the kind of woman I used to be. Not how I am now."

"Becky, I don't care about the woman that you used to be. Well, I do, in that it made you into the woman you are today. But your past is just that, past. If you have been forgiven by Jesus, and if you are now a child of his, then I have nothing to say about what you may have done in your past. That's over. I will never pass judgment. If you want to talk about it, that's fine, but I want you to know that I am falling in love with the woman you are now."

Becky caught her breath. Had she heard that correctly? Did he really say that? Tears welled up in her eyes, but she got them under control before she answered. "Oh, Coop, I do need to talk to you about it. If we are going any deeper with our relationship, I think it's only fair that I tell you what I've been through. At least some of it. It will help you understand me even more. And I wouldn't want any secrets between us."

So she proceeded to tell him about her affair with Derek. How she fell hard for him, and threw away all her common sense and whatever morals she thought she had. How he left her the minute he found out about the baby. How she felt humiliated, dirty, and ashamed. How only the grace of God had pulled her from a world of darkness and depression. She told him everything, and he listened with understanding and a genuine desire to know more about her. There was no judgment. There was no disgust. There was only acceptance and compassion.

"So that's my story, pretty much." Coop pulled her close, and she rested her head against his chest. He cradled her face in his hand and stroked her cheek gently with his thumb. "Do you want to know anything else?" Becky asked.

Coop hesitated just a second and said, "You never told me your favorite color."

She laughed a little which lightened the mood. "Blue. And my favorite movie is *The Notebook*. And my favorite verse is Romans 8:1. I love bacon. I don't like sushi. I sing in the shower, but not very well. Is there anything else you want to know?"

"Do you trust me?"

The question startled Becky, and she didn't quite know what to say. Coop went on, "I mean, with your past relationship with Jenny's father, I would assume that you might think that you can't trust a man again. So do you trust me?"

"Oh, Coop, yes I do. You are so completely trustworthy. I see honesty and integrity in you, and a desire to honor and serve God. Characteristics I've been needing, and looking for. Waiting for. I've learned from the mistakes I've made. That doesn't mean I'm perfect, or will never make a mistake again, but I think I am becoming a pretty good judge of character. I believe with all my heart that I can trust you."

Coop bent down and kissed her. She tilted her head and accepted his kiss with eagerness. Several kisses later, Coop said, "You know, as far as time goes, we haven't known each other very long. But I feel like I know your inner being, and you seem to know mine. I'd say 'it's a God thing,' but that sounds so trite."

Becky cuddled against him and said, "I know what you mean, though. I've felt God working in this right from the start. How else could it be that I feel so right with you? So safe and perfectly in the place God wants me to be? I've prayed so long that he would lead me to the right person, the one he has chosen for me. Or that he would make me content without a man. And here we are together. Yeah, I'd say it's a God thing."

He kissed her again, then said, "So is there anything you want to know about me?"

They went through the list. Color, green. Movie, anything John Wayne. Bacon over sausage, but just barely. He'd never tried sushi and had no desire to. Favorite Bible verse, it was impossible to choose.

Becky hesitated but felt she had to ask. "Tell me, how do you feel knowing that I'm not a virgin? Does that bother you?"

Coop took a deep breath and let it out slowly. He was trying to think of the best way to word his answer. "Wow! What a question!" He looked out over the pond to think. "I think God's perfect plan is for a married couple to learn about each other, explore each other's bodies, and learn together how best to please each other. And the union that forms is strong because of the time they spend together in that way. So if that's the case, it doesn't really matter if one has more actual experience than the other. It's the time they spend together that binds them to each other. Make sense?"

"Yes, actually, that makes perfect sense."

Coop laid her gently down on the blanket, leaned over her, and kissed her neck and ear. Then he started to tickle her, and she giggled and squirmed under him. "Besides," he said, "maybe you can teach me a few things!" She wrapped her arms around him and kissed him deeply.

The whinny of the horses got Coop's attention, and he said, "Hey, I'm afraid it's getting to be time to head home. I could keep kissing you forever, but I think they'd send the sheriff out looking for us." He pulled Becky to her feet, they gathered their things, and they mounted the horses. Becky again trotted in front of him, and Coop followed. "Thank you, God," he said. "Thank you."

Becky slowed and turned around in her saddle. "Did you say something to me? I heard your voice but not what you said."

Coop pulled up close to her and said, "I was just thanking God for you. You are an answer to my prayers."

"You too, Coop. You are an answer to my prayers too." She looked up toward Heaven and said, "Thank you, God."

CHAPTER 44

Party Prep

"Saturday! Saturday! Two more days till Saturday!" Jenny sang as she bounced around the living room. She could hardly contain her excitement.

Coop sat on the couch, surrounded by stuffed animals and books. He picked up a stuffed purple gorilla and talked to it. "Mr. Gorilla, what is happening on Saturday? Jenny sure seems excited. But I don't know why. What is she so excited about?"

Becky came in from the kitchen, where she was preparing spaghetti and meatballs for their supper. In her most effective gorilla voice, she replied, "Why, Coop, how could you forget? Jenny's birthday party is Saturday."

Coop tossed the gorilla up into the air, where it flipped several times while he said, "A party? Oh that's right. Jenny's having a party. How could I forget?"

Jenny ran to him and said, "You didn't forget. You're just teasing me!"

"You are right about that, Jenny. I didn't forget. In fact, I got you a present."

"Really?" Jenny looked around but found nothing. "Where is it?"

"Out in my truck. Let's go out and get it, okay?" He looked at Becky, who nodded and said, "Don't be gone long. Supper is almost ready."

When they came back, Jenny was holding a realistic-looking stuffed cat, complete with four little kittens. "Look, Mommy, Coop got me some cats! A mommy and some babies. They're so cute!"

"They sure are! Four kittens! What will you name them?"

Jenny thought a minute and then said proudly as she pointed to each kitten, "Paul and Silas, Mary and Martha." She giggled. "Like I learned about in Sunday school!

Becky asked, "So what's the momma kitty's name going to be?"

Without hesitation, Jenny said, "Marshmallow!" Coop and Becky burst into laughter. Delighted with herself, Jenny said, "Coop has Muffin. Hannah has Marmalade. Now I have Marshmallow."

This supper was the first time Becky had cooked for Coop. As he sat opposite of her at the table, Coop smiled contentedly. Becky asked him to pray, and he blessed the food, the hands that prepared it, and Jenny, whose birthday was coming soon. After the prayer, Jenny asked, "Are you coming to my party, Coop?"

"Not this year, sweetie. Your mom told me it's a girls-only party. You're going to do girly stuff, and I would just be in the way. But if it's okay with you, I'd like to take you and your mom on a drive Sunday after church. We'll go out to Dooley Lake, and I'll show you my favorite secret spot. We might even see some real animals while we're there!"

"Sure! That sounds like fun! Hannah's coming to my party, and Katie and Abby and Allison. We're going to paint our nails and do our hair. We're going to get beautiful!"

"See, like I said, girly stuff. Well, you girls have fun!" He winked at Becky. "I can't wait to see how beautiful you are on Sunday!"

CHAPTER 45

❦

The Trap Is Set

Saturday morning, Misty called in to work, told Al she was sick and she wasn't coming in for her shift. He wasn't happy about it, and said he was going to have to write her up for not giving enough notice. She said "Whatever" and hung up the phone. Things were all set at Billy's trailer, and Patch had the drugs safely stashed at his place. All that was left was to set the trap. And Misty figured she had just the right bait. She found her cell phone and made the call.

Coop was just coming out of his parents' bedroom when his cell phone vibrated. He looked at the caller ID and was surprised to see Misty's name show up. He wondered why she would be calling, considering the way she had last spoken to him.

Her call was just the first surprise. What she had to say was the biggest shock of all.

"Coop, hey, I was wondering if we could talk," she said clearly and calmly. "It's really important. I have some questions about what you were saying about God and forgiveness and stuff. I hope maybe you can help me understand this."

There was a moment of silence as Coop processed what had just happened. Was she asking him to explain the way of salvation?

Misty said, "I know when we last spoke, I was angry and hurt. But I've had time to think some, and, well, I don't blame you if you don't ever want to talk to me again, but I didn't know who else to talk to about this stuff."

Coop cleared his throat. "I'm curious. What happened? What caused you to think about salvation?"

"Somebody left this card on a table at the diner," she said. "It has Bible verses, and it says how everybody has sinned and that the wages of sin is death. And it talks about eternal life. I guess that means Heaven. But I have so many questions. I don't know anything about this stuff. It's all new to me. I don't even know how to pray. Can you help me? Can we talk about it? I don't know who else I can ask."

Coop closed his eyes and quietly mouthed, "Thank you, Jesus." To Misty, he said, "Yes, I'd be glad to meet you and explain it to you. We could go over to the church. I'm sure Pastor Green would be happy to meet with us. I can call him, and see when he's free."

Damn, thought Misty. *No way. He has to meet me alone.* Quickly she said, "Oh no, Coop, I couldn't talk to anyone else about my sins. I'm just so embarrassed. Can't it just be you and me? And if I don't understand what you're saying, we can go talk with the pastor another day. Please? Just you and me for now."

He fell for it. Misty couldn't have been more pleased. All was going according to plan. "Can you pick me up outside the diner, say four o'clock? We can go somewhere and just sit in the truck and talk. I have so many questions."

The trap was set. The bait was offered. Now to catch the rat.

CHAPTER 46

— ✣ —

Party Time

Jenny's party was a success. The cat cake was a big hit. The mani-pedi station entertained the girls for quite a while. Wrapping paper littered the floor, cake crumbs were scattered on the table, and nail polish spills were somehow miraculously restricted to the plastic mats provided to catch them. Becky looked around as Hannah, the last to leave, went out the door with her mother. Nancy had offered to help clean up, but Becky had declined. *What a mess,* she thought. But one look at her daughter—with her hair piled on top of her head, and bright orange polish on her nails—made her decide that it was all worth it. She picked up some wrapping paper and stuffed it into a trash bag.

As Nancy drove through town chatting with Hannah about the fun she had had at the party, she noticed Coop's red truck parked near the diner. Coop, wearing his black cowboy hat, was sitting in the truck as if he were waiting for someone. *That's kinda strange,* thought Nancy. Just then she felt a flutter low in her uterus. *The baby's kicking!* she thought excitedly. She placed her hand on her abdomen, hoping to feel it again. She concentrated on driving, talking to Hannah, and waiting for the next little kick. All thoughts of Coop flitted out of her pregnancy-focused brain.

Later, that same red truck was parked on a gravel road in front of Billy's trailer. Coop and Misty were deeply engaged in a conversation. He was using the verse card Nancy had left at the diner and looking up the Scriptures in his own Bible. It was a hot afternoon, and fortunately Misty had brought along her cooler with bottles of cold ice water. In the course of their conversation, Coop drank two bottles of water. Unknown to him, some of the bottles had been laced with Rohypnol, and each lid had been marked with a red dot, so Misty didn't accidentally drink one.

The conversation was going well, Coop thought. He had explained Romans 3:10 that says there is not one righteous person and Roman 3:23 that says everyone has sinned and everyone has fallen short of the glory of God. Misty seemed receptive and eagerly asked more questions. By the time he got to Romans 6:23, he was slurring his words and felt a little dizzy. His brow was sweaty and clammy.

Misty urged him to drink some more water, and he drained a bottle and dropped it on the floor of the truck. Misty handed him a third bottle, opening it for him because he wasn't strong enough to twist the lid off. He felt immediately cooler but listless and weak. He didn't know if his words were making any sense, and Misty kept asking him to explain things that he thought he had already explained. He tried to turn the pages in his Bible, but he felt like he couldn't even move his fingers. Lifting his arms became impossible. Keeping his eyes open was useless. He passed out, right there in the truck.

Misty signaled Patch, who came out of the trailer with Billy. Together they lifted Coop out of the truck and carried him between them. Anyone watching the scene would think that the guy in the middle was drunk, and his friends were helping him into the trailer. Misty held the door open for them, and then entered the trailer behind them.

They had planned out the whole sequence of photos, beginning with Coop sitting at the table, with Misty, wearing his black hat, perched on his lap. They posed his hands so it seemed that he was putting his fingers down the back of her shorts. Even though Misty was basically holding his head up, the pictures made it look like they were involved in a passionate embrace.

The photo session continued with different poses and a variety of stages of undress. Coop remained unaware of what was happening. His body did respond automatically when manipulated but he had no knowledge of what was going on. Had he known he would have, of course, ended it at once. But he was completely oblivious. The drugs had made him powerless and unconscious.

Billy had arranged cameras in each room and at several different viewpoints. He busied himself taking dozens of pictures, while Patch assisted with the photo composition. He hoisted Coop's body around like a sack of potatoes, posing him as realistically as possible.

They had practiced the day before, and Patch had a good idea of what he had to do to position Coop so that Billy could get the pictures just right. Misty helped too, with angles and facial expressions that made every picture look natural.

"We got enough. Let's get him out of here before he comes to," Patch said, and Billy started putting away the camera equipment. Misty caressed Coop once more and dressed him. She struggled with his boots, so Patch came over to help. He looked at her, now dressed in a thong and loose T-shirt, and reached his hand up to touch her, ready and hard with desire.

"You said we need to get him out of here," Misty said, pushing his hand aside. "We'll play later."

"Besides," said Billy, "I'm first.

As darkness fell, Billy and Patch took Coop back to his truck and placed him in the passenger seat. Coop's Bible was knocked to the floor, where a collection of water bottles had been tossed. Patch drove the truck a few blocks away, parked it with the keys dangling in the ignition, and pulled Coop to his place behind the wheel. He leaned Coop's head on the back of the seat, so it looked as if he were sleeping. Patch grabbed Misty's little cooler and starting walking back to Billy's trailer.

Inside, Misty noticed Coop's black cowboy hat left behind on the table. She put it on her own head again and said, "Oh well, guess I'll keep this as a souvenir."

Billy grabbed her and pulled her toward the bedroom, saying, "Come here, bitch. You owe me." He pushed her down on the bed. Coop's hat fell off Misty's head and rolled onto the floor. "Time to pay me for my services. I've been waiting a long time for this. Make it good."

"Oh, Billy Boy," she cooed. "I'm gonna give you something you'll never forget."

A few minutes later, Patch opened the trailer door. He heard noises and walked to the bedroom, where he found that Misty and Billy had already started their victory celebration without him.

CHAPTER 47

Worrisome Indeed

Marla Jean kept listening for sounds of Coop's truck pulling into the driveway, but she heard nothing. She didn't sleep well, worrying. She knew that her son had gone off to talk with that woman, Misty, the one with purple hair. The one he had been trying to witness to and who now seemed to be receptive to the gospel. She offered up a prayer for him, asking that the Lord give him the words to say and that he would return home safely with good news about the salvation of another soul.

But next morning, his truck was still not in the driveway. There was no message from him. That was so uncharacteristic. He always let her know when he was going to be late, even a few minutes. She asked Dana if she had heard from her brother, but she hadn't either. This was worrisome indeed. Maybe he'd had an accident on the way home. Maybe they should drive into town, checking the ditches for his truck. Maybe they should contact the sheriff.

One thing for sure, they weren't going to tell Walter that Coop hadn't come home last night. No need to upset him. And anyway, Coop would probably drive in any minute, with a perfectly logical explanation as to where he had been.

But why hadn't he called? There must be something wrong. Marla Jean and Dana held hands and prayed for Coop's health and safety. Dana got in her car and began to drive slowly toward town.

CHAPTER 48

─── ⌘ ───

Praying All the Way

Becky took Jenny to her classroom and went to wait for Coop near the church entrance. The crowd cleared as everyone dispersed to their classrooms, and she was nearly the only one left. It was time for class, and he still hadn't arrived, so Becky walked by herself to Sunday school. She found a seat near Nancy and looked nervously at her cell phone. There was no message from Coop. That might mean he was running late, or it might mean he was really busy and couldn't take the time to message her.

Nancy noticed her concern and asked, "Where's Coop?"

"I don't know. He hasn't called or texted me this morning. He didn't call after the party last night either. He said he would call and see how it went, but he didn't. I hope everything's all right."

"Maybe something's happened with his dad," Nancy said.

"I know, that's what I was thinking. I wish he would have messaged me."

Class started, and still Coop did not show up. Becky was distracted and kept checking her phone for word from him. Nothing.

Becky went into the church sanctuary, hoping he might be there waiting for her. But he wasn't. She sat by herself and tried to concentrate on the sermon, but her mind kept wandering. She said a prayer for Walter and the whole Smith family.

She gathered up Jenny from the children's area and walked hurriedly to the parking lot. Before they got to her car, she saw Dana sprinting toward her. She saw right away that Dana was upset about something. "Dana, what's wrong. Is your dad all right?"

Dana looked past her, hoping to see Coop exiting the church. Then she looked expectantly at Becky and asked, "Isn't Coop with you? He didn't come home last night. I was thinking he might have stayed at your place."

"No, he didn't stay at my place. He wouldn't. And I haven't heard from him since yesterday morning. I thought maybe he was with your dad. Your dad's okay?"

"Dad's fine. But we don't know where Coop is. He went out yesterday afternoon, and we haven't seen or heard from him since. I drove in looking for his truck in the ditches or something. But I can't find him. Maybe we should contact the sheriff."

Greg and Nancy walked by and noticed that Dana and Becky seemed upset about something. They went over to see what was wrong. Nancy confirmed that she had seen Coop parked out in front of the diner Saturday around four o'clock, like he was waiting for someone. Dana said, "Mom told me he was going to meet with that waitress,

Misty. She said she wanted to talk to him about God. Coop thought she was ready to hear about salvation. He went to witness to her."

"And he didn't come home all night?" asked Greg. "I don't have a good feeling about this. Have you tried calling him?"

"He's not answering. It's like his phone battery is dead. There's nothing. I'm really worried." Dana was visibly upset and Nancy gave her a hug.

"Greg, I think we should contact the sheriff. Would you do that for me, please?" Dana asked. "I think I'd fall apart, talking to him."

Greg called Sheriff Bert Bertell, who got into his cruiser right away and met them in the church parking lot. He asked a lot of questions, took down some notes, and said, "We don't usually get missing persons cases here. And when we do, we usually wait twenty-four hours before we start an investigation. That's standard. But since it's Coop, and we know this is not his typical behavior, and since I don't really have anything else to do today, I'll just do some driving around and see if I can find anything. You all go on home now, and I'll be in touch if anything turns up."

They thanked the sheriff and he said, "Don't worry about Coop. He can take care of himself. And there's probably not a thing wrong. There's usually a perfectly good explanation for things like this."

Greg and Nancy got back into their car, saying they'd be checking with them soon. Becky and Dana hugged each other and drove to their homes. Everyone was praying all the way.

CHAPTER 49

─── ❧ ───

Who Took the Farmer's Hat?

Coop woke slowly, with a pounding headache and drenched in sweat. He was hot, so hot. But no wonder. The truck was sitting in the sun, windows up, and heat building by the minute. He needed air. He needed water.

He wiped the sweat out of his eyes with the back of his hand. His shirt was plastered to his chest as if glued there by his perspiration. So hot.

Coop struggled to make his eyes focus. Where was he? He saw the keys in the ignition and turned them. The truck's air-conditioning kicked in but did little to cool him adequately. He rolled down the windows to let the heat escape.

Water. He needed water. There was a half-filled bottle lying on the seat beside him. It was hot, but at least it was wet. He guzzled it down quickly. Better, but not much.

Then his head started to pound. He unbuttoned his shirt and let it hang open, hoping it would help to cool him. His vision blurred again, and he closed his eyes.

What was happening to him? He felt a sense of doom, a foreboding of dread like he had never known before. No, no. He had to stay awake. He had to go home. He put his hands on the steering wheel and compelled himself to open his eyes. The world spun around him and he collapsed. His last semiconscious thought was *Oh God, help*. Then he passed out again.

He heard voices but could not force his eyes open. "Coop. Coop. Wake up, Coop."

Was it Becky? He wanted to see Becky. *Oh, Becky, don't go away. Becky, come back.* Coop drifted in and out of consciousness.

Sheriff Bertell pulled Coop from his pickup and laid him out in the grass, shaded by a stand of pine trees. He went to his car and came back with cold fresh water, which he helped Coop sip slowly. He wet his handkerchief with cold water and wiped it across Coop's face and shoulders. Slowly Coop came around. His head still hurt, hurt bad, but at least he could see better now. As things came into focus, he asked, "What happened?"

"That's what I'd like you to tell me. Your family is worried sick."

"I guess I fell asleep with the windows closed and slept past sunrise, and then it got hot. Maybe I had heat stroke or something. I don't know." Coop sat up and asked for more water. "I'd better call Mom." He pulled his cell phone out of his pocket and saw that the battery was dead. "Oh, that's great."

The sheriff said, "Don't worry. I'll call your mom and tell her I found you. Do you think you can drive? Maybe I should take you home."

Coop stood up and walked back to the truck. He was already starting to feel better, although his head throbbed, and he was still confused about what had happened. He squared his shoulders, buttoned up his shirt, and said, "I should be okay now. I've got a headache, but I think that's all. Maybe you could give me another bottle of water to drink on the way home?"

When the sheriff came back with another bottle of water, he found Coop walking around his truck, looking in the bed and in the back crew seat. He asked, "Are you looking for something, Coop?"

"Yeah. I can't find my hat."

CHAPTER 50

Young Love

"I can't figure it out, Mom. I was sitting in the truck with her, talking about verses in Romans. Things were going well, she was asking good questions, and my explanations were working. But I starting getting dizzy and sleepy. And next thing I knew, it was the next morning, and I was drenched in sweat and had this terrible headache. I can't remember anything in between."

"I think you were drugged," Dana said as she handed him a cup of steaming hot coffee. "I've heard about this thing called a date-rape drug. It's usually given to girls, though, by men who want to take advantage of them. And the girls don't usually remember a thing."

"That pretty much describes how I felt, so maybe you're right. But who would have done it? Misty? But why?" Coop shook his head as if to clear out the cobwebs. "None of this makes sense."

Marla Jean sipped her coffee and said, "What does make sense is that you are home safe now. And God answered our prayers. He kept you sheltered under his wings. I was so relieved when Bert called to say he had found you. How is your headache now?"

"Better since I took that Tylenol. And this coffee is helping too. I need a shower, though. I've never sweat that much in my life, even mowing hay in August!" He stood and put his coffee cup in the sink. "But first I need to call Becky."

Dana said, "I already called her, as soon as we heard from Sheriff Bertell. But I'm sure she'd like to hear your voice."

She answered on the first ring. "Oh, Coop! I'm so glad you are all right! We were all so worried. What in the world happened?"

"The funny thing is, I don't know. Dana thinks I was drugged, but I can't for the life of me figure out why Misty would do that. Anyway, I'm home and all is well. I'm just sorry you were worried. And sorry that our plans for this afternoon got messed up. I'll take you and Jenny out to the meadow sometime soon, I promise."

"Could you talk to Jenny a minute? She's been worried too."

Coop caught his breath. He sure didn't want to worry Jenny. "Of course."

Jenny took the phone. "Are you okay, Coop? Mommy said you were sick, and we couldn't go to that special place today."

"Sweetie, I'm okay now. I was very sleepy and had a big headache, but I took some medicine, and I'm going to be fine."

"I was praying for you. Mommy was crying. But we prayed, and she stopped."

"Thank you, Jenny. I felt your prayers. Hey, listen, I'm sorry we didn't go to the meadow today. But we will. I promise."

"Okay," Jenny said. "Bye. I love you."

"Oh I love you too, Jenny." Again Coop had to choke back his emotion. Both of those Emerson women were pulling on his heart. And he didn't mind it one bit.

Becky had the phone back and asked, "Coop, are you sure you're okay? Should you go to the doctor? urgent care or something? I could drive you over to Atkins. Maybe you should get checked out."

"Thanks, hun, but I'm fine. Really. I need a shower and some good sleep. And I need to stop in and see Dad for a minute. And I need for you to stop worrying. We'll figure all this out another day."

"Well, if you're sure. Call me tomorrow?"

"You bet. Goodbye, Becky."

"Bye, Coop." She wanted to add "I love you" but didn't.

CHAPTER 51

Detective on Duty

The next morning, Sheriff Bert Bertell pulled up the farm-house driveway. He wanted to see how Coop was feeling, and get some additional information from him.

"Sounds like you were drugged, if you ask me," he said. "I'd like to take a look at your truck, if I could."

"Sure," Coop said, and led the sheriff out to the pickup. Bert put on latex gloves and carried a plastic bag out with him. He collected several empty water bottles from under the seat and put them into the bag. He found Coop's Bible on the floor of the front seat, photographed it, and handed it to Coop. He dusted the steering wheel and door handles for fingerprints. He took lots of photographs.

"I didn't know you knew all this CSI stuff," said Coop. "That's pretty big time, for a small town like ours."

"Took some classes. I'm not a pro, but gathering this evidence should help, if we end up with a crime here. Don't usually get to use this stuff," he said, nodding in the direction of his camera and fingerprinting set. "But every once in a while, it comes in handy." He packed up his equipment and walked with Coop to the cruiser. "Sure do wish I would have told you to go to urgent care last night, though. They could have run some tests for drugs, but it's too late to be accurate now. Maybe we'll find something in the water bottles."

"Let me know what you find out, okay? I still don't remember much of last night. Like I told you, I was talking with Misty in the truck, and next thing I knew it was daytime, the truck was really hot, and I had a headache."

"Yeah, well, don't worry. I'll get to the bottom of this. So long, Coop."

Bert drove off and Coop headed to the barn. He felt half naked without his cowboy hat. But he knew he had an old baseball cap in the tack room. That would have to do.

Becky's white cowboy hat was hanging on a peg in the tack room too. She had put it there after their ride, saying she would need it again, because she wanted to ride with him again. He smiled when he saw it, remembering that special time they had spent together riding and talking, kissing and learning about each other. Was that just a week ago? So much had happened. More than ever, he wanted to hold her.

Sheriff Bertell walked into the diner and looked around. He saw the waitress, Misty, right away but went to the counter to talk with Al. They walked to Al's office and shut the door. Misty was serving a customer at a table in the corner and didn't notice.

Bert knew it would be a while before the DNA results would come back on the water bottles. While he waited, he would just keep an eye on things. No sense alerting the guilty party or parties. Wouldn't want them leaving town in a hurry.

CHAPTER 52

The Prodigal Son Returns

Michael Walter Smith hadn't been back to the Kansas farm for years. Today he was returning with his wife, Stacy, and two weeks' leave. He was surprised at how much was the same, yet so much was different. The driveway was still crushed gravel. The trees were much taller. The barn was still bigger than the house. But the house seemed much smaller than it used to be.

Michael was tall, though not quite as tall as Coop. His hair was cut short in typical Marine style, and he held himself in a straight and tall fashion. He walked right up to his mother and kissed her cheek. He hugged Dana and tousled Coop's hair. He introduced Stacy, looked around for Riley, and then remembered that his mom had told him about what had happened.

His mom had not told him what had happened to Coop, however. Marla Jean thought he should know about it, but there were other priorities just now. She led the way into the house, showed Stacy around, and took them to Michael's old room. It had been turning into a sewing and craft room years ago, but it had a sofa bed they could use. There was a closet with some space cleared for their clothes. Stacy looked around at the modest accommodations, and said, "Thank you. We'll be very comfortable here."

Michael went into his parents' room and was shocked to see the shell of a man that lay on the hospital bed. He sat on the edge of the bed, trying not to cause his father to roll or be uncomfortable. Walter moved his hand out from under the blanket and reached for Michael. "I'm glad to see you, son."

"Dad," Michael said, and couldn't say another word. They sat in silence for quite a while.

Walter whispered, "I prayed you would come in time."

"I'm here, Dad. I'm here."

Walter squeezed Michael's hand for a second but was too weak to hold tightly for long. He let his hand fall open.

"I'm so sorry, Dad. Sorry I haven't been here more. Sorry you are suffering like this. Sorry I can't do anything."

"Not suffering. Just waiting," Walter whispered weakly.

"Waiting? Waiting for me?" Michael asked.

"Waiting for the trumpet call. Listen."

"Trumpet? Is that something from the Bible, Dad? I think I remember a verse about a trumpet calling people to Heaven. Right?"

Marla Jean was watching from the doorway. She picked up Walter's Bible and turned to I Corinthians 15:52. "In a moment, in the twinkling of an eye, at the last trump: for the trumpet shall sound, and the dead shall be raised incorruptible, and we shall be changed." She closed the Bible. "He's really looking forward to Heaven. And he wants his whole family to be coming after him. He prays for you and Stacy a lot."

Michael turned to her and said, "Then you'll both be happy that we have been going to a good church on base. The chaplain has been preaching about sin and forgiveness and eternal life. A few months ago, something incredible happened. It was a full out revival in our church. Just like at camp meetings we used to go to when I was a kid. The Spirit of God moved through that church, and many people went forward to pray for forgiveness. And Stacy and I went to the altar together and gave our lives to Jesus. I know we have a lot to learn, we have wasted a lot of years, wandering in our own wilderness of sin. But that's over now, and we have turned our lives over to Christ."

Stacy came in from the hallway to stand beside Michael. "Yes, we did. And we're trying to learn about prayer and how to live a spirit-filled life. Michael grew up in a good and godly home, but Christ was a foreigner in the home where I was raised. So we're struggling, but we won't give up. We are pressing on. There's a verse about that somewhere. We have so much to learn. Anyway, you can rest assured that we will both be joining you in Heaven someday."

There wasn't a dry eye in the room. Michael hugged his mom. Stacy held Walter's hand. Marla Jean started to sing "Amazing Grace." They all joined in softly, even Walter was trying to sing. Dana and Coop came in from the kitchen and joined in the singing. "When we've been there ten thousand years, bright shining as the sun, there's no less days to sing God's praise than when we first begun."

Walter closed his eyes and fell into a peaceful sleep. Everyone tiptoed out of the room. In the living room, they stood close together and praised the Lord for his goodness, his faithfulness, and his promise of eternal life.

CHAPTER 53

Valley of the Shadow of Death

When Wanda and Judy arrived later that afternoon, they found Walter still sleeping, breathing shallowly and sporadically. The family gathered around his bed once more. Judy noted that it was good that Michael and his wife had arrived. "It seems that sometimes the person is just waiting for someone to come, or something to happen. When that person arrives, the patient can let go and is ready to move on."

The family was comforted by Wanda's words. "Go ahead and talk to him. It's thought that hearing is the last sense to leave. He will be able to hear what you say. He may not respond, but he will hear you."

Each member of the family took a turn sitting with their dad, talking about anything that came to mind. Memories, funny stories, farm life, regrets, and thankfulness. One by one, each child had a chance to recall a special time they had had with their dad. He didn't respond to any of the stories, but they trusted that he heard them. It brought them a comfort and a sense of closure.

Before she left, Wanda took Marla Jean and Dana aside and showed them how to administer the morphine that Walter would need to relax and be oblivious to pain. He was on a low dose for now, but the dosage would be increased as his bodily functions began to shut down. They wanted him comfortable. No reason at all that his last days should be filled with pain.

Some friends from church had organized a group of women to cook a few meals for the Smith family. They knew the stress that these next weeks would bring and wanted to help any way they could. Tonight's meal was chicken and dumplings, mixed vegetables, and a Jell-O salad. Coop prayed, "Lord, we thank you for this food, provided so kindly by your servants at the church. We ask that it strengthen us for the challenges in the days ahead. And thank you for Michael and Stacy and their safe journey here. And best of all, we rejoice in their decisions to follow you, Lord. Now the circle is unbroken. Amen."

In the darkness of the night, Walter rolled over in his bed and got twisted up in the sheets and blankets. His legs were tangled, and he tried desperately to free himself. He began digging at the bedding and was trying to crawl from his bed to Marla Jean's. "Get out. Get out," he said over and over.

Marla Jean woke and tried to help him, but he was confused and pushed her away. She tried to free his feet, but the sheet was wrapped around his ankles several times. She turned on the light on the side table, and that woke Walter somewhat. "Get out," he said again, but his struggling subsided, and he lay in the bed panting. He turned from side to side as if trying to figure out where he was.

His eyes had a blank stare that frightened Marla Jean. She got him a dose of morphine; he needed something to calm him.

Coop and Dana met in the hallway outside of their parents' room. Michael and Stacy joined them quickly. They wondered what this meant. What was going on?

They quietly stood in the doorway, looking in. Marla Jean was holding Walter, rocking him like a baby, and reciting the twenty-third Psalm. As the children came into the room, they joined her. "Yea, though I walk through the valley of the shadow of death, I will fear no evil: for thou art with me, thy rod and thy staff they comfort me."

Walter calmed and went to sleep.

CHAPTER 54

—— ❦ ——

Mail Call

Before breakfast, Dana went out to the mailbox. They had forgotten about getting the mail yesterday, and the box was full. Several people from church had sent cards saying they were thinking about the family and praying for their comfort. The choir director, Kaye, sent a card signed by all the members of the choir. Doc Larson and his wife sent a beautiful card with a picture of a collie. The family sat around the table, eating together and chatting about the goodness of their church friends.

"Look, Coop," said Dana, handing a large manila envelope across the table to him. "This is addressed to you. But it's not mail, there's no postage on it. No return address either. They must have just put it in the mailbox."

"That's odd," Coop said as he sliced the envelope open with his knife. He slid out a piece of paper and read it to himself. His face turned white. He looked into the large envelope and saw that there was something else down at the bottom. He excused himself from the table and went to his room.

Coop studied the paper again.

> Pay me $25,000 or your reputation will be ruined. I have more pictures. Hundreds. I'm going to put them out on the internet if you don't pay me what I want. Won't your friends and family be interested in seeing what the high and mighty, hell and brimstone preaching perfect Coop has been doing with his free time? $25,000. Get it now. Details will follow.

He slid his hand deeper in the envelope and pulled out a proof sheet of thumbprint-sized photos. They were small, and Coop had to look closely to determine exactly what he was looking at. Once he did, he sat down hard on the bed, put his head in his hands, and called out to his Lord. "Oh, God, no."

Becky was about to leave for work. Jenny was ready to be dropped off at Grandma's. With Marshmallow and her little kittens tucked under her arm, Jenny went out the door first. As she stepped outside, she saw a large manila envelope lying on the doorstep. "Look, Mommy! I think somebody left me a birthday card!"

CHAPTER 55

❦

Small-Town CSI

Bert Bertell had been sheriff of Winslow for almost thirty years. He liked the small-town vibe and the relatively low crime rate. He had the respect of most of the locals, who were pretty law-abiding citizens for the most part. Speeding tickets and minor vandalism topped the list of common criminal offenses. Once he had organized a search party to find a lost child, who had turned up walking to Grandma's house. And a couple of times he had helped drive some cows home after they had broken through a fence. But crime, real crime, was pretty foreign in Winslow.

The last few years, however, had seen an influx of a rougher crowd. Most of them were bikers, with seemingly nothing better to do all day than cruise the streets, make noise, and hang out in the trailer court.

Bert hated stereotypes. To lump all bikers together as lazy troublemakers was unfair to those hardworking, decent citizens who just happened to ride motorcycles. Bert knew a few of that type, and had never had any trouble with them. This new bunch, though, well, he didn't have a good feeling about them.

And especially after talking with Al at the diner. Al told him that a couple of bikers had been hanging out around a waitress at the diner. The girl's name was Misty, but Al didn't know the names of the two guys that often came in. He'd kept an eye on them, but he didn't get too close. Just didn't like the look of them.

Bert knew that Misty was the name of the woman Coop Smith had gone to see on Saturday afternoon. She might be the last person to have seen Coop before he had mysteriously blacked out. That made her a suspect, and possibly those two men were also persons of interest.

When his computer dinged to announce the arrival of e-mail, Bert sat down at his desk and turned his attention to his inbox. He found the e-mail from the lab and opened it. "Yup. Just like I thought. Rohypnol. Otherwise known as the date-rape drug." He printed off the report and put it into the file on his desk. There weren't many other papers in the file yet, but he'd be collecting the fingerprint report soon. In the meantime, it was probably a good time to go talk with Coop some more. Too bad about his dad's illness. This was a difficult time for the Smith family, and now this new situation could just make matters worse. Well, it had to be done.

CHAPTER 56

Confrontations

Coop's phone lit up, and he checked the caller ID. Becky. Good. He needed to talk to her. He could use her prayers right now.

"Hi, Becky. I'm glad you called. I need to talk to you."

Her voice seemed strained, and she stuttered a bit. Right away, Coop could sense that something was bothering her. "Well, I need to talk to you too. There's something really strange going on. I need you to explain some things to me."

Coop's heart sank a bit. He could tell she was upset. "Sure, Becky, what's the matter?"

"Not on the phone. Could you come over here? I called Doc Larson and took some time off. We have to get this cleared up. Jenny's at Mom's. So we can talk about this in private."

"It sounds important. I'll be right over. I have to make a phone call and check on Dad. But I can be at your place in forty-five minutes."

"Okay. Thank you," Becky said and hung up the phone. She sat at her kitchen table, looking at the picture that had been delivered mysteriously to her front door. Her stomach churned, and she felt like she might throw up. The handwritten note said, "And you thought he was a good boy."

Becky turned the picture upside down. She couldn't stand to look at it.

"Was I wrong about him? Did he fool me all this time? I thought he was the man you were leading me to, Lord. I'm so confused now. Maybe I can't really trust him. Maybe he's just like Derek, saying all the right words, acting the right way. Just to get me where he wanted me. But God, I thought he was the answer. I was so sure you were bringing us together. Maybe I can't trust myself. Maybe I'm not as strong as I thought I was. I just don't understand."

She put her head in her hands and prayed, "Lord Jesus, I'm afraid. Help me. Help me, Lord."

Coop closed his bedroom door, so he couldn't be overheard. He scrolled through his phone contacts and found her number. He said a prayer for calm and dialed her number.

She didn't answer.

He sent her a text. *What in the world are you doing? You're crazy to think I can get $$$ just like that. And where did these pictures come from anyway? Did you drug me?*

He put his phone into his back pocket and put the pictures and note back into the envelope and carried it with him. He sure didn't want his mother to find those pictures. Or his sister. Or anybody.

He peeked into his dad's room, told his mom he was going to Becky's, and left. On the porch he reached for his black cowboy hat, and then remembered that he couldn't find it. *Great. What else could go wrong?*

He met Sheriff Bertell pulling into the driveway. He stopped the truck and rolled down his window to talk. "Got the toxicology screen back," the sheriff said. "You were drugged, Coop, just as I suspected. I need to talk to you about the events of that afternoon. Can we go somewhere to talk? I don't really want to upset your folks."

Coop thought a minute and asked if he could make a phone call. He called Becky. "Hey, Becky, I just ran into Sheriff Bertell, and he told me that he knows I was drugged on Saturday. He needs to talk to me about things, so I'm going to be a little late getting over to your place. Can I call you when we're done? Then you and I can talk."

"You were drugged?" Becky asked. "Oh, thank goodness."

"Huh? Being drugged is a good thing?"

"Well, it does help to explain what I found on my porch today."

"What did you find?"

"A picture of you and that waitress, Misty, in a very compromising position. I couldn't understand how you could do that, and I was really hurt and confused when I saw it. But if you were drugged, well, that explains it a little."

"Oh no, I can't believe she did that. I'm so sorry. Becky, she sent me some pictures too. And she's demanding money, or she's going to send the pictures to the Internet. Hey, listen, can the sheriff and I come over to your place?

We need to talk this out in private. I don't want to do it here at home, with things so bad with dad."

"Of course, you can come here. Maybe we can figure this out together."

"Thanks, Becky. I am so sorry you've gotten dragged into this." Coop wished he could hug her. Or turn back time. "We'll be over soon."

CHAPTER 57

The Lost Has Been Found

Becky sat the coffee pot on the table when she heard Coop's truck pull into the driveway. She watched from the front window as the sheriff parked his cruiser in the street. She saw him reach over to the seat beside him and put his hat on his head. When he got out of the car, she noticed that he was carrying a folder in his hand. The sheriff met Coop at the sidewalk, and they walked together to the front door. Becky noticed that Coop was carrying a manila envelope similar to the one she had lying on the kitchen table. She also noticed that he wasn't wearing his cowboy hat.

Coop had been praying all the way to Becky's place. He asked for calmness and clarity. He asked for a swift solution to this mess, if it be the Lord's will, and patience if the answers didn't come quickly. But mostly he asked for forgiveness. He knew God would forgive him; that was his nature. He prayed that Becky would forgive him.

Becky answered their knock and welcomed them in. Coop introduced the sheriff and said, "Becky is my girl-friend. I want her to know what's going on. I have no secrets from her. She got something delivered to her house this morning too. This has to fit together somehow. Let's sit and talk about it all." He led the way to the table. Becky poured three cups of coffee and sat down beside the sheriff. She was able to look directly into Coop's eyes. Her envelope lay on the table between them.

"First things first," said the sheriff. "I need to get your fingerprints, Coop. I've sent off the water bottles for fingerprinting, and we need to have yours on file for comparison and elimination." He set up the fingerprinting equipment and got to work. He took Becky's too, just for principle.

The sheriff took Coop's complete statement and asked a lot of questions that Coop couldn't answer. No, he couldn't remember anything past the time he was sitting in the truck with Misty, talking about salvation and drinking water she had brought along. No, he hadn't seen any men. No, he didn't know where they had taken him, but he had these pictures that might help identify the place.

Coop hesitated to take the picture sheet out of the envelope. He looked at Becky and said, "I'm sorry, Becky. I don't want to upset you."

"It's okay, Coop. I got a picture too." She nodded at her envelope on the table.

Coop took the blackmail note out of his envelope first. He let the sheriff read it, then passed it over so Becky could read also. She raised her eyebrows and clicked her tongue. "She actually thinks she can get away with this? That woman is crazy! What are you going to do, Coop?"

The sheriff took the note back. "Well, one thing's for sure, you are *not* going to pay this money."

"That's what I told her. I said I couldn't get ahold of money like that."

Sheriff Bertell was interested. "You talked to her? When was this?"

"I tried to call her, but she didn't answer so I left a text. Just before I met you on our driveway. Here." He took his phone and scrolled to the texts. "Here, I still have the text on here. She hasn't answered me yet, though." He found her number and immediately noticed that she had just answered. He opened it and said, "Oh look, a text just came in. It says 'Sell a cow or something. I want the money in 48 hours or I release the pictures.'" He handed the phone over to the sheriff.

Sheriff Bertell read the texts and took a picture of the messages between Coop and Misty. He reached for Coop's envelope and looked at Coop. "May I?" Coop looked toward Becky, who lowered her eyes and nodded her okay.

The sheriff withdrew the sheet of photos. He put on his reading glasses and brought the page close to his eyes. "Really small. Hard to see details. Might have to get these enlarged. Do you recognize this place, Coop? Anywhere you've ever been before?"

"No, it doesn't look familiar at all. But the pictures are so small, it's hard to tell."

Becky pulled the picture out of her envelope. "Here, try this one. It's an enlargement. You might recognize it easier."

Coop drew his breath in quickly when he saw the picture. He wasn't used to looking at pornography, and this picture could certainly be classified as that. There was Misty, practically naked, sitting on his lap straddling him and kissing him. He turned the picture over and covered it with his hands. "I don't recognize the room, but I did just solve one mystery."

"What's that?" asked the sheriff.

"I found my hat."

CHAPTER 58

Together

The sheriff put the photos and notes into his file folder with the handwritten notes he had taken. He thanked them for their time. He told them he was sorry they had to go through this, but it should be resolved soon. Meanwhile, if Coop or Becky got any more messages or pictures, he needed to know right away. And Coop wasn't to worry about the forty-eight-hour deadline. He expected they'd be wrapping this up before the deadline got here. He left his phone number with each of them, gathered his things, and left.

As soon as the sheriff left, Coop took Becky in his arms, holding her close and stroking her hair. "Oh, Becky, I am so, so sorry. Can you forgive me? I would never do anything to hurt you. Please believe me. I don't remember a thing. I know it sounds absurd, but really, I do not remember. I would not do that. I hope you know. You can trust me. I have no memory of any of that."

Becky pulled away and put her hand over his mouth. "Shhh," she said. "Don't say another word. There's no need for me to forgive you. You didn't do anything wrong. All that was done *to* you. I believe you were drugged, kidnapped, and had no part in it, except as a target for Misty and whoever else was involved." She took his hand and led him to the couch. They sat together, arms wrapped around each other.

"I will admit, I was hurt when I first saw the picture they sent me. I was angry for a minute, and then I started thinking. It was so unlike you to do something like that. It just didn't fit your character. I had to believe there was more to this story. I prayed, told God my fears, and he put me at ease. I recalled the verse about the Lord being a stronghold in the day of trouble, and I asked him to hold on to me. And to come close and hold you too."

"Thank you for praying for me. I was very confused when I first woke up in the truck, and even more confused when I got those pictures. I didn't know how it could have happened. The last thing I remember was sitting with her in the truck, talking about leading her to the Lord. Then *bam*, all this."

"Well, the sheriff seems to think he can get to the bottom of this pretty fast. So don't worry. We'll take it one day at a time."

"I hope he can. I would hate for those pictures to get out to the public."

"Coop, anyone who knows you will know that you were set up somehow. This is not something that you would knowingly participate in. Your reputation is spotless, and we all know that. Trust me. No one would believe that you did this willingly."

"I hope you're right." Coop thought for a while, and a shudder came over him. "I would sure hate for my mom to see those pictures. Or Dana. Or you, Becky. I don't want you to have those images in your mind. Oh honey, can you ever forgive me?"

"Benjamin Cooper Smith!" she said with exaggeration. "I told you! There's nothing to forgive. Now stop. We move on. Don't dwell on the negatives or the what-ifs. We'll deal with whatever comes our way. Together. And with the Lord's help, we'll have peace about it."

"Together?" Coop asked. "I like the sounds of that." He kissed her softly on the head.

"You once told me that you'd take care of me. But sometimes you need to let me take care of you too. Together we can be a great team. You said that once too." Becky sighed and Coop pulled her closer.

His phone, sitting on the kitchen table, began to vibrate. Fearing that it might be Misty, Coop stood reluctantly. Looking at the caller ID, he breathed a sigh of relief. It was Dana.

"Coop, you need to come home quick. It's Dad."

"I'll be there as fast as I can. Bye."

Coop looked at Becky. "Come with me. Dad's at the end."

CHAPTER 59

Welcome, Good and Faithful Servant

Becky stood beside Coop as the family stood in a circle around Walter's bed. Marla Jean held Walter's hand and kept her eyes on his face. Dana began to sing an old hymn, "Blessed Assurance," and the others joined in. Walter took a breath and then was silent. Dana started "What a Friend We Have in Jesus," and Walter took another breath. Marla Jean leaned close to him and said, "I love you Walter." He made a vocalization, raspy and unclear, but to everyone in the room it sounded like it could have been "I love you too." The song ended, and the room was silent except for some muffled sobs. Michael moved close to his mother and put his arm around her for support. Becky took Coop's hand, and he squeezed it tight.

Wanda and Judy checked Walter's vitals for the last time. They noted the time of death on his chart. Wanda closed his eyes and pulled the bedsheet up to his chin. "We'll leave you now, to have some final moments with him. You just take your time. Judy will call the funeral home and arrange transportation. But there's no rush. Take as long as you need to say goodbye."

The family held hands and Coop prayed. "Lord God, thank you for giving us this wonderful man to be our father and Mom's husband. Thank you for his godly leadership for our family. Welcome him now into your presence, where he has longed to be. Comfort our grieving souls, and give us strength to get through the days ahead. In your name we pray. Amen."

Stacy said, "Do you know the song 'It Is Well with My Soul'?" Everyone nodded. "I don't know all the words, but could we sing it?"

Marla Jean said, "It was one of his favorites. He wants it sung at his funeral."

Coop's deep voice started the song, and soon they were all singing. The words swelled, and tears flowed as they sang. "Whatever my lot, thou hast taught me to say, it is well. It is well with my soul."

"Just imagine," Becky said. "He's breathing heavenly air!"

Dana added, "Full deep breaths of heavenly air. No coughing. No struggling to breathe deep enough to talk. Perfectly wonderful air, filling his lungs. I'm so happy for him now!"

Marla Jean smiled. "And he went with almost no pain. That was my prayer, that he wouldn't suffer. God spared him that. He went peacefully, with all of his family here. That meant a lot to him, I know." She looked at Michael and Stacy. "I'm so glad you made it in time." She turned to Becky. "I'm glad you were here too."

Becky went to her and gave her a hug. Dana bent over her father and gave him a final kiss. "Give Riley a hug from me," she said, with tears flowing down her cheeks. One by one, the others said their goodbyes and left the room. Marla Jean stayed behind and sat with Walter's body a while longer.

In the kitchen, they chatted quietly. Becky asked Dana, "Is there anything I can do? What do you need?"

Dana looked around blankly and couldn't answer. Her mind wasn't processing much just yet.

"I know," said Becky. "How about I call Pastor Green and let him know? He'll want to tell others at the church, I'm sure. And he'll probably want to meet with you all to plan the service."

"The service is pretty well planned already," Dana said. She was gaining her composure. "Dad and Mom talked about it months ago, got everything worked out. But yes, you could call Pastor please. That would be a big help right now. I don't know what else to do. I'm kinda numb."

Wanda and Judy walked in, and Judy said to Dana, "A numbness is quite normal. It will feel unreal for a while." Dana nodded in acknowledgement. She couldn't talk.

"I've called the funeral home, and they should be here in about forty-five minutes, to transport him," Judy said. "But they won't rush you. Take as much time as you want. Do you want us to stay until they arrive? Or would you like us to leave?"

Marla Jean came into the kitchen and said, "You can leave. We'll be just fine. And thank you so much for all you have done. For Walter and for all of us." She was amazingly composed and seemed to have overcome her grief, for the moment at least.

Shortly after the nurses left, the drivers from the funeral home arrived. Michael showed them into the bedroom, and they prepared Walter's body for departure. As the stretcher rolled out the door, Michael and Coop stood on either side of their mother. Dana, Stacy, and Becky stood together, crying softly.

CHAPTER 60

Cops on Call

Bert Bertell might be a small-town sheriff, but he knew how to get things done in a big-town way. After he talked with Coop and Becky, he got busy.

He looked for fingerprints on the photo sheet and the enlargement and was able to lift a couple of good samples. He sent those off for identification right away.

The fingerprint results from the water bottles had come in by fax while he was talking with Coop. The report showed that the water bottles had two sets of prints, besides Coop's. Using the fingerprint database, he was able to identify Misty and Patch, whose real name turned out to be Randall Hornsby, who had a record of assault with a deadly weapon and a history of drug use, as well as possession with intent to distribute. Misty had a record too for shoplifting in Wichita and several cities in California.

Sheriff Bertell was able to get a search warrant for the homes of both Randal "Patch" Hornsby and Melissa Madison, otherwise known as Misty. He held off on processing the warrants, though, because he was waiting to see if any prints from the second man would show up, maybe on the photos. He didn't have to wait long.

Next morning, the report was in. William "Billy" Wilson had left his fingerprints on the sheet of small photos sent to Coop and the enlargement sent to Becky. His prints were in the database because of a record of burglary and breaking and entering.

Sheriff Bertell contacted the sheriff in Atkins, the next town over, and was able to ask for his assistance. He needed two men, he said, to assist with serving warrants in Winslow. He wanted to hit all three locations at once so that none of the suspects could warn the others. The time was set for that very afternoon, at four o'clock. They would meet at Sheriff Bertell's office, discuss Coop's case and the evidence gathered so far, go over the warrants, and look at some mug shots. They discussed the procedures to be followed, and Sheriff Bertell said, "Let's go men. Get this done, get it done right, and get it over with. Coop Smith deserves our finest efforts."

At the appointed hour, three law officers approached three residences, armed with warrants and government issued fire arms. Deputy Lefty Jones entered the home of Misty's father. Misty was not there, and her father was cooperative. Not surprised that his daughter was in trouble with the law, he sat at the kitchen table, with his hands folded in front of him. As expected, Deputy Jones found drugs in Misty's room. Evidence was photographed, bagged, and tagged. He also photographed the entire room, which included, oddly enough, a man's black cowboy hat sitting on the dresser. Knowing that it was an important part of the evidence, Lefty photographed it and carefully placed it in an evidence bag.

Deputy Jones left his assignment and drove to the trailer park, where he was to meet his boss, Sheriff Feldman, and assist with processing the scene at the trailer of William Wilson.

Sheriff Mark Feldman, from Atkins, knocked on the door of Billy's trailer, identified himself, and entered without incident. As a precaution, Billy was handcuffed to the refrigerator door. Sheriff Feldman photographed the entire trailer. Billy remained silent. He was busy thinking about how he could get out of this mess.

Before Sheriff Feldman finished processing the scene, Deputy Jones arrived to assist. When they discovered the camera equipment, they gathered it as evidence. Billy, still silent, was secured in the sheriff's car.

Patch's trailer was nearby, and Deputy Jones had noticed Sheriff Bertell's cruiser parked there when he had driven past on his way to Billy's. The two officers from Atkins parked their cars behind Sheriff Bertell's and approached the trailer just as gunshots rang out. They drew their weapons and entered cautiously.

On the floor, clutching his leg and screaming in pain, lay Randal "Patch" Hornsby. "Watch him," Bertell said to the deputy. "Don't let him up."

"I've been shot, damn it!" yelled Patch. "Get me to a doctor."

"Well," said Sheriff Bertell, "if you hadn't tried to pull a knife on me, I wouldn't have had to shoot you. Now we can add resisting arrest to your list of charges."

"I need a doctor!" Patch yelled louder. "Help me!"

"You're not dying. Shut up. You'll see a doctor soon enough," said Deputy Jones, pointing his revolver at the man who was bleeding on the floor. He tossed Patch a dish towel and said, "Here, put some pressure on it. Maybe the bleeding will stop."

The two sheriffs searched Patch's trailer and found Rohypnol in the bathroom cabinet and other drugs scattered throughout the bedroom. Other than some makeup on the bathroom counter and clothing items in the closet, there was no sign of Misty. Sheriff Feldman and Deputy Jones helped Patch get into the deputy's car. He was secured with handcuffs, and the deputy drove him to urgent care in Atkins.

Billy, sitting in Sheriff Feldman's cruiser, wondered what charges would be made against him. Blackmail? No, he really hadn't had a part in that. That was all Misty's doing. Her idea, her plan. Drugging Coop? Nope, not guilty. That was Patch and Misty. Kidnapping? Ya, there's that. Taking the pictures? Was that really even a crime? True, he had stolen the camera equipment from a pawnshop in Atkins. So guilty of robbery, a minor offense. Maybe he could make a deal. If he talked, they might let him off easy.

CHAPTER 61

─────── ✦ ───────

Lion on the Loose

Misty left work and was headed to Patch's place. She was in a good mood, lighthearted and cheerful. She was about to be rich. She'd pay off those school bills, move to NYC, and have the life she always dreamed of. Away from this stupid ho-hum town. Away from farmers and preachers and cows and cornfields. Yep, Coop's time was running out. Only twenty hours until his deadline. She would message him tonight, with instructions about where to leave the money. She'd leave him the camera card, take his money, give Patch his share, and be gone.

She rounded the corner and slowed her steps when she saw a police car outside Patch's place. This could be trouble. She changed directions and went between two trailers, keeping out of sight as much as possible. Then she saw two more cruisers go by and stop at Patch's trailer. Damn.

She walked toward Billy's trailer, still picking her way between trailers and among cars and bikes parked haphazardly in the yards. She saw Billy's bike on the side of his trailer and assumed he was inside. She knocked on the door and entered. The place was deserted. Not a good sign. Looking around, she recognized right away that the camera equipment was missing. That didn't necessarily mean anything, but it could mean something. She searched for the camera card, hoping to find it hidden somewhere, but there was no sign of it.

So what does this mean? If the police have been here, they probably have the cameras and the card. They might have Billy, who was unstable at best. They might have Patch, and all the evidence that was in his trailer. The drugs. Oh shit, things were falling apart. *I've gotta get out of here,* she thought and looked around in desperation. She saw the key to Billy's bike on top of the microwave. She grabbed it and put it in her pocket.

Misty went to Billy's bedroom and found some money hidden in a drawer. She took it. She grabbed some cans of beer from the refrigerator and threw them into a bag, along with some leftover burgers from Billy's supper last night. At least she'd have some food.

Misty opened the door slowly, to be sure that there were no cops around. She went to Billy's bike, put on Billy's helmet, started the bike, and drove slowly away. No need to stir up attention.

Sitting in the sheriff's car, Billy caught a glimpse of a bike driving away from the trailer court and said, "Damn it. She's got my bike."

Misty rode to her dad's place, packed some of her things, grabbed her tip money, and went to the coffee can in the kitchen, where her dad kept cash for emergencies. *Hell, if this isn't an emergency, I don't know what is.* She looked around the house and said, "Well, so long, Pops. See ya around."

She went to the diner and quietly walked to the cash register. Al was in the back, and the only waitress in the place wasn't paying her any attention. She took all the cash out of the register, turned, and left.

Once on the bike she went north out of town. She didn't know where she was going. Just away. Far, far away.

CHAPTER 62

Predictions

Wednesday evening, instead of going to the single-moms' group at church, Becky and Jenny went out to the farm. The family was gathering around the table for supper, which had been supplied by members of the church. With four extra people to be seated at the table, an extension leaf had been added. There was barely room to maneuver in the kitchen.

They talked about the funeral arrangements and went over final details. The viewing would be Friday evening; the funeral was Saturday at ten o'clock. The pallbearers had been confirmed, the music chosen, and special verses selected.

Marla Jean leaned around Coop, so she could talk to Becky. "I'd like you to sit with the family, if you would please, Becky. Walter would have liked that."

Becky said, "I'd be honored to do that." She looked down at Jenny and said, "I'm not sure what to do about Jenny. She's never been to a funeral before. Is five too young?"

Marla Jean said, "I know your mother is planning to come. Maybe Jenny could sit with her."

"That's a good idea. We'll talk about it."

Jenny pulled on her mother's arm. "Mommy! I'm five! I'm a big girl!"

Everyone smiled and Becky said, "Like I said, we'll talk about it."

Coop hesitated but decided that now was the time to tell his family about his situation with Misty and the blackmail note. He spoke cautiously, so as not to be too graphic in front of Jenny. The grown-ups caught on quickly and asked a few questions for clarification. Marla Jean's face paled, and she shuddered. "Thank the Lord your father didn't know about this."

Dana was indignant. "I just knew she was trouble. I knew it. You should have stayed away from her from the very beginning. I told you she was bad news."

"But she has a soul, Dana, and I have a commission from the Lord to spread the gospel to the lost. I tried. And despite everything, I'll still pray for her. The seeds I planted may be watered by someone else, and that's fine. I still hope and pray that she'll accept Christ someday."

Becky added, "That's amazing, Coop. To still care about her salvation, I mean, it would be so easy to be angry and bitter and even to hope she gets what she deserves. That's really showing mercy."

"Well, I wonder what happens next." Marla Jean pondered the situation. "Will there be a trial and everything?"

"Sheriff Bertell seems to think they can get this all cleared up quickly, and we'll put it all behind us," Coop said, and looked at Becky. "Then we can move ahead with life. Make some plans for the future."

Dana noticed Becky's slight blush. She said, "Nobody would have believed anything bad about you anyway, Coop. You have a reputation around this town, and anybody who knows you would not believe you'd do something like that. The whole thing was a ridiculous plan from the start."

"I know, and I appreciate you saying that. But I'd still hate for those pictures to be made public and maybe plant doubts in someone's mind. It's not just my reputation I was thinking about, but my witness. I wouldn't want anyone to be turned away from Christ because they saw how I had fallen. Kinda like 'If Coop calls himself a child of God, and still got sucked into this, then why didn't God save him from this mess?' I wouldn't want my mistakes be a hindrance to others."

"You just have to put it into God's hands, Coop," said Marla Jean. "God knows your heart, and your intentions were good. Other people who know and love you will believe that you were not responsible. And as far as that goes, only God has authority to judge, and he loves you unconditionally. Remember what Romans chapter eight says. "There is now *no condemnation* to those who are in Christ. That's you, Coop. You are not condemned by God, so don't worry about what others might think."

Coop looked at Becky, and Becky was already smiling really big. "That's Becky's favorite verse," he said, "and I think it's mine too."

Michael spoke up, "I'd forgotten how good it is to sit around a table and talk of favorite verses, and God's unconditional love, and other spiritual matters. I didn't appreciate it growing up, but I sure do now. It's good to be home."

"I just wish your father was here, to talk about spiritual things with us again," Marla Jean said. "I'm sure he's looking down and smiling at us right now." The room grew silent.

"Hey, I've been wondering," said Dana. "Do you think Patrick met him at the pearly gate? And would he be a child, like when he died? Or would he be like twenty-five years old or something? And would Dad recognize him? I wonder what Dad did when he saw Jesus? Can you just imagine?" Dana was almost giddy with excitement.

Coop answered, "Good questions, Dana. And I don't think we'll ever know, until we get there ourselves."

"Isn't there a song that says, 'we'll understand it better by and by?'" Becky asked. "I've heard Mom singing that."

"Yes, it's an old hymn," Marla Jean said. "I was playing it on the piano a short while back. Your dad always liked to hear me play."

"He'll still be listening, Mom," said Michael.

After everyone had eaten their fill, Dana said, "Mom, you just relax. Us girls will take care of the dishes. I'll even let Becky help this time. She's practically family now!"

Stacy looked at Becky and asked, "Are you and Coop engaged? I hadn't noticed a ring." She reached for Becky's left hand as Becky said, "No, we aren't really. We've only gone on one official date. Dana likes to stir up things!"

"Call it wishful thinking if you want," said Dana. "Or maybe predicting the future!" She picked up some dishes off the table and said, "Come on, let's get these dishes done. We can talk more while we're cleaning up."

Jenny wandered out to the porch, where Coop and Michael were sitting and reminiscing. She climbed up on Coop's lap and cuddled into him. He stroked her hair and said, "Well, hi there. Make yourself comfortable." Jenny giggled.

Michael said, "She looks quite comfortable with you. You'd make a good father, Coop."

"What about you, Michael? Are you and Stacy going to have kids? Not to pry or anything, just wondering."

"Actually, we're thinking about adopting. We visited an orphanage when we were stationed in Japan last year, and we've been talking about it ever since. When my enlistment is up in a year, and we figure out where we are going to live, we'll get the ball rolling. So maybe Jenny will have a cousin in a couple of years."

"Or a baby sister," said Jenny, just as Becky, Dana, and Stacy joined them on the porch.

"What in the world are you guys talking about?" Becky asked with a surprised chuckle.

"Babies, Mommy, we're talking about babies."

"Well, then, I think you better go into the house and gather up Marshmallow and her babies. It's getting late, and we need to get home. Some of us have to go to work tomorrow." Becky looked around the porch as Jenny got up off Coop's lap. "It's been great spending time with you all tonight. Nice to get to know you better. I guess I'll see you all on Friday night." She turned to Coop. "You let me know if you need anything, okay?"

Coop stood and said, "I'll walk you to your car."

As they were kissing good night, Coop's phone vibrated, and he answered when he recognized the sheriff's number.

"Sorry to bother you so late Coop, but I have news you may want to hear," the sheriff said.

"News? Great. Hey, Becky is here too. Let me put you on speaker, okay?"

"Sure." Bert paused a second and then went on. "We have arrested Patch and Billy. Patch was hurt in a struggle and went to the hospital. But he's going to be okay. He's being held under guard at the hospital room. Probably released tomorrow, and put in jail. Billy is here in the Winslow jail. I think he's ready to talk. I'll work on him tomorrow, after he's had a lovely night's sleep on a hard bed with a pot to pee in. Oh," he said, "sorry, Becky."

"What about Misty?" Coop asked.

"She was last seen headed north on a stolen motorcycle. We have an APB out for her. She can't get far. We might even have her by morning."

Coop breathed a sigh of relief and said, "That's all great news. Thanks for letting us know. Becky says thank you too."

"Oh and, Coop, I was so sorry to hear about your dad. When is the service? I want to be there. He was a good man."

Coop gave him the details, and they said goodbye. Then he hugged Becky and said, "I'm so glad that's over. Now we can move on. What a relief."

Becky drove home, with a sleeping Jenny in the back seat. She recalled the conversations of the evening. She admitted she felt really comfortable in this family. And she was curious about what Coop meant when he said "Now we can move on."

She parked her car in the carport, but before she got out, she closed her eyes and thanked God for Sheriff Bertell and the quick resolution to Coop's troubles. She once again thanked God for Coop and asked for direction and guidance. She put their relationship into his hands.

As Coop walked into the farmhouse, he stopped and gazed up at the sky. The moon was just rising over the top of the barn, and the sky was sparkling with stars. He inhaled the familiar scents of farm and dirt and animals and night. He sighed in total contentment. "Oh, God, I don't know what to say. Thank you does not seem adequate. You have protected me, blessed me, and been with me all along my life. I'm so glad to know that you will make the path clear for me in the days ahead, and even the years ahead. I trust you. I love you. I thank you."

CHAPTER 63

—— ✑ ——

The End of the Road

At a big truck stop east of Atkins, Misty bought a pair of scissors and cut her hair. She figured she'd buy some hair dye later and change her look completely, but for now, this would have to do. She strolled casually through the store, snatched a few candy bars, and stashed them inside her knapsack. She bought a soft drink and went to a table to sit and think. It was getting dark, and she really needed to find a place to sleep. Maybe a trucker would like a companion. And maybe he would give her a ride east. The bike only had a little gas left. If she couldn't find a trucker, she'd have to buy some gas. If she did find a trucker, she would just abandon the bike. The cops were probably looking for her on a bike anyway. Best to ditch it as soon as possible.

She looked around the truck stop, hoping to find a likely-looking trucker, someone who looked lonely. Or horny. She made eye contact with a man in his forties. He seemed like a possibility, and he was sure looking her over good. Misty walked over to his table, started up a conversation, and before long she was climbing into the sleeper of his cab. She'd worked out a sweet trade.

The driver, Craig Cashman, had been listening to his radio scanner and was aware of an APB out for a woman on a motorcycle. He noted her description: long black hair with purple streaks, tattoo of flowers and vines on her right arm, bike model, and license plate number. He'd been watching for her as he drove along the highway. He always liked to help the police. Be a hero. Maybe get his picture in the paper.

So he had spotted her a few miles back, and followed her into the truck stop. He watched her go into the bathroom with long hair and come out with short. He noted the tattoo and knew he had the right gal. He had notified the local police just minutes before she walked over to him and offered herself in exchange for a ride. Just enough time to collect before the cops showed up. Pretty sweet deal.

"I gotta use the bathroom before we hit the road," the driver said. He left the truck and headed toward the building. Misty watched as he adjusted his jeans and tucked in his shirt. At the door, he stopped to talk to two police officers who were coming out. He looked at something the officers showed him and nodded in the direction of his truck.

"Well, crap," Misty said as she opened the driver's door and slid out. She crept between trucks, always moving farther and farther away from the building. She circled around and got back to where she had parked the bike. Fortunately, no one was there, and she was able to put on her helmet and jump on the bike before anyone noticed.

She heard the trucker yell out, "Hey, there she goes," and soon the policemen were in their car, in hot pursuit.

Flying down the highway, with police lights and sirens right behind her, she was desperately searching in the darkness for a side road, a farm road—something, anything—to get out of their line of sight. There. At the base of a hill, a gravel road took off through farm fields. She made the turn while the police car was down in the valley on the back side of the hill. Hopefully, they didn't see her leave the highway. She breathed a sigh of relief.

But it was short-lived. The police car made the turn and closed in on her. The bike was unstable on the gravel, but the car was bearing down on her fast. The headlight on the bike barely lit the ground in front of her. Gravel was flying, and dust was billowing. The police car was closing in.

The deer came out of nowhere. Misty tried to avoid hitting it, but to no avail. The bike crashed into the side of the deer, and Misty was thrown off. The frantic deer, trying to escape, kicked in desperation and struggled to get up from the heap of metal that had landed on him. Misty, lying off to the side of the wreckage, found herself being pummeled by deer hoofs.

By the time the police officers reached the wreckage, the deer had gone crazy with fear and pain. Trapped partially under the motorcycle, trying desperately to free himself, he kicked and kicked at anything. His hooves connected with Misty's chest, and she felt some ribs crack. She tried to crawl away, but found that her arms wouldn't pull her weight. Another whack from the deer punctured her kidney. One blow of a hoof hit her squarely in the head, and she was knocked unconscious.

Just before she passed out, she heard a gunshot. The deer was dead. Misty was barely hanging on.

CHAPTER 64

We Are Family

The church was filled with friends of the family. The service was a wonderful memorial to a man who had been a pillar of the community, a friend to many, and an honest man who shared the gospel with farmers, neighbors, store clerks, and the mailman. Several people rose to speak in honor of Walter's memory.

Becky sat beside Coop in the family row. Jenny sat beside her, wide-eyed but quiet. After they had talked about it, Becky decided that Jenny would probably be okay sitting with her. She really was mature for a little girl.

Pastor Green was teaching on Psalms 116:15 "Precious in the sight of the Lord is the death of his saints." The verse was written on the back of the funeral card. There was a picture of Walter on the front, taken before the cancer had hollowed his cheeks or taken the sparkle from his eye. Becky thought again of how much Coop looked like his father.

A woman stood at the microphone and sang "It Is Well with My Soul." Becky heard Stacy sniffle and wipe her eyes.

Dana was also teary-eyed. Becky handed her a tissue and got one for herself.

The congregation rose to sing "When We All Get to Heaven." Everyone in the family row joined hands. Becky felt Coop's strong grip and felt comfort. On the other side, Jenny held her hand and swung her arm to the beat of the music. Becky smiled. Standing between these two made her feel complete.

The casket was carried solemnly down the center aisle, followed by the family. It was a short walk to the cemetery at the side of the church. Walter Allan Smith was buried under the shade of a large oak tree. Dead at the age of fifty-one, but alive in heaven for eternity.

As they turned to leave, Jenny slipped over to the side of the grave. She waved and said, "Bye-bye. See ya later." Then she walked to Coop and said, "Your daddy's in Heaven, isn't he?"

"Yes, sweetie, he is."

"Then he's not really gone. We get to see him again."

"That's right, Jenny," Coop said. "One day, all of us will be there with him. And we'll be with Jesus too."

"Great. I'll like that," said Jenny. She turned to Becky and said, "Let's go to the farm. I want to milk Bessie."

"Oh goodness, Jenny, we can't today. We have our good clothes on and—"

Coop interrupted. "Jenny, we'll do it soon. I promise. But right now, I have to be with my family."

Jenny asked, "But aren't I your family? I love you."

Coop smiled down at her and said "And I love you too, sweetie."

"I love Mommy and she's my family," Jenny said. "I want you to be my family too."

Coop looked at Becky and said, "Out of the mouths of babes…"

Becky looked puzzled, but before she could say anything, they were interrupted. Doc Larson and his wife came over to speak with Coop and his mother. He greeted Becky with a smile and a nod. Becky touched Coop on the shoulder and said, "I'm going to get Jenny home. She's had enough excitement and should get a nap. Will I see you at church tomorrow?"

"Yes. And we *will* finish this conversation." He kissed her on the top of her head. "See you tomorrow."

Driving home with a smile in her heart, Becky hummed the tune "I Could Sing of Your Love Forever."

"Sing it, Mommy, sing it." They drove the rest of the way home, singing the words over and over.

CHAPTER 65

———— ⌘ ————

A Man of Good Character

A week later, Michael and Stacy left to go back to Arizona. They had already made plans to return in December, so the family could celebrate the Lord's birth together. Becky and Jenny came out to the farm to say goodbye. Stacy and Becky walked around the yard and talked a few minutes. "I feel like we're already sisters," Stacy said. "Being married to a Smith is a good thing. Michael and Coop were raised right. Strong values, honest, faithful. They are good men. You'll do good to marry into this family."

"You're jumping the gun a little, aren't you?" Becky asked. "I mean, he hasn't even asked me yet."

"*Yet*. That's the word. *Yet*. But he will. I just know." Stacy hugged her and added, "In fact, I bet you'll have a ring on your finger the next time we see you!"

They laughed and turned toward Michael and Coop, who were loading suitcases into the rental car Michael had gotten at the airport when they arrived. Was it only two weeks ago? Marla Jean and Dana stood on the driveway, ready for last hugs and kisses. It was a hard goodbye, but they all knew they would be together again soon. Christmas wasn't that far away.

Stacy leaned out the window and said to Becky, "See you soon. And remember what I told you." Michael drove the car away, and Coop leaned down to Becky and asked, "What did she mean? What did she tell you?"

"Oh, nothing. Just silly girl talk. Stacy thinks she can predict the future. Just like your sister!"

Coop took Jenny off to the barn to milk Bessie. Becky took pictures of the fun. When Muffin the cat came into the barn, Coop squirted some milk right into her mouth. Jenny laughed with delight.

Jenny noticed the ladder to the haymow and asked if she could climb up there. Coop said, "Yes, if your mother says it's okay."

"Let's all go up," said Becky. "I can take some more pictures." They climbed the ladder, Becky first, then Jenny, with Coop following. Once they got up, Jenny found hay bales to climb on. She climbed almost to the peak of the barn roof. Coop went up after her and showed her how to jump down to some bales a little lower below. Becky was snapping pictures of their antics.

Coop said to Jenny, "Stay right here." He grabbed hold of a thick rope that was hanging from the ceiling. Holding on tight, with his legs wrapped around the rope, he jumped and went swinging through the air. Becky took more pictures. Jenny jumped up and down in the hay and said, "My turn! My turn!"

Coop stood on the floor of the haymow, holding the end of the rope. He helped Jenny grab a hold just a little above the ground. He said, "Hold on tight," and gave Jenny a ride through the air. She laughed and laughed.

"It's Mommy's turn," Coop said as he set Jenny down on a hay bale. "Watch this!" He took the rope over to Becky, told her to climb up onto a stack of bales, and get ready for a ride. Coop climbed up too and stood behind her. "Trust me?" he said.

"You know I do," Becky answered, and before she knew it, Coop had surrounded her body with his own. His hands were on the rope above her head, and his legs were wrapped around hers.

He said, "When I say 'let go,' let go!" He backed up, lifted his legs, and jumped. Together they went swinging back and forth. Then Coop yelled, "Let go!" He let go and Becky let go too. They fell together into a thick pile of hay and lay there together, laughing. Coop rolled over onto Becky and kissed her. When they separated, Becky was breathless. She wasn't sure if it was because of the swinging ride, or the closeness of Coop lying on her. Maybe both. But she liked it, that's for sure.

Jenny was still sitting on the hay bale, smiling.

As they climbed down the ladder and walked through the barn, Coop said, "I want you to come back tomorrow after church. We can have Sunday dinner here, there's still a lot of leftovers from all that food the church ladies brought. Then we can ride out to the lake, hike to the meadow, and see what animals show up. Sound good?"

Jenny was excited, but Becky said, "Are you sure? You don't have to entertain us every minute, you know. I mean, obviously we like coming out here. But you might have chores, or some other things to do. And your mom might need you. The house is going to be really quiet without Riley, your dad, and now Michael and Stacy gone too."

"Exactly. That's why you should be here. To bring some life into the house. To bring some joy into *my* life."

"Well, if you're sure." She turned to Jenny and said, "We'll have to bring some clothes to change into after church."

"Yay! We're going to the meadow. The special place! Yay!" Jenny went off skipping to the house.

"Gather your things, honey. We will be going home soon."

Coop took Becky's hand as they followed along to the house. "She's such a good kid," Coop said. "Full of life, lots of fun, smart, and adventurous. Just like her mom! I really love hanging out with her. And if you hadn't noticed, I love hanging with you too."

"She sure likes being here. Well, I do too. It's a great place."

Coop said, "It's a great place to raise a family."

"It must be," Becky said. "You and Michael and Dana have turned out pretty good!"

"All credit to Mom and Dad, fresh air and sunshine, chores and responsibilities, and the Lord. All good things."

"I wish I had known your dad better. But I think you are a lot like him. A man of good character."

"A good father." Coop turned to Becky, took both her hands in his, and started to speak. But suddenly Jenny's voice called out from the porch, "Mommy, I can't find Paul. I got Marshmallow and Silas and Mary and Martha, but I can't find Paul."

"I guess we better go look for Paul," Becky said. "I wonder if he's in Rome, or Corinth, or maybe Ephesus."

"Clever girl," Coop said and kissed her nose. "Let's go find Paul."

CHAPTER 66

———— ✺ ————

Perfection

Sundays with Coop were beginning to feel normal. Coffee, Sunday school, church, and a big dinner at the farm. Jenny obviously loved the activity around the farm. All the animals delighted her. As they were walking toward the truck to ride out to the meadow at Dooley Lake, Jenny begged to feed Nell and Slick some carrots first.

"Remember how to hold the carrot in your hand?" Coop asked, and Jenny demonstrated a flat hand. "Perfect! Here you go!" he said, as he laid a carrot on her palm. "I'll make a farm girl of you yet!"

"Mommy, I want to be a farm girl," Jenny said as Nell took the carrot from her hand. "I want to milk Bessie and feed carrots to the horses every day."

It was the perfect opening, Coop thought. He turned to Becky and said, "Would you like to be a farmer's wife?"

But Becky ignored the obvious direction Coop was heading. She avoided the question by saying, "I grew up on a farm. I like farm life. It's hard, but has so many rewards. And I love the connection to nature and the dependency on God. It actually makes me feel closer to him, being out here in open country."

Coop sighed, called Jenny, and they all got into the truck. Jenny sat in the middle and sang Sunday school songs all along the way. Becky and Coop joined in, and the time passed quickly. A short ride took them to the park and the lake. They exited the truck and hiked toward the lake. Coop was looking for an unmarked path and soon led them down a trail that was barely visible. Just a grass path through the brush, over several small hills, to a stand of trees. The trees grew close together, and Coop maneuvered slowly through an opening that was practically invisible. Suddenly the trees thinned, and they stood gazing into an open meadow surrounded on two sides by tall pine trees. The fourth side was a steep rocky cliff with trees along the top ridge. Water trickled from the rocks and formed a small stream at the bottom. The stream flowed toward Dooley Lake.

Becky drew in her breath and Jenny said, "Oh! Pretty!"

"Coop, this is beautiful. So private and quiet and peaceful. I see why you say it's such a special place."

They spread a blanket on the meadow grass and sat in silence, enjoying the beauty and peace. They listened to birds singing in the trees and heard cardinals calling back and forth. They watched a large bird circle in the sky high above the cliff and suddenly make a dive down and grab something, maybe a rabbit, from the meadow. They saw a mother fox and several kits playing in the distance. They watched white puffy clouds float through the bright blue sky and tried to imagine shapes, animals, airplanes, and angels. It was a blessed time, just the three of them, making memories.

"It's just beautiful here, Coop. Perfect."

When Jenny went off to gather wildflowers, Coop grabbed Becky's hands in his and said, "Becky, I agree that it's really nice here, but it's not perfect. It could only be perfect if you agreed to be my wife." He reached inside his shirt pocket and pulled out a small box. "I love you, Becky. I want you by my side for the rest of my life. I dream of making a good life with you, serving the Lord together, growing our family, and bringing up our children in our Christian home. I'm asking you to marry me. Please."

He opened the box to reveal a diamond engagement ring. He took the ring and placed it near the tip of Becky's ring finger. "Will you be my wife?"

With tears in her eyes and a big smile on her face, Becky nodded yes. Coop slipped the ring on her finger, and she threw her arms around his neck. "I love you, Coop. God has brought you to me, and I know we are meant to be together forever. This life and the next. Yes, I will marry you! Yes!"

Jenny came up to them with an armful of wildflowers while they were kissing. Coop pulled himself away from Becky and said, "Jenny, I love you. When your mommy and I get married, you will be my little girl forever!"

Jenny looked at her mother and said, "Married? You are having a wedding? I already got the flowers!"

EPILOGUE

Chaplain Barb Olsen walked down the hall of Atkins General Hospital with Pastor J. D. Green and Nancy Martin. Chaplain Olsen was filling them in on a patient they were about to visit. "She has been in ICU for several weeks. Lots of internal injuries, broken bones, and other serious trauma. Although she has a father in Winslow, she's had no visitors since she was admitted. She was in a medically induced coma for a while, because of the extreme pain she was in. It helped her to rest more comfortably. But now that she's conscious, she has been talking a lot about a near-death experience she had. It's very interesting actually, and has opened up opportunities to talk with her about the Lord."

"I've heard that people sometimes say they have seen a bright white light, and they felt the Lord calling to them. Is that what happened to her? How interesting to talk with her about that, and assure her that the Lord is indeed calling her," said Nancy.

"Well, no, it wasn't exactly like that with this woman. It was actually the opposite. She says she saw the pit of hell, and she felt the heat of the fire. It seems to really have had an effect on her. I'll let her explain more when you see her. She is very eager to talk about it. She also keeps repeating verses from Romans, particularly 'For all have sinned' and 'The wages of sin is death.' So she has some knowledge of the Scriptures. Someone has planted the seeds. Now she needs nurturing and care. I think she's really ready to hear the good news of salvation and eternal life."

"Excellent," said Pastor Green. "Sounds like the field is ripe and harvesttime is at hand. We'll be happy to talk with her and pray with her about the steps of salvation."

"I must tell you also," said the chaplain, "she is under guard because of some criminal activity she has been involved in. So there will be a police officer stationed at her door at all times. He knows you are allowed to be with her. You just need to check in with him whenever you visit."

"Okay. Is there any danger to us, do you think?" Pastor Green was concerned not only for himself, but also Nancy and her unborn child.

"Well, certainly not at this time. She is in traction for broken bones and can't even feed herself at this point. But she wants to talk. She needs to talk."

As they approached the room and greeted the officer stationed at the door, Pastor Green offered up a prayer. "Lord God, be with us now as we speak with your child in this room. May our words be a reflection of your love and mercy. Open her heart to receive your gift of salvation. If it be your will, let Nancy and me water the seeds that have been planted. We praise you, o Lord, for what we know you are longing to do in the life of this young woman. Thank you for the opportunity to be bearers of your good news. Amen."

They walked into the hospital room and the chaplain said, "Melissa, I'd like to introduce Pastor Green and Nancy Martin. They've come to talk with you."

"Oh good! I need someone to talk to. I have the most amazing story to tell you. Frightening, really, but eye-opening for sure! I never believed in Heaven and hell before my accident, but now I think it's all true. I'd love to talk to you about it. Maybe you can answer some questions I have. There's so much I don't understand about God and Jesus and the plan of salvation and eternal life. I need to know more." She smiled brightly at her visitors and said, "Oh, by the way, you can call me Misty."

ABOUT THE AUTHOR

Under His Wings is Rosemary Fisher's first adventure as a published author! The idea for the story came to her in the middle of the night, and Rosemary feels it was God-given. It was a story that had to be written!

The writing started out as a creative outlet during the COVID-19 quarantine. Rosemary had no intention of publishing, but friends who read her manuscript encouraged her to take that next step. Rosemary hopes the Scriptures and songs within her novel will bring you peace and comfort during difficult times.

Reading, Scripture, gardening, and music have brought much enjoyment to Rosemary throughout her life. Growing up in a small town in Iowa, she considers herself a country girl. It's only natural that her first novel would be about family life on the farm.

Rosemary is a retired teacher, having dedicated over forty-five years to the education of young children as a teacher, family-home childcare provider, and director of a childcare center. She has taught children from infancy through second grade, in addition to raising two sons and two stepdaughters. She particularly loved her years working with infants and toddlers in her home family day care in Maryland, and her time with Early Head Start as a Child and Family-Development Advocate in Missouri.

Rosemary and her husband, John, live in Columbia, Missouri. With their four children and eight grandchildren scattered throughout the United States, they have devoted their retirement years to training and loving their beautiful collie, Regina Rose.

CPSIA information can be obtained
at www.ICGtesting.com
Printed in the USA
BVHW080845060521
606646BV00003B/209

9 781098 083151